Praise for Gini Hartzmark's previous Kate Millholland novels

FATAL REACTION

"Exceptional: Hartzmark paints a fascinating picture of the world of drug research with characters who are believable, varied, and likable (even the villains are the kind you love to hate). The intensity of the complex plot never wavers, and the ending explains just enough to satisfy without being too pat."
—*Publishers Weekly*

FINAL OPTION

"A cleverly plotted and convincing inside look at freewheeling financial crooks and wizards . . . Hartzmark keeps the story moving swiftly to an explosive conclusion."
—*San Francisco Chronicle*

BITTER BUSINESS

"A page-turner."
—*People*

Please turn to the back of the book for an interview with Gini Hartzmark.

By Gini Hartzmark
Published by The Ballantine Publishing Group:

PRINCIPAL DEFENSE
FINAL OPTION
BITTER BUSINESS
FATAL REACTION
ROUGH TRADE

ROUGH TRADE

A Novel

Gini Hartzmark

IVY BOOKS • NEW YORK

An Ivy Book
Published by The Ballantine Publishing Group
Copyright © 1999 by Gini Hartzmark

www.randomhouse.com/BB/

Library of Congress Catalog Card Number: 98-93447

ISBN 0-8041-1829-9

Manufactured in the United States of America

First Edition: January 1999

10 9 8 7 6 5 4 3 2 1

To Michael

Acknowledgments

I'd like to thank Dee and Lee Hartzmark and Debby Jacobs for contributing to my football education and faithfully keeping me up to date as the Cleveland Browns' saga unfolded. Thanks also to Heather Raaf, Chuck Zellmer, Sid Dworkin, Mark Schwartz, Don McIntyre, and Steve Wasserman for pitching in with their special areas of expertise. Additional thanks to Donald Maass, Susan Randol, Teague Von Bohlen, and Lisa Collins for their help in shaping the manuscript and Jane Lassar and Barb Varney for helping me get a feel for Milwaukee. As always I am in debt to Dawn Machen and Leigh Trainer for keeping my life on track so that I can write books.

Finally I ask forgiveness of the good people of Milwaukee for allowing me to give them a football team only to threaten to take it away.

CHAPTER

1

In my line of work you get used to other people's distress the same way that doctors grow inured to other people's pain. I know that sounds cold, but that distance is important. It's what makes it possible to wade in and do what needs to be done. Don't get me wrong. I'm not pretending that what I do should be compared with easing suffering or saving lives. I am a deal lawyer, not a doctor. But that doesn't mean I'm not a specialist. Believe me, when the bank has you by the balls, you don't call a urologist. You call me.

That still didn't mean that Beau Rendell wanted me to be there. No one who fancies himself the master of his particular universe wants a woman less than half his age telling him how he's screwed up. Even his son, Jeff, who'd practically begged me to come, now seemed miserable to find that I was actually here. Not that I blamed him. After all, my presence could mean only one thing. The situation with his father had finally deteriorated to the point where they both needed lawyers.

For secrecy's sake we were meeting at Beau Rendell's house in River Hills, an exclusive suburb of Milwaukee. The two sides stared at each other across the glass and chrome travesty that passed for a dining room table, Jeff Rendell and I on one side; his father Beau, the owner of the Milwaukee Monarchs football team, and his longtime

1

lawyer and drinking buddy, Harald Feiss, on the other. Outside it was raining. Cold, fat drops smeared the large plate-glass window that looked out over the sodden backyard. It had been coming down for days, and the ground had long ago exhausted its ability to absorb the water, which lay in frigid pools that filled the low spots in the grass. I could only imagine what it would be like at the stadium that afternoon when the Monarchs took the field against the Vikings. No doubt things would get ugly.

Even though I usually don't follow football, I knew that *ugly* was a word that had been getting a lot of use in connection with the Monarchs. So far, this season, like the several before it, had been a disaster. Plagued by losses on the field as well as off, Beau had surprised everyone by firing the team's general manager and replacing him with his son, Jeff. Now, in addition to a string of humiliating defeats, discord reigned in the team's front office—a situation that had been reported in embarrassing detail in the press.

But what the media didn't know—and what Beau was desperate that they not find out—was that the Monarchs were also on the verge of bankruptcy. With his seventieth birthday fast approaching and one heart attack already behind him, Beau Rendell had made one last desperate attempt to finally buy the championship that had so long eluded him. Using his shares of the team as collateral, he had borrowed heavily to sign a pair of franchise players. One had broken his back his first time in a Monarchs uniform and the other had ended up in jail for aggravated assault. However, both continued to collect their multimillion dollar salaries.

Through it all, the Milwaukee fans had done what they do best—filled the stadium and steadfastly supported their team. Unfortunately, the same could not be said for the bank. During the preseason Beau had defaulted on the loan. Under the terms of his agreement he then had ninety days to correct the default. As of today, he had ten days left to come up with the $18 million payment. If he couldn't produce the cash, the bank would make the situation public, call the loan, and force the team into bankruptcy. In a country where toppling the mighty is second only to football as a form of public entertainment, I knew that the same press that had kept Beau Rendell on a pedestal for the last thirty years would be only too happy to report every detail of his fall.

Still, I had to confess that sitting at the head of his own table Beau Rendell did not look like a desperate man facing an impossible situation. Actually, he just looked pissed. He might be on the ropes, but he was still very much a man who expected to get what he wanted. Normally I'm glad to see people like Beau finally get what's coming to them, but not today. Beau's son was married to one of my closest childhood friends, and I knew that whatever forces stood poised to flail her husband's family would end up raining their blows down on Chrissy, too.

I honestly don't think I would have made the trip for anyone else. I was in the middle of a particularly complex transaction, a high-profile deal for difficult clients, and I had no business being out of the office, much less Chicago. As it was, the fear that something would happen while I was away—something that would expose my absence and provide ammunition for my critics—was already making my nerves sing like a high-voltage wire.

As we waited to begin, there was no small talk and the atmosphere in the room was almost unbearably strained. I found myself wishing for a cup of coffee, not just for the caffeine, but to have something to occupy my hands. Unfortunately, Beau wasn't the domestic type and the last of the Mrs. Rendells had been handed her divorce papers nearly a decade ago. I briefly considered getting up and making some myself—at least it would have gotten me

out of the room for a while—but Beau was definitely of
the generation that equated domesticity with weakness. So
I kept my seat.

When the doorbell rang, Jeff got up to answer it, leaving Harald Feiss and me to glare at each other. Feiss was
a contemporary of Beau's, thrice divorced, who still fancied himself something of a swinger. I found I disliked
him less for his hair plugs than for the preening air of self-
importance that hung about him like the scent of stale gin.

Beau ignored us both. He was busy meticulously dia-
gramming plays on the yellow pad in front of him. While
the trend in the NFL was to give increasing autonomy to
the head coach, this concept was nowhere in evidence in
Milwaukee. Beau Rendell was a football man, an owner
from the old school, and when it came to the Monarchs,
he was the one who called the shots . . . at least for ten
more days.

Katharine Anne Prescott Millholland—I was named for
an heiress, an eccentric spinster, a lumber magnate, and an
opium baron. In my family they never let you forget who
you are—or where you come from. The fact is that in the
ever-dwindling universe that is Chicago society, my
family still sits at the top. My mother, Astrid E. Millholland, is arguably one of the most socially prominent
women in the country. Indeed, when someone once asked
her what the *E* in her name stood for, she replied, "Estab-
lishment." Her middle name is really Eunice, but you get
the picture.

Chrissy Rendell, on the other hand, was hardly to the
fund-raiser born, which is one of the reasons ours has always been such an unlikely friendship. Her father was an
orthodontist, a man who, my mother never tired of pointing out, made his living putting his hands in other people's
mouths. Chrissy's mother was a socially ambitious woman,

as anxious to find a way into the suffocating confines of North Shore society as I was to find a way out. She was relentless in her efforts to push the two of us together, though I'm sure that Chrissy had little interest in befriending a sharp-tongued and sullen thing like me, even if I was a Millholland. Even then she was already everything I would never be—lighthearted, beautiful, and every bit as at ease in the world as she was in her own skin. But we did have one thing in common—our mothers—overbearing women who imposed their rigid expectations for us with the same zealous discipline with which they conducted their own lives.

I have no doubt that by high school Chrissy's mother had come to regret her efforts to bring us together. I know that my mother spared no breath in putting the blame for our transgressions squarely on Chrissy's shoulders—not that either of us cared. We were much too busy running wild. By graduation Chrissy had a collection of little black dresses roughly the size of postage stamps and a well-developed preference for commodities traders over high school boys. I, on the other hand, shook up the North Shore by dating Stephen Azorini, whose father was suspected (correctly) of having ties to organized crime.

Of course, we've both straightened out since then, a fact that neither of us seems able to quite get over. Chrissy is not just married, but a mother now, her party-girl days behind her. I have a corner office and a reputation as a corporate gunslinger to uphold. But it is less the idea of how far we've come that is disconcerting, but rather, as the years have passed, how much higher the stakes have grown.

I got married the summer after law school, but I was a widow before my first anniversary. My husband, Russell, was diagnosed with brain cancer three weeks after our honeymoon. Chrissy's daughter, born last year and named Katharine in my honor, is deaf—undeniably grown-up problems for two girls who were once in too big a hurry to grow up.

Now this.

There are few businesses as public and as personal as an NFL franchise. Most people have no idea who runs Ford or General Motors, but a surprising number can tick off the names of the men who own the nation's football teams. When Chrissy married Jeff Rendell, she knew that she was not only marrying the Monarchs' heir apparent, but stepping into the public eye, as well. In Milwaukee the Rendells have always been treated as a kind of minor royalty. And if she occasionally missed the urban electricity of Chicago or felt suffocated by people's rigid expectations for her in her new hometown, she had nonetheless always been careful about holding up her end of the bargain.

No one knows where their life will lead them, but surely the Monarchs' current problems were more than Chrissy or anyone else had signed on for. Through a combination of hubris and circumstance, risk and miscalculation, Beau Rendell had brought his family to the cusp of disaster. While I'm sure that Chrissy was prepared to remain at her husband's side come what may, I was equally determined to steer them from the precipice—if I could only figure out a way.

A hundred years ago they would have hidden away their daughters when Jack McWhorter rode into town. Now, when he shows up in his private jet they practically offer their daughters up to him, debutantes and brewery princesses, all hoping to snag Milwaukee's most eligible bachelor. Even though I am inherently suspicious of blatantly handsome men, I must confess that when he walked into the room, I had to suppress the fleeting impulse to if not exactly hurl myself at his feet, then at least to bat my eyelashes.

Stray raindrops glistened among the strands of his jet-black hair, which he wore slicked back, no doubt something he'd picked up in L.A. along with his tan. His shirt was custom made and in a carefully chosen shade of blue that matched his eyes, which were hooded, hard, and glittered with self-assurance.

Like so much of the money in Milwaukee, Jack Mc-Whorter's came from beer. His family owned a food service and concession company that supplied the stadiums and arenas in a half a dozen cities with not just popcorn and hot dogs, but the small river of brew the fans washed them down with. Jack was in charge of the company's West Coast operations and as such divided his time between Milwaukee and Los Angeles. However, it was his California connections that brought him to Beau Rendell's dining room today.

Jack had come on behalf of the Greater Los Angeles Stadium Commission, a quasi-government agency whose mission was to bring professional football back to the City of Angels. He was an interesting choice of emissary. Not only had his family's company long held the concession contract at Monarchs Stadium, but he was a contemporary of Jeff's. As I sat there about to watch him make his pitch, I couldn't help but wonder whether his masters in Los Angeles assumed that with Beau beaten and near ruin, the reins of the Monarchs organization had already been passed to Jeff. If so, I figured they still had a thing or two to learn about Beau Rendell.

McWhorter began by telling us what we already knew. With the ignominious departure of both the Rams and the Raiders, Los Angeles had become a National Football League city without an NFL team—a situation that the municipal movers and shakers were prepared to pay handsomely to correct.

"Believe me, no one wants to see the Monarchs leave

Milwaukee," Jack confided. "This is a great town, a football town. I should know. I grew up here. But things change. There are the realities to consider. It used to be that all that you needed for a successful franchise was fan support. Market size. Then it was television revenues. Now it's stadium economics. Before free agency all you had to do was fill the seats, but nowadays less than thirty percent of a team's revenue comes from ticket sales. Today you need revenue from parking, concessions, season ticket licenses, and skyboxes just to make ends meet."

One look at Beau Russell was all it took to see that Jack was already pedaling uphill. The Monarchs' owner did not look like he was enjoying being lectured to by a man whose knowledge of football was limited to how many hot dogs he could expect to sell at the game. Harald Feiss wasn't listening at all—a fact I found particularly annoying. As Beau Rendell's closest business adviser he, more than anyone else, knew that the Monarchs were in no position to close the door on any viable offer. But of course, if Harald Feiss knew anything at all about business, the Monarchs wouldn't be in this mess in the first place.

Perhaps sensing that he was losing his audience, Mc-Whorter produced copies of a term sheet outlining the specifics of what L.A. was prepared to offer to bring the NFL back to Southern California. There was a copy for each of us, individually numbered in the top right-hand corner. It was a familiar lawyer's trick, useful for keeping track of sensitive documents and making sure that stray copies didn't find their way into the wrong hands. The front page was also stamped "confidential" in big red letters. Given the subject matter, they could just as easily have been labeled "dynamite."

It took me only about ten seconds of adding up the numbers to realize that what I was holding wasn't just a proposal but the team's salvation. Los Angeles wasn't offering a deal, they were offering a bribe—a football palace, a new stadium whose every square foot was designed to make Beau Rendell money. To sweeten the deal they were even offering a one-time $100 million "moving fee" to help the team defray the costs of the transition, which Beau would be free to spend any way that he saw fit. All he had to do was sign the agreement with L.A. and his troubles would be over.

From beside me I could sense the relief move through Jeff's body and hoped that he wasn't wearing it on his face as well. Any way you looked at it, this was going to be a complicated transaction. Even though the terms L.A. was offering seemed extremely favorable, there was still much that needed to be negotiated and the longer we were able to keep the Monarchs' financial situation under wraps the better. Desperation is never an advantageous position from which to strike a bargain.

Beau, no stranger to playing his cards close to his chest, maintained a cypher-like demeanor. He let Jack finish and then dismissed him with the neutral promise that he would confer with Jeff and Harald Feiss before coming to any decision. It wasn't until the door had closed behind McWhorter that the owner of the Milwaukee Monarchs let us know what he really thought of L.A.'s offer. Beau Rendell fixed his eyes upon his son directly across the table, picked up the copy of the term sheet, held it up, and tore it into little pieces.

"Just so that you and I understand each other," he proclaimed coldly. "I'll die before I move this team."

CHAPTER

2

In the aftermath of his father's performance with the Los Angeles term sheet Jeff maintained an incendiary silence—one that I, half friend, half lawyer, felt uncomfortable trying to breach. Instead, I suggested we save our discussion for the relative privacy of his office at the stadium, a suggestion he seemed eager to embrace. Following behind him in my own car as we headed downtown I hoped that the drive would give him a chance to calm down and collect himself. Beau's refusal to even consider L.A.'s proposal moved things one step closer to catastrophe, which meant that Jeff and I had much to discuss.

As we passed through one pristine suburb after another I was struck, not for the first time, by how much Milwaukee seems like a cleaner, kinder version of Chicago, a sort of metropolis in miniature perched on the edge of Lake Michigan. It was almost as if God, foreseeing what a sprawling mess Chicago was destined to become, decided to let the Germans try their hand at doing better. The result was a small big city, beertown to Boston's beantown, true to its blue-collar roots and, in deference to its Teutonic heritage, almost fanatically clean.

Kickoff was still almost an hour away, but the parking lots surrounding Monarchs Stadium were already crowded with fans. Despite the dismal weather, the team's depressing record, and their even gloomier prospects against

Minnesota, a carnival atmosphere reigned. A lot of it had to do with the fact that over the years Monarchs fans had developed their own variation of the tailgate party, with die-hard supporters gathering before every game in their own version of a Monarch's court. Dressed in approximations of medieval garb, they ate turkey legs and called each other thou, as in "Will thou pass me another beer?"—which they drank from tankards the size of turrets.

There was even an actual monarch, a three-hundred-pound welder who ruled the bleachers from beneath a crown of beer cans and moth-eaten ermine robes. Home games found him attended by his court: his Rubenesque queen, an assortment of swaggering knights who demonstrated their fealty (and foolhardiness) by baring their chests in all weather, and a leering, gap-toothed jester in purple tights and a cockscomb cap.

As I waited in the shadow of Monarchs Stadium for the guard to wave me into the players' lot, it occurred to me that if the team was looking for a physical symbol of their problems, this was it. Built as part of the city's unsuccessful bid for the 1932 Olympics, it was a structure that was simultaneously imposing and decayed. Big enough for the opening and closing ceremonies of an Olympiad and designed as an oval to accommodate the track-and-field events, it was a spectacularly flawed venue for football. Not only were the sight lines terrible, but over the years moisture seeping through the concrete had caused the structure to crumble, leaving gaping holes and rusted, exposed girders. The Monarchs had played there for thirty-one consecutive seasons, during which time, Beau never tired of pointing out, the johns had never worked right.

I eased my battered Volvo in between a Ferrari and a Porsche, both red, and trailed Jeff into the dark bowels of the stadium. He led the way through a series of narrow corridors, up a service elevator loaded with pallets of hot dog buns, and along a series of dimly lit concourses that smelled of spilled beer. The team offices were in the uppermost reaches of the stadium and consisted of three adjoining double-wide trailers suspended from the roof and accessible from the concourse below via a series of poorly lit metal staircases barely wide enough for one person to pass.

Jeff's office adjoined his father's, and both were jammed with Monarchs memorabilia and done up in the team's colors. The walls were painted a mustardy yellow, no doubt meant to invoke gold, and the indoor/outdoor carpeting was the color of grape jelly. Taken together the effect was of an old bruise. On the wall opposite Jeff's desk was an enormous board on which was written the name of every player in the NFL, along with his team, the length of his contract, and his reported salary. A quick look at the totals told me that the Monarchs were carrying the third highest salary load in the league. It was, I reflected, a high price to pay for last place.

Jeff sat down behind his desk, and I settled into the visitor's chair. Up to this point our relationship had been one that could best be described as once removed in that it had always been dictated by or conducted through Chrissy. That was only natural seeing as he was my best friend's husband. However, now that I was being thrust into the middle of the Monarchs' financial crisis, I found myself taking stock of him afresh.

In his early thirties, Jeff Rendell still had the kind of lantern-jawed, Clark Kent good looks that made you want to whip off his glasses and run your fingers through his hair—just to see what developed. However, compared to the men who Chrissy'd been involved with in the past—pro athletes and soap opera stars—Jeff was stunningly ordinary.

Everything else I knew about him I knew second-hand. From Chrissy I'd heard about his disjointed childhood marked by a succession of opportunistic stepmothers and his own adolescent transgressions. From the sports pages I'd followed the course of his near epic disagreements with Coach Bennato, Monday morning volleys of accusation and blame acrimonious enough to have been picked up and reported in the national press.

One thing was clear from all this: football had always been the one constant in Jeff Rendell's life. He'd grown up in the sport the same way that acrobats are raised to the circus. He'd spent his childhood on the sidelines and in the locker room and gone to work in the team's front office straight out of college. He'd literally known no other world.

I understood, perhaps too well, about the burdens carried by the children of prominent parents, but at least I'd had the chance to put some distance between myself and the world in which I'd been raised. While no one could ever blame Jeff for not striking out on his own—there aren't many people who'd turn their back on the chance to be a part of an NFL team—I worried whether a lifetime spent in his father's shadow had adequately prepared him to stand up to him now.

"Do you want to know what I've been thinking about the whole way down here?" asked Jeff, morosely rocking back and forth in his desk chair. "I've been thinking my father must have a death wish."

"Why is that?"

"It's the only explanation. What he's doing makes just about as much sense as dousing himself with gasoline and striking a match. I mean, what does he think is going to happen in ten days?"

"Do you think there's a chance he's already figured a

way out and he's just not telling anybody?" I asked, being well acquainted with Beau's reputation for secretiveness.

"I have absolutely no doubt *he* thinks he has," replied Jeff. "He's been running around town for weeks holding hush-hush meetings and dropping hints to the press, but believe me, he's just deluding himself."

"Why do you say that?"

"Because I've been talking to people, too. Dad's living in the past, when a handful of guys with cigars got things done with a handshake. Everything's *bigger* now, things have moved past him. Baseball, basketball, even fucking soccer is cutting into football's appeal. Football isn't even just a game you sell tickets to anymore, it's a gigantic entertainment industry encompassing everything from television to athletic shoes. Player salaries are stratospheric, and stadiums cost more to build than skyscrapers. Dad thinks that just because he's the owner of the Milwaukee Monarchs he's not going to get hammered, but he's wrong."

"So why not just sell the team?" I asked. "Isn't the going rate for an NFL franchise something like $300 million?"

"We could probably get a little more. Unfortunately, by the time we retired our debt and paid capital gains taxes, there'd still be nothing left."

"I had no idea your level of debt was that high."

"We've borrowed against everything but our socks, and that's only because nobody will give us anything for them."

"Then what about selling part of it, taking on a minority partner?"

"We already have two."

"You're kidding. Who?"

"Harald Feiss and Coach Bennato each have a minority interest in the team."

"I didn't know that."

"Nobody does. Dad got them to agree to take the shares in lieu of salary. That's how tight things are."

"What if you sold a thirty or forty percent ownership in the team? There've got to be plenty of sports-crazed tycoons out there who'd be willing to spend $100 million to own a piece of a franchise like the Monarchs."

"Sure. Provided my dad didn't own the other sixty percent. The guys you're talking about didn't get where they are by being stupid. Nobody's going to pony up that much dough without being absolutely certain that Dad isn't going to just piss it away again. They're going to want to make damn sure that they have a say in how the team is going to be run."

"Surely there are worse things."

"Not to my Dad. I guarantee you he'd lose the team before he agreed to that."

"Well, then what's he thinking? He can't just be waiting for the bank to take the team away from him."

"Oh, I guarantee he and Feiss have been trying to cook something up."

"With whom?"

"I know they've been meeting with a group of suburban developers who want to build a new stadium out in Wauwatosa. They want to use it as an anchor for a big shopping and entertainment complex. . . ."

"And?"

"And it's a terrible idea. Nobody wants to drive out into the cornfields to see a football game. Monarchs fans don't want to shop for shoes and catch a movie after the game. Besides, everywhere they've already tried the suburban stadium idea it's failed miserably. They're shutting down the Pontiac Silverdome, and last I heard, they're turning the Richfield Coliseum into a prison. People want downtown stadiums."

"So what are the chances of the team cutting a deal with the city?"

"And having a check for $18 million to take to the bank in ten days? After Dad publicly backed the mayor's opponent in the last election? I'd say they're the same as our winning the Super Bowl this season—somewhere between zero and none."

"Even if the city realizes that the alternative is losing their football team?"

"You heard what my father said. He's not moving the team."

"I'm not saying that he necessarily should. But you and I both know that's how the game is played. Teams squeeze their home cities in order to get them to ante up a new stadium, or else they threaten to move to a place that will. Grant you, most of the time it's just blackmail—millionaire team owners squeezing the taxpayers for subsidies that will allow them to make even more money—but the irony of it is that in the Monarchs' case it wouldn't be. You really may have no choice but to move the team."

"Unfortunately, Dad doesn't see it that way. Harald Feiss has got him convinced that just because Dad plays golf with Gus Wallenberg and invites him to watch the games from the owner's box that the bank won't make good on its threats."

"Who's Gus Wallenberg?"

"The president of First Milwaukee Bank."

"The bank that holds the team's note?"

"Yeah. It's one of the few private, family-owned banks left in the city. But just because they haven't let themselves be bought up by one of the big national chains doesn't mean they don't have to compete with them every day. Believe me, Dad's deluding himself if he thinks that Gus cares about anything but the money. He isn't going to cut us any slack."

"Why don't you let me talk to Wallenberg?" I suggested. "Maybe I can find some way to restructure the loan or at least convince them to give you some more time."

Jeff shook his head.

"Come on," I pressed. "I do this kind of thing all the time. Bankers love me."

"Believe me. It's no use."

"At least let me give it a shot. You never know. Maybe they'll be more willing to listen to an outsider, someone who hasn't been part of the problem up until now."

"You don't understand. If I thought there was even a one-in-a-million chance, I'd take you to talk to them right now. But I guarantee you there's no way they will give us anything—not one more day, not one more dollar. Nothing. Not even the benefit of the doubt."

"How can you be so sure?"

"Because on October 3 my father paid $11 million to buy Tamecus Johnson's contract from the New York Jets."

"Tamecus Johnson? Isn't he the wide receiver who was arrested for possession of cocaine while he was with Dallas?"

"Cocaine in Dallas, cocaine and a concealed weapon in New York, and DUI and resisting arrest three weeks after he signed with us. At last count he's been in rehab seven times."

"Let me get this straight. Your father paid to sign this guy *after* he was already in default with the bank?" I was beginning to see Jeff's point about his father having some kind of death wish.

"Yep. Dad went out and spent $11 million that he should have paid to the bank to acquire the biggest drug addict in the league. So now do you believe me when I say that when it comes to the bank, we are well and truly fucked?"

* * *

While Jeff made arrangements to have copies of the team documents I needed packed into boxes and brought down to my car, I went off in search of Chrissy. Even if Jeff and I both agreed that moving the team to L.A.—or at least threatening to do so—was the only way for the Rendells to get out of this mess, the first thing I needed to do was review the various agreements and covenants that governed the team. It made no sense to push the issue with Beau until we knew for certain that such a move was even possible. Of course, I was also secretly hoping that I might find something else, a loophole or some other point from which to maneuver, that had heretofore been overlooked by Feiss.

Not that I had any idea when I was going to actually find the time to do any of this. My plate at the office was already hideously full, and my life, well, let's just say that I was going through one of those periods where I preferred not to think about the catastrophe that passed as my personal life. That said, there was still no way that I was going to leave Milwaukee without stopping to at least say hello to Chrissy—especially not today. It wasn't just that the whole mess with the Monarchs had me worried and feeling protective of her. On some level I felt responsible for the situation in which Chrissy now found herself.

The truth is, before she met Jeff Rendell, Chrissy had been engaged to someone else. Malcolm Partiger was wealthy, successful, and devastatingly handsome. He was also thirty years her senior. Their whirlwind romance was emblematic of Chrissy's place in the fast lane and when *People* ran a full-page photo of her showing off her four-carat engagement ring her only regret was that her parents, especially her mother, hadn't lived long enough to see it.

Malcolm's attorney waited until the day before the wedding to present Chrissy with a prenuptial agreement. With no one else to turn to, she came to me for advice. I was a second-year law student at the time, every bit as idealistic about love (I'm sure some would say naïve) as I was about the law. But that didn't prevent me from speaking my mind.

Stepping back from the sense of injury and outrage that had been my first reaction, I told Chrissy that I found not just the document but its timing troubling. Oddly enough, money wasn't really the issue; Malcolm was actually being more than generous. The issue was control. If Chrissy signed the prenup, she was not just agreeing to a less than equal partnership, but ceding to her husband the power to make all the important decisions in their life.

Throughout the entire drama Malcolm was cordial and curiously silent. No doubt he assumed that a girl like Chrissy, if just left alone with her wedding dress for long enough, would eventually come to her senses and sign. Perhaps if she'd picked another maid of honor, she would have. As it turned out, half an hour after she was supposed to descend the curved staircase of the Four Seasons Hotel, dressed in a confection of taffeta and tulle, Chrissy marched down the stairs in her going-away suit and announced to the three hundred assembled guests that there would be no wedding.

It was an act of bravery, a victory for what was right as opposed to what was expected, but in light of the Rendells' current predicament I couldn't help but wonder whether it hadn't also turned out to be a quixotic act of folly. Malcolm had gone on to marry a starlet, a leggy blonde, and together they had become a staple of the magazines that chronicle the doings of the rich and beautiful. Despite her protests to the contrary, I knew that Chrissy had to wonder how her life would have turned out if she'd chosen differently that day.

I made my way through the team offices to the owner's skybox that hung, suspended from the top level of the sta-

dium, directly over the fifty-yard line. There I found my
friend doing what she'd done every game day since her
marriage—acting as hostess for the dozen or so invited
guests in her father-in-law's box. Waiters were cleaning
up the remains of a catered lunch, and several of the VIPs
had already taken their drinks out onto the balcony overlooking the field.

Sensing a new arrival, Chrissy turned toward the door
with an automatic smile of welcome on her face, a smile
that was instantly transformed into something much more
genuine when she saw that it was me. As always, I was immediately struck by how beautiful she was. Dressed simply in black pants and a cashmere sweater of Monarchs
purple she easily eclipsed every other woman in the room.
It wasn't just that she was tall, thin, and blond. Chrissy
carried herself like a duchess and her features possessed
a sly asymmetry that drew you in and held your interest.

She would have been beautiful no matter what: dressed
in rags, soaking wet, after an entire day of weeping . . .
though no one would ever see her that way, not even me.
Chrissy had long ago discovered that her face could serve
not only as a magnet but a shield. No doubt some people
saw her devotion to the mirror as vanity, but I knew
better—her wardrobe was her armor and her flawlessly
applied make-up often the only buffer between herself and
an increasingly intrusive world.

As she crossed the room to meet me I caught Jack
McWhorter following her progress from beneath veiled
lids. I immediately thought of Jeff and found myself wondering what it must be like to be married to a woman so
beautiful that men couldn't help but watch her greedily
with their eyes. But then again, perhaps the inevitable
envy was part of the appeal.

We hugged like sisters. Her body felt thinner to me than

last time I saw her and I found myself worrying about how all the team's troubles must be affecting her.

"I'm so glad you're here," she whispered under her breath as she took me by the elbow and steered me toward the door. "That way you can keep me from killing him."

"Killing whom?" I demanded, craning my neck to look back over my shoulder at the other people in the box.

"Gus Wallenberg, of course."

"He's here?" I demanded, surprised.

"That's him over there with Beau, the one with the mustache who sort of looks like Hitler. I wish he would just choke."

"What's he doing here?"

"Beau invited him if you can believe it," she continued as she drew me out the door, down the corridor, and into an adjacent box, which was vacant—another symbol of the Rendells' distress. Since the completion of the city's new baseball stadium, there were no municipal funds left to renovate the football venue, and the corporate boxholders had defected in droves, lured by plush luxury boxes that actually afforded a decent view of the game. This one was now apparently being used to store dozens of stacking chairs. Chrissy boosted herself up and perched on top of them.

"So how did the meeting go this morning?" she asked. "Are we moving to La-La Land?"

"Have you talked to Jack? How does he think it went?" I countered.

"We didn't really have a chance to talk about it. Why? What happened?"

"Let's just say that your father-in-law didn't exactly embrace the idea."

"Do you mind explaining what that means in plain English?"

"He tore up the proposal and told Jeff he'd die before he moved the team."

"Then I wish he would," she announced, fiercely.

"Would what?"

"Die," replied Chrissy. "I wish he would die."

"You know you don't mean that," I replied, genuinely shocked. Chrissy was fun-loving and nonjudgmental by nature. This wasn't like her at all.

"You don't understand," she blurted. "We're going to lose everything." The last statement was delivered in something very close to a sob.

"What?"

"You heard me. If the team goes bankrupt, so do we. Jeff, me, the baby . . . personally we lose everything."

"How is that possible?"

"Easy. The team hasn't paid Jeff a salary in eleven months. We've borrowed every penny we can against our house just to cover our living expenses. The rest we've lent to the team so that they could make payroll. Can you believe it? Jeff and I are in hock up to our eyes so that his father could keep paying players whose weekly paychecks are more than most people make in a year. We haven't paid our own bills in months."

"My god, Chrissy, why didn't you tell me?" I said, reaching for my purse. "I'll write you a check right now."

"For $18 million?" she countered, bitterly. "Unfortunately that's what it's going to cost to get us out of this mess."

"What about for your bills?"

"What would be the point? Either we move the team, in which case everything's going to be all right, or . . ."

"Or what?"

"Or it'll be like pissing into a forest fire—a complete waste."

I took her by the hand.

"It'll be all right," I said. "I promise."

For a second we eyed each other with the ferocious intensity of fifth graders swearing a blood oath, but it quickly evaporated into awkwardness. Nothing in our careful upbringings had ever prepared us for how to gracefully navigate this moment.

"Oh my god!" exclaimed Chrissy, as if suddenly remembering something. She hopped lightly off the pile of chairs. "There's something I've been meaning to show you and the way things have been going, who knows if I'll have another chance."

"What is it?"

"You'll see when we get there," she replied, giving me the same mischievous look I recognized from high school, the one that had landed me in the headmaster's office on more than one occasion.

I followed her down the stairs and through the labyrinthine back corridors of the stadium. As soon as we'd strayed from the main concourse I was astonished by how a structure that held more than eighty thousand people could suddenly seem so empty. I trailed her down a dim corridor illuminated by a series of naked light bulbs hung at intervals from dripping pipes overhead. I suddenly found myself thinking about rats. A building this old was sure to have thousands of them. After years of feasting on dropped popcorn and spilled beer they were probably as big as goats.

We walked faster, hurrying toward our destination, though as we traversed the bowels of the aging stadium I couldn't even begin to imagine what it was. Eventually I became aware of a noise, a kind of continuous roar like the sound of machinery or running water. As we walked, it grew louder, and I realized that it was voices, the mingled voices of the thousands of Monarchs fans.

Chrissy led the way down two flights of stairs, around a sharp corner, and through a set of heavy double doors marked AUTHORIZED PERSONNEL ONLY. We banged through them and suddenly found ourselves back in the world of bright lights and fresh paint. There were trainers carting armfuls of towels and huge coolers of Gatorade, and tense-looking young men clutching clipboards and wearing headsets. Off to one side were three sportscasters, each standing in his own halo of TV lights, speaking to the camera, each oblivious of the others.

I saw the players coming just in time to step out of the way. Chrissy and I stepped back and pressed our backs against the wall to let them past. The players, enormous men made even more so by their equipment, emerged from the locker room at a trot, shouting. Chrissy took my hand and led me in their wake up the ramp and through the tunnel toward the light. As soon as the first one hit the field the roar obliterated everything else. I heard the groan of the bleachers as the sellout crowd rose to its feet and raised its voices in unison.

"Isn't this amazing?" demanded Chrissy, shouting to be heard over the din.

You hear so much about an adrenaline rush, but this was something different. An adrenaline rush is what you get when you have a fight with your boss or a truck cuts you off in traffic. This was like some kind of powerful drug, like having firecrackers go off in my blood. As I stood there in the tunnel watching the Milwaukee Monarchs take the field, the hair on the back of my neck actually stood on end.

In an instant I understood everything. I thought of Beau Rendell and knew just why he didn't want to give any of it up, and more importantly why he was afraid to move the team. As I listened to the roaring adulation of the fans, I knew that somewhere above me Beau Rendell heard it, too. I wondered whether, high in his box, he was thinking

the same thing: What would it be like when the energy behind all of the cheering and adulation suddenly turned
to hate?

CHAPTER
3

When I arrived back in Chicago and got to the office, I was disappointed to discover that the corporate law fairy had not paid a visit in my absence and made the Avco file disappear. It was the deal from hell and it was never going to go away. I'd been working on the initial public offering for Avco for so long that it was getting hard to remember a time when the company and its problems had not consumed me.

Avco Enterprises billed itself as an entertainment company. It was the brainchild of a pair of creepy Eurotrash twins, Avery and Colin Brandt, who'd started out in the adult video business and ended up owning a string of adult entertainment restaurants called, of all things, Tit-Elations. The restaurants were scattered across the Midwest in places like Muncie, Indiana, and Portage, Ohio. Their plan was to take the company public, raise $40 million, and turn Tit-Elations into a nationwide chain.

It was just what the world needed.

My only consolation was that the porno brothers (as I called them behind their backs) and their tawdry enterprise had been forced on me. They were really Stuart Eisenstadt's clients. Stuart had been a partner in a smaller firm that Callahan Ross had acquired lock, stock, and copy machine in one of its periodic buying binges. How he managed to convince Callahan Ross's notoriously puritanical management committee to allow him to handle the deal in the first place was totally beyond me, although I secretly hoped that blackmail was involved.

Of course, once they'd given their okay, the managing partners immediately came down with a case of the vapors and began slapping conditions and restrictions on Eisenstadt, the most onerous being that I, with my extensive experience with IPOs, take the lead on the transaction. This was exactly the kind of passive-aggressive bullshit for which the management committee was famous. Eisenstadt was furious and I must confess I was feeling pretty cranky myself. I suspected that they'd tapped me for the case expressly because they knew it would make my flesh crawl. I just couldn't decide whether it was some kind of test of my loyalty or a payback for my subversive attitude and general lack of rah-rah spirit regarding the firm. In my more cynical moments I decided it was both.

Like most shotgun weddings, this one had been rocky from the start. While Stuart and I had so far managed to remain at least superficially cordial, it would also be fair to say that we had quickly developed a healthy sense of loathing for each other. Since day one Stuart worked hard to systematically sabotage my relationship with his clients, who even without his help seemed to bring out the absolute worst in me.

It didn't help that the Securities and Exchange Commission had ridden us hard from the beginning, making no secret of the fact that they intended to make the process as difficult as possible for us. Because the SEC feared flack from the religious right, Avco's bid to go public had been exposed to the most rigorous regulatory scrutiny. So far we had managed to get through due diligence, the underwriting agreement, the red herring, the SEC's idiosyncratic computer system, EDGAR, the comfort letter, seven

drafts of the registration document, the blue-sky memo-
randa, and five separate SEC comment letters, each of
which we had to meticulously reply to, specifically ad-
dressing every one of the SEC's concerns.

I had long ago passed the punch-drunk, burned-out
stage of being totally fried that marks the end of a long
case. Now I was at the point where I hated the clients, the
deal, and myself. The only good thing that could be said
was that after nearly a year, we had to be approaching the
end. I alternated between feeling delirious at the thought
that we might soon close the deal and sick with fear that
the SEC would manage to devise even more impediments.

I rounded the corner to my office expecting to find my
secretary, Cheryl, waiting for me. Instead, I saw Stuart
Eisenstadt sitting behind my desk, casually flipping through
my files.

"Where's Cheryl?" I demanded, shrugging off my coat
and trying to keep the edge out of my voice. Our latest—
and I prayed final—answer to the SEC was due in Wash-
ington by nine the next morning, and I had asked my
secretary to come in, even though it was a Sunday, to enter
the final changes in the draft.

"I sent her home," replied Stuart, rising from my chair,
picking up the silicon breast implant I used as a paper-
weight, and beginning to knead it in his hand. It had been a
present from my roommate, who gave it to me when I first
told her about the Avco IPO. It was actually one of the
more tasteful presents I'd received. Ever since the word
got out about representing Tit-Elations, a veritable tide of
gag gifts, mostly from adult novelty stores, had washed up
on my desk.

"Why would you do that?" I demanded. "Now who's
going to do the reply?"

"My girl Teri can handle it," Stuart assured me. In an office where half the guys make Steve Forbes look sexy,

Stuart was considered unattractive. "It didn't make sense to have two girls sitting around filing their nails, seeing as I had no idea where you were or when you'd get back."

"Let me explain something to you, Stuart," I said. "For one thing, when this deal closes, we're going to hand the client a check for $40 million and our bill for $250,000. They're going to kiss our feet, not quibble about a couple of hours of secretarial overtime. For another thing, I can't speak for Teri, but Cheryl isn't a girl, she's a highly intelligent twenty-eight-year-old woman who, on top of working for me, is in her second-to-last semester of night law school where she is at the top of her class. She's the one who's done all the work on the original document, and for that reason I want her to be the one to enter the changes. Unfortunately she lives forty-five minutes from here, so now instead of one secretary waiting at sixteen dollars an hour we have two lawyers waiting at six hundred."

"That's okay," Stuart replied, nonplussed. "We still haven't gotten the changes back from the client yet."

"Tell me you didn't send it to them," I groaned, trying to decide whether to burst into tears or leap over my desk and strangle him with my bare hands.

"Of course I sent it. They said they wanted to see it again. Why wouldn't I?"

"Because between the two of them the Brandt brothers have yet to see a sentence written in the English language that they don't think needs changing if only for the sheer joy of changing it. Avery is illiterate and Colin is so anal compulsive that he thinks that if he just gets all the commas in the right place, the SEC will forget that he's running a bunch of sex clubs and let him collect his $40 million, not to mention give him a gold star for neatness."

"They're the clients, Kate," intoned Eisenstadt, doing a good job of pretending to be affronted.

"They're morons, Stuart," I shot back in disgust,

"morons who are paying us big bucks to save them from themselves."

While I waited to hear back from the Brandts I summoned Sherman Whitehead to my office. Sherman was the associate who I counted on to do the grunt work on most of my cases. He had a nasal voice, an irritating manner, and an adolescent habit of blurting out the first thing that came into his head. With his acne scars and thick glasses he was practically a poster child for the socially disadvantaged and thus was never permitted in the presence of an actual client. The other lawyers in the firm avoided him, as well, preferring to send him their assignments by E-mail. The truth is that he made them nervous. Scratch the surface of even the most urbane lawyer and you'll find a nerd screaming to get out. Sherman reminded them too much of what they might have been if their wives hadn't worked so hard to shape them up.

Fortunately, what Sherman lacked in social grace he made up for in brain cells. Unburdened by any kind of personal life, he also did the work of ten without complaint and indulged in none of the ass kissing and back stabbing that characterized most of the other young lawyers in the firm. Besides, his appetite for detail and his ability to deal with the kind of mind-numbing, number-crunching, go-on-until-you're-dead minutiae that characterizes so many financially complex deals was nothing short of amazing.

"So, have we gotten the updated financials from Avco yet?" I inquired as Sherman perched on the edge of the associate's chair, nervously intertwining his fingers and awkwardly crossing and uncrossing his legs.

"I've called their accounting guy at least twenty times. He promised me on his mother's grave that I'll have them on Monday."

"If he doesn't deliver, I want you to go there personally

and get them even if it means sitting on him until they cough them up. We're past the point of bullshitting on this. I don't want to be this close to closing this deal and have the SEC come back to us saying that we haven't given them everything they asked for."

"I'll take care of it."

"Good. In the meantime I want you to start in on something else." I pulled out my car keys and tossed them to Sherman, who didn't even come close to catching them. He was probably the kid who, in gym class, was so uncoordinated he'd trip over the paint on the floor. "There are a couple of document boxes in the trunk of my car. I want you to go through them for me."

"Should I set up a case file?" he asked, stooping to retrieve the keys.

"Not yet. I also don't want you to tell a single soul about this." I pulled out my copy of the L.A. term sheet and slid it across the desk to Sherman, briefly summarizing the Monarchs' financial situation. "I want you to take a close look at the lease agreement between the city and the team."

"What am I looking for?"

"Anything that would prevent the Monarchs from moving the team."

"You mean like a specific performance clause?"

"Exactly."

As a rule, a contract cannot force a party to do what they do not want to do, it can only make them pay damages if they fail to perform as specified. If you rent an apartment, the lease states the amount you must pay in rent. It may also prohibit certain behaviors like keeping pets or causing damage. What it doesn't say is that you must actually live in the apartment. A specific performance clause was the exception to that rule. Just like the name implied, if one is included, it means that the parties agree that a specific action will be performed. In recent years they had become standard in most agreements between professional sports teams and the municipalities that owned the stadiums they played in. It was a way of obligating teams to play all their home games in the stadium throughout the duration of the lease period. But the Monarchs' lease had been signed nearly a decade ago. I prayed that their agreement with the city predated this trend.

"Anything else?" asked Sherman, whose other admirable quality was his disinclination for small talk.

"Yes," I replied. "If you find a stray $18 million salted away somewhere, be sure to let me know."

I spent the rest of the day fighting over commas with the Brandts, who seemed determined to interject themselves into a process they didn't understand with the same instinct that drives a dog to mark its territory. While deep down I knew that Stuart was right—they were the client and therefore paying for the privilege of being as irritating as they pleased—it didn't make it any easier to be lectured on the finer points of syntax by flesh-peddling high school dropouts for whom English was a second language.

By the time I slipped the final pages into the fax machine, it was well past midnight. Naturally, Stuart Eisenstadt was long gone. Exhausted, I put Cheryl into a cab with instructions to sleep in the next morning. Then I began to make my weary way back home.

As a rule I like the small hours of the morning. The darkness softens the edges of the city, and the deserted streets seem to offer up the illusion of freedom. But tonight I felt restless and dissatisfied, unable to savor even the minor satisfaction of having gotten the Avco letter out on time.

No doubt a good part of my disenchantment was personal. There seemed to be a great deal in my life right now that was either unsettled or outside of my control. After Russell died I had drifted, almost without thinking, back into what could best be described as an arid relationship of convenience with Stephen Azorini. No longer the black sheep of North Shore Country Day, Stephen was now the eminently presentable CEO of a successful, high-tech pharmaceutical company that was also my most important client. We accompanied each other to business dinners and charity balls, with most of these evenings ending in Stephen's bed. This had now been going on long enough and publicly enough that almost everyone assumed there was a level of commitment and affection between us that frankly did not exist.

Stephen loved his business first and himself second, while I was still in love with my dead husband and in no hurry to offer up my heart again. While hardly the stuff of Hallmark cards, it worked, or at least, it had until recently.

In a moment of weakness Stephen and I had bought an apartment together, a once-palatial Lake Shore residence in one of the city's premier buildings that had fallen into disrepair. Perhaps I'd mistaken my love for the apartment (which, even in shambles, was almost heartbreakingly beautiful) for affection for the man, or maybe I'd secretly hoped that it would bring us closer together. Instead, the strain of undertaking the massive and expensive renovation had only seemed to etch the empty spaces in our relationship into sharper relief.

Of course, the lawsuits didn't help. The new apartment occupied the top two floors of a landmark David Adler building on East Lake Shore Drive. Unfortunately, we did not discover until after we'd begun replastering that there was a structural problem with the roof—specifically the thousands of tons of dirt, grass, and trees that our downstairs neighbor had put on top of it to construct a rooftop play area for his children. He'd erected an impressive urban oasis, a sylvan aerie in the very heart of the city. Unfortunately, it was also about to come crashing down through our ceiling.

The downstairs neighbor in question was Paul Riskoff, the abrasive and notoriously combative real estate tycoon. When negotiations broke down, we'd been forced to file a lawsuit against him and obtain a court order allowing us to remove the hazard on the roof. We'd also taken separate actions against the city building inspector who'd initially granted the permit allowing Riskoff to construct the garden (no doubt after his palm had been generously greased), the inspector we'd hired who had failed to detect the problem before closing, and the entire condo board who'd thus far sided with Riskoff. Naturally, none of this had endeared us to our future neighbors.

Since then we'd made steady progress renovating the apartment, and while I still had faith that it would be stunning when all the work was finally completed, I had recently found myself wondering, without any great sense of tragedy, which of us was going to end up moving into it once the last of the paint had dried.

I pulled into the alley behind the Hyde Park apartment I still shared with my roommate and reflected that it had been more than a long day. I was glad to be home. The apartment had originally been Claudia's, rented the day she arrived from New York to begin her surgical residency at the University of Chicago. It was a huge, rambling wreck of a place, reduced to near tenement status by a succession of student renters and in no way improved during our stewardship. The floor tilted wildly, and there were only three windows that opened and closed in the whole place. It hadn't been cleaned since our last cleaning lady quit more than a year earlier.

I unlocked the door and checked the front hall for signs of Claudia's diminutive sneakers, which she invariably kicked off the instant she walked through the door. Unsurprisingly the mat was empty. Now that she was pursuing a fellowship in trauma surgery at Northwestern Memorial, she'd begun spending nearly all her time at the hospital. Still, I was surprised by how disappointed I was to find her not at home. I was more than just physically tired; I was feeling emotionally exhausted and I really didn't want to be alone.

I jumped at the sound of the telephone and hurried across the living room to answer it. By the time I reached the receiver, the adrenaline was already starting to flow. No one calls with good news at two o'clock in the morning.

I picked it up.

"Hi, Kate. It's me, Jeff. I need a favor." It was his usual greeting. During the day it was Chrissy who called. These nocturnal communications were Jeff's specialty.

They'd started almost as soon as Chrissy and Jeff had gotten back from their honeymoon. After all, I was more than just Chrissy's best friend, I was a well-connected Chicago attorney who knew how to keep her mouth shut. I could be useful.

Chicago is only an hour's drive from Milwaukee, even less if you happen to be behind the wheel of a Ferrari. It is also a much better place to party than buttoned-up Milwaukee, especially if you're a twenty-year-old millionaire with more testosterone than common sense. In the cynical world of pro sports it is a given that boys will be boys, and the Monarchs preferred that their boys did their playing in Chicago, away from the prying eyes of the fine, upstanding citizens of Milwaukee. Unfortunately, it is also axiomatic that semiliterate, unsocialized gladiators will occasionally get themselves into trouble.

"Oh, please," I groaned, "no more crimes against women, not after last time."

"Don't worry," Jeff replied. "There were no women involved."

"What is it then? Did some hero wrap himself around a tree and get picked up for DUI? Why don't you call Glen Morrissey? He usually handles those for you guys."

"I don't think he'd come. We haven't paid him for the last two. Besides, this isn't a DUI."

"Then what is it?" I asked, scrabbling through the four days' worth of unread mail that had accumulated on the table for something to write on.

"A player named Jake Palmer. He's the offensive lineman they call Jake the Giant."

"I don't care what position he plays. Just tell me what he did that makes him need a lawyer in the middle of the night."

"I'm a little fuzzy on the details, but apparently he and a bunch of special-teams players decided to drive down to Chicago after the game and drown their sorrows over the loss to Minnesota."

"You guys lost again?"

"Crushed would be a more accurate description. The final score was 27 to 3. I don't know how Bennato has the balls to call himself a football coach."

"So tell me about this guy Palmer," I prodded.

"He and a bunch of special-teams boys drove down to Chicago and hit the bars. I guess somehow or other they ended up at The Baton."

"At The Baton?" I demanded incredulously. "How do a bunch of football players manage to just somehow end up at the most notorious transvestite bar in the city? I'm surprised they'd even let them in the door."

"Apparently not as surprised as Palmer."

"Oh, no."

"Oh, yes. I guess he started buying drinks for some dishy blonde he picked up at the bar. At some point he must have gotten sleepy, because he put his head in her lap. I gather that's when he discovered that—how shall I put this?—things were not exactly as they seemed."

"And let me guess," I practically hooted. "A disturbance broke out." I imagined a three-hundred-pound Gulliver from the University of Alabama warding off the blows of the assembled homosexual population of Lilliput and burst out laughing.

"It's not going to be funny if the press gets hold of this," cut in Jeff. "It's not like we don't already have enough trouble on our hands."

"I'm sorry. What's he been charged with?"

"So far nothing. They took him to the Eighteenth District, but he hasn't been booked. One of the cops recognized him and called me. Luckily he's a fan."

"I suppose you promised him fifty-yard-line seats the next time you play the Bears. . . ."

"Are you kidding? I'd let him bang the entire cheerleading squad if I thought it meant keeping this out of the papers."

CHAPTER

4

The last time I'd made a trip to the Eighteenth District it had almost turned me off not only to football but the entire human race, too, when I realized that people like Darius Fredericks were a part of it. Fredericks had been the Monarchs' first-round draft pick that season, a talented wide receiver who'd gotten himself into some kind of trouble in college—trouble that had been hushed up as he led his team to a national championship. As a pro he also did not disappoint. His first year as a Monarch he made a record-tying one hundred twenty-six receptions and nearly killed a nineteen-year-old call girl in his hotel room after an away game against the Bears.

It had been snowing that night, too.

I'd driven to the Eighteenth District police station in a blizzard and arrived to find Fredericks cocky, unrepentant, and signing autographs for cops and fellow prisoners alike. He'd treated my arrival as he might a plumber coming to unplug his sink—inevitable and unremarkable. As I explained the arrangements I had made for a criminal attorney to represent him, he'd looked bored. We had been talking for several minutes before I realized that the speckles on his expensive silk shirt were not polka dots, but blood. When I left the Eighteenth that night, for the first time in my career I had felt ashamed of being a lawyer.

The surprising thing isn't that he did it. Big men beat the faces of women into hamburger every day. The surprising thing is that he ended up doing time for it. It helped that it was an election year, and that he drew a political and feminist judge. And to their credit, both the Rendells and the league refused to pull any strings to help him get off.

Suddenly I felt like the only person awake and working on the face of the planet. Whoever said misery likes company knew what they were talking about. I picked up my car phone and punched in Claudia's pager number. She called back just as I was passing Soldier Field. I explained my errand and she agreed to meet me at the corner of Fairbanks and Superior. She was already outside and waiting when I got there, a tiny figure in a down parka standing in the light of the emergency room entrance sign, rolling on the balls of her feet to stay awake.

"Don't you think it would be more efficient if they just kept these guys in jail between games?" inquired my roommate as she slid into the passenger seat. She threw back her hood to reveal a face that was deceptively young looking, as pale and unlined as a child's.

"Rough night?" I asked.

"Not too bad. Carrelli is in New York delivering a lecture, so it was torturer's night out."

Carrelli was the head of Claudia's training program, and from what little she had told me about him he made the power-hungry partners at my office look like a bunch of nuns. He was a sadistic egomaniac who believed that the trauma of the surgical training program should in no way be limited to what had been suffered by the patients.

"Sundays are usually pretty quiet anyway," continued my roommate, "though we did have a little bit of excitement this afternoon—a crush injury from a car accident on lower Wacker Drive. A twenty-six-year-old kid spent three hours with his arm pinned under a flipped pickup truck. I got to go out and help with the field amputation. What did you do today?"

"Made the world a better place for topless dancers and dirty old men."

"I can't believe you're *still* working on that strip club deal."

"Still. Always. Forever. I'll be trading faxes and wrangling with the SEC when I'm in the nursing home."

"So what did tonight's football felon do?"

"He's not a felon, at least not yet. Hopefully he's not going to end up being charged with anything."

"Are you going to answer my question and tell me what this guy did, or are you going to give me a lecture on the finer points of the law?"

"He got into a fight with a bunch of drag queens at The Baton."

"Wow," exclaimed my roommate, obviously impressed. "The football players versus the transvestites. It's a wonder he ended up in jail instead of in the hospital."

The Eighteenth District police station is a dismal box of a place erected in the architectural style once favored by urban-renewal advocates in the sixties. On Chicago Ave. just east of Dearborn, it sits just beyond the glittering prosperity of Michigan Avenue. Whether it is because real estate is still at a premium here or because its patrons usually arrive in the back of a blue and white, there is no parking lot at the station. Instead I found an illegal spot in the alley that ran behind the currency exchange next door.

Apparently, it was a busy night. As we passed through doors of heavily scratched bullet-proof glass, we made our way past two hookers in matching patent leather halter tops, being released into the custody of their pimp; an old woman, obviously drunk, decked out in a grimy bathrobe, high heels, and a blond fright wig; and a muscle-bound tough with his hands cuffed behind his back, wearing an immaculately white tennis visor in the latest gangland fashion—turned upside down and backward as if he was hoping to collect rain. There were also a dozen or so theatrically sobbing drag queens nursing their wounds with their wigs askew, demanding either their lawyers or a trip to the ladies' room in disconcertingly deep voices. I hadn't seen so much running mascara since Tammy Faye Baker went off the air.

We pushed through the scuffed and narrow lobby and made our way to the battered linoleum counter. I gave my card to one of the officers behind the desk, who took one look at it, offered up a conspiratorial grin, and ushered us behind a barrier marked POLICE ONLY. He led us down a dark and narrow hallway where the phones pealed, unanswered, while laconic plainclothesmen lounged against the walls and talked in groups, their handcuffs dangling from their belts. Claudia and I followed the sergeant to the second floor by way of a dark staircase that looked like a perfect place for a mugging.

Apparently the cops had stashed Palmer in somebody's office. When the sergeant opened the door, the first thing that hit me was the smell. It was like a mixture of sweat and the inside of a bottle of Jack Daniel's. Jake Palmer lay inert on a torn vinyl couch, emitting whiskey fumes, while a half a dozen cops craned their necks to catch a glimpse of him over each other's heads like gawkers at the scene of an accident.

"I thought the idea was to try to keep this quiet," I complained.

"I don't know, lady," he replied. "A guy this size is pretty hard to miss. Plus, he wasn't exactly this quiet when they brought him in."

Oh, great, I thought to myself. In my experience beauty shops and bingo parlors had nothing on police stations when it came to gossip. Nothing like a couple of hundred men, driving around in cars all day, talking to each other on radios for passing information around.

"I tell you what," I said, handing him another one of my cards. "I want you to get me the name of every officer who was on duty tonight, and I'll make sure that the team takes care of them the next time the Monarchs play Chicago. I'm talking tickets, locker room passes, the VIP treatment—provided, of course, that in addition to no charges being brought, nobody talks to the press."

"Sure thing," he said, palming my card with a grin. When the list came back, it would probably have a hundred names on it, but I figured that was Jeff Rendell's problem. My problem was how to get a three-hundred-pound man out of the police station and into the backseat of my car. While I glumly contemplated the alternatives, Claudia elbowed her way in for a better look.

Jake Palmer was simply enormous. His head, shaved bald, hung backward over the arm of the couch. His mouth hung open, exposing white teeth and a pink, orcalike tongue. His feet seemed roughly the same size as Claudia, who laid her tiny hand against the massive cylinder of corded muscle that supported his head, checking for a pulse.

She turned to the cop standing closest to her. "When I wake him up, I want you to be ready to help him to his feet," she instructed in the quiet manner of one who is used to giving orders and having them followed without question.

"And how do you think you're going to be able to do that, sweetie?" he asked, unable to conceal his amusement.

"That's Dr. Sweetie to you," Claudia replied, unfazed.

She dug into the pocket of her jacket and pulled out a small ampoule of smelling salts.

I had to admit that it was an elegant and audacious plan.

She broke it open quickly, held it directly under Jake the Giant's nose, and then neatly stepped out of the way. He was on his feet in an instant, roaring like he'd been stung, and looking around for someone to take it out on. For an instant I had to fight the urge to run, and I immediately discovered a newfound respect for bullfighters, rodeo clowns, and anybody else who was willing to get into the ring with three hundred pounds of thundering flesh.

Fortunately, this wasn't the first time the cops of the Eighteenth had been called upon to wrestle a drunk. Eventually, using the same technique that is used for herding angry elephants, they managed to get him on his feet and set him moving toward the door. However, getting him into my Volvo was a whole new adventure.

As soon as we got him out on the sidewalk and into the cold air, he seemed to take notice of where he was and started bellowing about police brutality until I was sure that we were going to draw a crowd. He also took a swing at one of the officers who had the good sense to duck. Surprisingly it was Claudia who got him into the car. She grabbed his arm and twisted it with a well-practiced snap behind his back and used it as a lever to maneuver him into the backseat. I wondered whether this was something they taught in medical school or whether it was just something you had to pick up on the job.

I thanked the cops profusely, hopped behind the wheel, and stepped on the gas. It wasn't until we were rolling that I realized that I had absolutely no idea where we were going. When I stopped at the red light at Michigan and Chicago, Jake the Giant reached over the seat and tapped me on the shoulder. It was like being hit with a ham.

"Who the fuck are you?" he demanded in the unmodulated bellow of the truly plastered.

"My name is Kate Millholland. I'm the attorney sent by the team to pick you up and take you home."

"There's no way I'm goin' back to Alabama!" he screamed. Every time he opened his mouth, he seemed to emit an alcoholic breeze. I could hear him scrabbling in the dark for the door handle and prayed that he was too drunk to find it.

"We're not taking you back to Alabama," I assured him hastily. I was still wondering where exactly it was that we were going to take him.

"Where do you live?" asked Claudia.

"Great house, real big, all full of marble and shit. You want to come and check it out, baby? You want to come over, go skinny-dippin' in my hot tub?"

"I'm afraid I'm going to have to decline that very kind offer," replied my roommate, who as a rule preferred to deal with people while they were safely under anesthesia.

"I'm sure he lives in Milwaukee," I sighed, wondering why this simple fact had not previously occurred to me.

"Then what are we going to do with him?"

"Let's just take him back to the apartment. He can sleep it off on the couch."

"Surely you're kidding."

"Do you have a better idea?"

Her silence formed an eloquent reply.

We rolled down the windows for the rest of the ride. Even if the cold air didn't actually sober him up, I hoped it would at least keep him from throwing up. The inside of the Volvo, which I used interchangeably as a garbage can, was already disgusting enough without adding the eruptions of an offensive lineman to the mess.

By the time we arrived in Hyde Park, Jake the Giant was sound asleep and snoring.

"Can't we just let him sleep it off in the car?" inquired Claudia as we pulled into the parking space behind our apartment.

"I don't know," I replied dubiously. "It's pretty cold. What if he dies of hypothermia?"

"You're right. I guess the Monarchs would be pretty pissed off if you accidentally killed him."

"That's not it," I replied, grabbing one of Palmer's legs and starting to pull. "I was just thinking that once rigor mortis set in they'd have to saw the damn car in half in order to get him out."

The next morning I slept through my alarm, and by the time I finally got out of bed, both Jake Palmer and Claudia were already gone. I might have imagined the entire episode except that the blanket we'd used to cover him was still there, lying neatly folded on the end of the couch. He'd also left an autographed football card on the kitchen table along with five crisp, new one-hundred-dollar bills. He'd probably taken a good look at the apartment and decided we could use the money.

I took my time getting ready, deciding that I deserved it, and took a detour to the Starbucks across the street after I parked my car at the office. Juggling two hot lattes and my briefcase, I arrived upstairs and set them all on top of Cheryl's desk. From the pocket of my coat I extracted the money that Jake the Giant had left and handed it to my secretary.

"What's this?" she asked, her head cocked to one side.

"Donation to your scholarship fund. Bring in your pad and I'll tell you where to send the thank-you note." I picked up my coffee and stopped in my tracks. "Before you do that," I added, "do me a favor and get Jeff Rendell on the phone for me."

"He already called. There was a message on your voice mail when I got in."

"What did he say?"

"Just thanks for picking up the package."

"Some package."

I hung up my coat, gave my hair a distracted pat, and made my way to my desk, which was already lined with dozens of pink message slips arranged by Cheryl in order of importance. I picked up the first one; it was from my mother reminding me that Stephen and I were scheduled to meet the following afternoon with the decorator to make our final selections of fabrics and wallcoverings. Stephen had already canceled or rescheduled four times.

"I want you to call Rachel over at Azor and tell her that if Stephen isn't back from London tomorrow afternoon and at the meeting with the decorator as promised, his ass is grass," I said.

"Do I detect a hint of irritation in the famously unruffled Millholland manner?" demanded my secretary impishly.

"I swear, if I have to face my mother and Mimi and talk about wallpaper all by myself, I really am going to kill him."

My phone rang, and I pushed it across my desk to my secretary. I make it a policy to never answer my own phone when my mother is in town. Cheryl shot me a look.

"Oh, come on," I pleaded. "If it's her, just tell her I'm in a meeting or something."

"You are such a baby," replied Cheryl, who was happy to talk to her own mother every day. But then, of course, her mother was a normal person. "Good morning, Ms. Millholland's office," she chirped with exaggerated cheerfulness. She listened briefly, her smile slowly dissolving into an expression of concern. "She's right here," she said. Then she put her hand over the receiver. "It's Chrissy Rendell," she whispered, and handed me the phone.

"Hi there," I said.

"Oh my god, Kate, I'm so glad you're there." She sounded breathless and upset, her words practically tumbling over each other.

"What's wrong?" I demanded.

"I just got home from the grocery store. When I walked in the door, the phone was ringing and I rushed to answer it. It was a reporter."

"Oh, no," I groaned. It was hoping too much that of all the people at The Baton last night there wouldn't be at least one who would talk. "How bad is it?"

"It's terrible," she sobbed.

"Why don't you just try to calm down and tell me everything that's happened."

"I don't know how it happened. Nobody told me anything. All I know is that he's dead."

"Dead?" I demanded. Suddenly I felt sick. I should never have let Jake out of my sight. I thought of the blanket and the football card and wondered where he'd gone after he left my apartment. "How did he die?"

"The reporter didn't know."

"Where did it happen?"

"At the stadium. They found him at the bottom of the stairs leading up to his office."

"Whose office?" I inquired. Football players didn't have offices, at least not at the stadium they didn't.

"His office," she replied.

"Who are we talking about?" I was starting to feel confused.

"Beau."

"Beau's dead?" I demanded incredulously.

"Yes. Who did you think we were talking about?"

"What can I do?" I asked automatically, not yet able to let the implications of the news sink in.

"Just come," whispered my best friend from the time we were both thirteen. "Please, just come."

CHAPTER

5

In an instant everything changes. An event, a piece of information, and suddenly your world shudders, convulses, and reconfigures into something else. Whenever Chrissy and Jeff looked back, they would remember this as being the day, the nexus around which everything had shifted. I knew that I should have felt more sorry, but as I threw my briefcase into the back of my car all I could think of was that by dying, Beau Rendell had taken the easy way out.

Of course, Chrissy didn't want me to come because she needed my sympathy. I'm sure there were people in Milwaukee who were already lining up to offer their shoulders for her tears. No, she and Jeff needed me for something else. People in their position are afforded many things, but the luxury of time for grief is not one of them. When Beau threw off his mortal coil, he left his son in a world of trouble. I was one of the handful of people who not only knew, but was also in a position to do something about it.

Under the best of circumstances the drive to Milwaukee is nothing but a boring gauntlet of tollbooths, cheese shops, and outlet malls. Today, desperate to get there and cursing every orange construction cone, it was also an agony. By the time I arrived at Beau Rendell's house, the street was already lined with cars. I parked mine at the end of the block and hoped that I wasn't violating a community ordinance against rust.

River Hills is an exclusive community where the residents live in splendid, pseudorural isolation. The houses were enormous, the lots ran to acres, and the grocery store parking lot looked like a Range Rover dealership. Beau Rendell's house was considered the local eyesore. He'd built it twenty years ago when he was between wives, hoping to erect a swinging bachelor pad. Now, of course, it looked hopelessly dated, as if someone had consulted Hugh Hefner for ideas about what was hip. I wondered who would buy it now that Beau was dead.

Inside the color scheme was black and white, and as I pushed open the front door, I felt like I was stepping inside a pair of dice. I pulled the door shut behind me and made sure that it was locked. Most likely the people who had already arrived were friends of Beau who had come to pay their respects, but I knew that it was only a matter of time before the curious started showing up.

I found Chrissy in the kitchen looking perfect. She was dressed in a simple black pantsuit, and with her blond hair pulled into a tortoiseshell clip and her flawlessly understated makeup, she looked like a tasteful advertisement for grief. She was staring at the innards of an old-fashioned percolator looking as though if she just stared at it long enough, it might give up its secrets.

"Have you ever made coffee in one of these things?" she asked, as if picking up the thread of a conversation that had only recently been interrupted.

"Is that what that's for?" I asked. "I thought it was a small still. The crowd out there looks like they would prefer gin. Who are all those people?"

"I don't know most of them. I think they must be neighbors. Of course, Coach Bennato's wife, Marie, was the first to arrive. She and their weird daughter, Debra, brought along a lovely tuna casserole. I don't know when they even had time to make it. They must have cooked it in the car on the way over. . . ."

"Well, put that thing away. You don't have to entertain anybody today. Where's Jeff?"

"He's still down at the stadium. Harald Feiss called a couple of minutes ago and said that they'd be leaving soon."

"So do they know what happened yet?"

"According to Harald, they think Beau either had a heart attack and fell down the stairs, or he fell down the stairs and had a heart attack. I guess at this point it doesn't matter. . . ." She began slowly winding the cord to the coffeepot into a careful bundle, a task that seemed to require all of her attention. "I know it sounds awful to be even thinking about money at a time like this," she continued finally, in a small voice, "but I guess that's what happens when you don't have any."

"It's not awful," I assured her. "Under the circumstances it's the most natural thing in the world."

"So what's all this going to mean?"

"Financially? It's hard to say without knowing what Beau's testamentary plans were."

"You mean like his will?"

"Yes, that and any irrevocable trusts he might have set up. Who handled his estate planning, do you know?"

"I'm sure it was Harald Feiss. He handled all of my father-in-law's business and financial affairs."

"I know that Beau relied on him heavily for advice," I began, carefully, "and the last thing I want to do is put pressure on you and Jeff, but the two of you should probably decide fairly quickly how you feel about continuing that relationship."

"We both think that Harald's an ass," said Chrissy simply. "If Beau had had someone who knew what they were doing advising him, he'd never have gotten into this mess in the first place."

"Then you're going to have to decide who you want acting on your behalf. I guarantee you that Harald is expecting to take charge of things, especially until after the funeral. He'll see it as a kindness—"

"Will you do it?"

"Do what?"

"Help us."

"Of course, I'll help you," I replied without hesitation. "But no matter what, handling Feiss is going to be a delicate business. Don't forget your father-in-law wasn't just his closest friend, but his most important professional connection. This has to be disastrous for him on every level. No matter what, you want to keep him on your side. Not only is he a minority shareholder in the team, but he's the person who has the most intimate knowledge of Beau's business affairs. To put it another way, he knows where all the bodies are buried."

"Yes," replied Chrissy, "but that's only because he's the one who buried them."

In the end it was Coach Bennato not Harald Feiss who brought Jeff back from the stadium. They slipped into the house through the garage after having somehow managed to avoid the news crews who'd begun to congregate on the front lawn hoping to get footage of the still-arriving mourners, or better yet, the grieving family, to air during the five o'clock news. Both men had the empty, sheep-like look that I have come to associate with sudden grief. Pale-faced and shaken, even their tread was gingerly, as if in the aftermath of calamity they had suddenly lost their faith in everything including the ability of the floor to remain solid beneath their feet.

"You'd better take him upstairs and make him lie

down," said Bennato to Chrissy, a note of something very close to warning in his voice.

Chrissy nodded wordlessly and took her husband by the hand. Jeff, bewildered and completely undone by grief, was apparently in no condition to resist. Chrissy put her arm around her husband's waist and, as if helping an invalid, led him from the room murmuring words of comfort and encouragement.

Coach Bennato, no stranger to Beau's kitchen, immediately made for the liquor cabinet. As he opened the doors it was pretty clear that Beau Rendell would have never died from thirst. Bennato selected a bottle of Balvenie single malt Scotch from among the dozens of bottles and helped himself to a generous dose. Although legendary for his nerves of steel, as he poured his drink his hands shook badly, like an alcoholic in need of a drink or a temperate man suffering from shock. He knocked it back in a single shot and quickly poured himself another.

Now that we were alone I found it strange to see Coach Bennato in person. He was much bigger than I'd imagined from all the shots of him pacing up and down the sidelines. He also seemed older and, if anything, less genial. In person you could see that the wrinkles in his face were as deep as channels and that his knuckles, like his nose, bore the signs of having been broken more than once during his career as a player.

The man himself was a mass of contradictions. One local sportswriter who described him best said that Bennato had the face of a parish priest, the vocabulary of a sailor, and the temperament of Attila the Hun. Mercurial, methodical, and prone to sweeping fits of both rage and generosity, he had at some point in his long career been the winningest and losingest coach in the league. He'd been hated, loved, reviled, and carried off the field in triumph.

He was a cagey and complicated man. Born in Palermo,

in either a tenement or a manger depending on who was telling the story, he immigrated to America with his parents when he was three. His father found work in the oilfields and he spent his childhood moving from one dusty wildcatting site to another along the Texas panhandle, proving himself with his fists in every new town.

Legend has it that it was a judge who ordered him to play football. Bennato was fourteen and had been hauled before him after one scrape or another and he'd been given the choice of working his aggression out on the gridiron or in juvenile hall. I had no idea whether the story was true. He played second string in college, spent an undistinguished season in the pros, and immediately went into coaching, landing a spot as an assistant to Joe Paterno in his first year at Penn State.

After three years at Penn State, Bennato returned to Texas and landed his first head coaching job. Apparently his fiery temper served him well, and after ten years as a head coach he had two national championships under his belt and a reputation for fashioning winning teams out of losers. Celebrated for his ability to turn green young men into effective gladiators as well as for giving rich boosters something to open up their wallets for, by all accounts he was on top of the world.

Then a second-string quarterback said something Bennato didn't like, and Bennato grabbed him by the throat, an action that was only remarkable for the fact that it was captured on national TV. The very same people who stood up and cheered when the players knocked each other down and ground their opponents' faces into the mud recoiled in horror at this display of violence. The boy's family sued. The university, eager to avoid the publicity of a trial, pressured Bennato to avoid the courtroom at any cost. The ensuing settlement forced him into bankruptcy while the scandal sent him into obscurity—which is where he remained until four years later when Beau Rendell offered him a coaching job.

"Who are you?" demanded Bennato, setting down his glass and apparently realizing for the first time that he was not alone in Beau Rendell's kitchen.

"Kate Millholland," I said, extending my hand. "I'm a friend of Chrissy and Jeff's."

"Tony Bennato," he said, taking my hand and giving it a rough tug. "If you're a friend of Chrissy's, then maybe you should be the one to go upstairs and give her this," he continued, pulling out a business envelope bearing the Monarchs logo and handing it to me.

"What is it?" I demanded, lifting the flap and looking inside. It was full of small white tablets, dozens of them.

"Sleeping pills. The team doctor wants Jeff to take two of them now. The rest are for later."

"He doesn't need them," I said, handing the envelope back to the coach.

"You don't understand—" protested Bennato, refusing to take them back.

"Yes, I do," I cut in. "Sleeping won't help anything." I knew what I was talking about. If I'd taken every sleeping pill that was pushed on me after Russell died, I would have been out longer than Sleeping Beauty.

"You're not listening to me," protested Coach impatiently. "He has to take them."

"He'll be fine now that he's with Chrissy."

"I'm not concerned about whether he's fine or not," snapped Bennato. "The cops are going to be here pretty soon, and when they show up, I think it'll be better for everybody if Jeff's sound asleep."

"Why do you say that?" I demanded, not sure I wanted to hear the answer.

"Let's just say that things got a little out of hand at the stadium."

"In what way?"

"I was in the front office when they found him. Beau said he wanted to see me about something so I left practice and went upstairs. When I got there the security guard had just found him."

"Where was he?"

"Lying at the bottom of the stairs that lead up to his office. I guess the guard was making his normal rounds and literally stumbled upon him lying in the dark on the D concourse."

"Dead?"

"Probably, but there was no way of knowing at the time. The security guard called the paramedics and I went and got the team doctor out of the training room."

"Where was Jeff?"

"At first we couldn't find him. We turned the place inside out, looking for him. It turns out he was in the john washing his hands."

"So when did things get out of hand?" I asked.

"When we told him about what had happened to his father."

"Why? How did he take it?"

"He went berserk," replied Bennato with no attempt to conceal his distaste.

"What do you mean?"

"He ran downstairs to where the paramedics were working on Beau, yanked them off of him, and shoved them aside. Then he grabbed his father by the front of his shirt and started shaking him."

"Maybe he was trying to revive him," I suggested.

"I don't think so," replied Bennato, taking another sip of Scotch and rolling it around as if he was trying to wash away the bad taste in his mouth. "Not unless you think he was trying to wake him up by screaming, 'You asshole! You asshole!' " at the top of his lungs.

* * *

I found Jeff in his old bedroom lying curled up on his side on the bottom bunk of his childhood bed. Chrissy knelt on the floor beside him, stroking his hair. The room itself was a time warp of purple and gold. There was shag carpeting on the floor and curling posters of Monarchs players gone by on the walls. I wondered when the last time was that he had crossed the threshold.

I was obviously less appalled by Jeff's behavior at the stadium than Coach Bennato was. From my perspective, given the Rendells' financial straits, it was as understandable as it was regrettable. Unfortunately, neither the paramedics nor the scores of front office personnel who must have witnessed the outburst had any idea of what had been behind it. They were probably on the phone right now peddling their eyewitness accounts to the tabloids.

However, it did raise another issue, one that hadn't occurred to me until I spoke to the Monarchs coach, and that was what, if anything, to tell the police about the team's financial situation. The police conduct a routine investigation of every unattended death, and in the case of someone as prominent as Beau Rendell they would go out of their way to make sure that every *i* was dotted and every *t* was crossed. They were sure to have questions about what had prompted Jeff Rendell's outburst over his father's body, and they would be expecting answers.

Even though the door was open, I knocked softly on the doorframe. Jeff did not seem to hear, but Chrissy looked up, her eyes wide with distress.

"I'm sorry to interrupt," I said. "But I need to talk to you guys for a minute."

"What is it?" asked Chrissy in a whisper.

"I need to ask Jeff whether he talked to the police at all while he was still down at the stadium."

Jeff shook his head.

"What would the police want with Jeff?" inquired Chrissy.

"They're going to want to talk to everyone who was anywhere near Beau before he died. They have to try and piece together what must have happened by talking to anyone who was at the stadium this morning."

"I don't want to talk to anyone," said Jeff, practically in a whimper.

"I don't think you should," I replied. "At least, not until we've worked out what to tell them about what's happening with the team and the bank."

"Oh, god, I never thought about that," gasped Chrissy. "If you tell the police about it, you might as well put the whole thing up on billboards. Someone will leak it."

"That's why I agree with Coach Bennato. It's best if Jeff doesn't talk to the police right now. Let them find out more about how Beau died. The more they know, the fewer questions they'll have left. I guess the team doctor prescribed some sleeping pills for Jeff," I ventured, opening the envelope, taking out two of the pills, and handing the envelope to Chrissy. "I think it's best if you hold on to these," I said. It didn't seem like a particularly good idea to give handfuls of barbiturates to someone in Jeff's frame of mind.

Jeff propped himself up on one elbow. "Why don't you get me a glass of water so I can take these things?" he asked his wife.

"Sure thing, sweetheart," she replied, giving him a quick kiss on the forehead before getting to her feet to fetch it.

Jeff waited until she was out of the room before he spoke, and then it was in an urgent whisper.

"Did Bennato tell you how I acted when they told me what happened to my dad?" he asked miserably.

"You went into shock," I replied.

"I went insane."

"Don't say that," I said. "Besides, there's nothing you can do about it now."

"I need you to do something for me."

"Anything," I replied, meaning it.

"I need you to keep something," he said, pulling something from his pocket and thrusting it into my hand. "Don't tell anyone else you have it," he whispered quickly, as Chrissy stepped back into the room.

I silently made a fist around the jagged edges of the object. It was a key.

CHAPTER

6

I put the key in my pocket and made my way downstairs, not quite sure what to do next. In the kitchen, Harald Feiss had replaced Coach Bennato at the Scotch bottle, but from the look of desolation on his face I found myself wondering if there was enough alcohol in the world to soften the blow of what he was going through.

What are you doing here?" he asked unpleasantly, spying me over the top of his glass.

"I came as soon as I heard."

"Business must not be too good if you have to drive all the way to Milwaukee trying to drum up clients."

"Listen, Harald. You were Beau's good friend. I'm Chrissy's. Let's just leave it at that. Sometimes at a time like this, things get said that people later wish they could take back."

"So, with your vast experience, you're lecturing me on behavior?" he demanded sarcastically.

"Harald, take my word for it," I replied in my most conciliatory tone. "It is not my intention to say anything that would hurt or offend you, especially not today."

Feiss, apparently mollified, reached for the bottle and refilled his glass. I suspected that he was the same kind of alcoholic as my father, the kind who drank constantly but was seldom drunk.

"Chrissy and I were talking earlier, and she said that

you handled all of Beau's affairs, including his estate planning."

"Yes, I did."

"So how did he leave things?"

"Everything goes to Jeff."

"Absolutely everything?"

"Yes. Everything."

"Who's the executor?"

"Jeff."

I was grateful that it wasn't Feiss, but I tried not to show it. "So how did he leave it? Is there an *in vivo* trust in effect or any other mechanism that would limit tax liability?"

"Originally there was, but we were forced to dissolve it as a condition of the loan agreement with First Milwaukee. Gus Wallenberg insisted that if he was going to lend Beau the money, the Monarchs' assets not be sheltered in a trust."

"You mean he wanted to make sure that the bank had a clean shot at the assets if Beau couldn't make his payments."

"You'd have to ask Wallenberg. I don't know what his thinking was, I only know what's in the agreement."

"But you do know what Beau was thinking. You were his closest confidant. He may have kept secrets from Jeff, but he didn't keep any from you. So what I want to know is what was he planning to do to keep the bank off his back?"

"He was about to sign a deal to move the team into a new stadium in the suburbs."

"How close was he?"

"The developer was in the process of drawing up the contracts. As soon as they were signed, Beau would have gotten the check."

"How big a check?"

"Enough to satisfy the bank."

"I assume the developer would be willing to deal with Jeff."

"The question is will Jeff be willing to deal with them?"

"I'm sure at this point Jeff just wants to keep all of his options open."

"That's not what it sounded like this morning."

"What do you mean?"

"You haven't heard about the scene this morning?"

"Are you talking about Jeff's behavior when he found out about his father's death?"

"No. I'm talking about the shouting match he had with Beau just before he died."

Great, I thought to myself. And the hits just keep right on coming. Out loud I asked, "What did they fight about?"

"The bank, moving the team. Gus Wallenberg was on his way down to the stadium to talk about the financing for the new stadium. Jeff wanted his dad to show Wallenberg L.A.'s offer in order to put pressure on the bank."

"And did he?"

"By the time Wallenberg showed up, Beau was already at the bottom of the stairs."

"So do you know whether Jeff got his father to agree to try to negotiate with the bank for more time?"

"You'll have to ask Jeff, but I can tell you from the way that it sounded, I'm pretty sure they didn't agree about anything. Where is Jeff, by the way? I haven't seen him."

"He's upstairs, asleep. He took a sleeping pill so I'm sure he'll be out for a while."

"Good."

"Why do you say that?"

"Because when he wakes up, he's going to have to deal with the fact that the very last thing he probably told his father was that he could take his football team and shove it right up his ass."

* * *

The police showed up while Harald Feiss was standing on the front lawn, bathed in klieg lights, issuing a statement on behalf of the family that no one had authorized—not Jeff, who was still deep in pharmacologically induced slumber, nor Chrissy, who was standing beside me silently fuming as we watched from an upstairs window. As soon as the police pulled into the driveway, I ran outside to intercept them. Thankfully, the reporters were too busy hanging on Feiss's every cliché to notice. No one ever accused TV journalists of being newshounds.

Two men with neat ties and shiny shoes got out of a white Caprice, flashed their badges at me, and identified themselves. They were both middle aged, rheumy eyed, and remote. The taller of the two said his name was Eiben. He had a lean, pockmarked face and a brush cut. He spoke with the kind of bland courtesy that's taught in customer service training courses. The other man's name was Zellmer. He was older, thicker, and wore his thinning gray hair in a comb-over that was remarkable if only for its ambition. Everything about them said cop.

I led them down the garden path and through the garage into the house so that they wouldn't bump into anybody. Then I ushered them into the bookless room that Beau Rendell had called his library. It had white shag carpeting, black leather furniture, and a wet bar. All it was missing was a painting of Elvis on black velvet.

"We're here to speak to Jeffrey Rendell," said Eiben, looking around and taking it all in.

"I'm sorry, but I'm afraid that's not possible right now," I replied, doing my best to sound apologetic.

"I'm not sure I understand. When we spoke to his attorney at the stadium, he promised to make him available to be interviewed when we came out this afternoon."

"Unfortunately, he's been given a sedative on doctor's orders. He's sound asleep."

"Now why would he need a sedative?" inquired Eiben earnestly, as if he really wanted to know.

"I don't know. You'd have to ask the doctor."

"I'm asking you."

"I don't like to speculate, but maybe it has something to do with the fact that Jeff was very upset by his father's death."

"How upset?"

"I don't know," I shot back. "How upset would you be if your father had just died?"

"My father died when I was four," deadpanned Eiben. "He got drunk and fell down a well. When do you think that Mr. Rendell might be available to make a statement?"

"I would think sometime tomorrow."

"Would you mind explaining to us exactly what your relationship is to the Rendells?"

"I'm a personal friend of Jeff and his wife. I'm also their attorney."

"So who was this guy Feiss we talked to this morning?"

"He was Beau Rendell's lawyer and business adviser."

"That's a lot of lawyers. I guess it's the money that attracts you guys—kind of like maggots and old meat."

"What a delightful metaphor," I replied in my best imitation of my mother at her most charming. "I hope you don't mind if I use it sometime."

"So I take it you knew the Rendells pretty well," he continued, ignoring my attempt to be irritating.

"I guess you could say that."

"So how would you characterize the deceased's relationship with his son?"

"Jeff and his father were very close. They had worked together every day for nearly a decade."

"Would you say they got along?"

"No better or worse than a lot of fathers and sons."

"Would you say that Jeff and his father argued a great deal?"

"I'd say that Beau argued with everyone. I'm sure you read the sports pages."

"You can't always believe everything you read in the papers," observed Zellmer sagely.

"True. Beau was the Monarchs' owner. His son was the team's general manager. Owners and general managers disagree all the time about what's best for the team. Jeff's personal relationship with his father was a close one."

"So you wouldn't be surprised to learn that Jeff Rendell and his father had a violent argument this morning?"

"I told you, Detective. Owners and general managers invariably disagree, often acrimoniously, and especially when a team is doing as badly as the Monarchs are this season. So, to answer your question, no, it wouldn't surprise me in the least."

The two detectives exchanged a quick glance, like the shorthand of two people who have been married a long time, and they rose to their feet in unison.

"Well, thank you for your time," said Eiben, patting his pockets and extracting a business card. "You've been very helpful." He handed it to me. "Please make sure that Jeff Rendell gets in touch with us as soon as he's able."

"Of course," I replied.

"Do you mind if we have a look around on our way out?" asked Eiben.

"Not if you have a search warrant."

"Well then, I guess we'll be on our way."

"Let me show you out," I said, following them through the kitchen and walking them back out to their car. In the little time we'd been talking, the wind had picked up and the temperature had dropped at least ten degrees. I blew on my hands and watched the detectives as they got into their car and drove away. In spite of the cold I stood there long after they'd disappeared from sight.

No pun intended; Milwaukee was a town where the Monarchs were king. For years the Rendells had been among its most prominent citizens. All things considered, I'd expected a lot more bowing and scraping with profuse apologies thrown in for intruding at this terrible time of tragedy. Indeed, the more I thought about it, the more I found the detectives' hard-nosed and businesslike approach profoundly disturbing.

There are no secrets for the dead, especially the rich. Lawyers and accountants turn their lives inside out like a pair of pants, looking for loose change. As I made my way to Beau's study I consoled myself with the fact that wherever Beau was, at least he was no longer in a position to object. Not that anyone familiar with Beau's current balance sheet would have mistaken him for wealthy. Still, Chrissy was so furious at Feiss for presuming to speak for the family that she asked me to have a look through Beau's papers. At least that way there would be someone who would be able to tell if something turned up missing later.

Beau's study was a large, masculine room that was part office, part refuge, and part shrine to football. The massive credenza was crowded with power photos, honors, and awards. Autographed footballs sealed in Lucite sarcophagi, trophies, and plaques of every shape and size filled the bookshelves. Signed jerseys of famous Monarchs players were stretched, framed, and displayed on the walls like fine art.

Of course, all these were just token symbols of the much larger prize. When it comes right down to it, an NFL team is the biggest, best, and most testosterone-induced trophy of them all. After all, there are only thirty of them, and together the owners form the most exclusive old boys' club in the world. This was the place where Beau had come to savor it. Looking around, I suddenly understood the desperation he must have felt at the prospect of having to give it all up.

The room still smelled of his cigars. The soft leather of his chair still bore the impression of his body. On his desk beside the telephone was a roll of blueprints held together with a red rubber band and a pencil that lay exactly where it had left his hand. What had he been thinking, ten days away from losing it all?

I sat myself down in his chair and unrolled the blueprints, expecting to see the architect's drawings for the proposed new stadium in suburban Wauwatosa. Instead, I was surprised to find a set of ambitious renderings for the proposed renovation of the existing Monarchs Stadium downtown. Curious, I laid them flat and examined them one by one.

From what I could tell, it looked like a daring plan, one that called for the existing structure to be almost totally rebuilt and the field to be lowered eight feet. This would make way for a new deck of luxury seating. In addition, the present-day lower deck would be ripped out and replaced with restaurants and restrooms. I loved the concept, but then again, concepts are cheap. I wondered if the city also had a plan for how to pay for it.

I looked in the folder that lay underneath the drawings and found my answer. Inside was what looked like a scribbled term sheet, probably handwritten during the course of a meeting, which outlined a proposal that cobbled together a package of deferred tax credits, income from a naming fee for rechristening the renovated stadium, additional parking revenues, and an 8 percent sin tax on tobacco and alcohol. Quickly adding the numbers in my head, I realized that with a little bit of creative massaging, they might be stretched to cover the deficit with the bank, as well. Unfortunately, there was no way of telling whether what I was looking at represented what Beau had asked for or what the city was offering.

I made a mental note to call the mayor's office, pleased at the prospect of possibly having another variable to play with. Then with a sigh I turned my attention to the rest of Beau's desk. A cursory look through the first drawer was enough to tell me that it contained the story of a man pushed to the very edge of ruin. All the files were neatly labeled and arrayed in chronological order. The checkbooks were reconciled to the penny. I found it heartbreaking to see the full scope of the disaster laid out in such an orderly fashion.

I found records from five different banks, each with multiple accounts in the names of the various holding companies through which he conducted business. They were all shockingly overdrawn. Beau had also margined his stocks. Loan documents filed with the secretaries of state in Illinois and Wisconsin revealed heavy borrowing by Rendell using everything from NFL TV rights to athletic equipment as collateral. Although league rules set strict limits on how much could be borrowed against the team, they didn't limit borrowing by the Stadium Corporation, which Beau also controlled, and the Monarchs had taken full advantage of the loophole. My heart leapt as I stumbled across a file containing a $2 million life insurance policy, but further examination revealed that it had already been completely borrowed against years ago. Even his credit cards were maxed out, and the dunning letters had acquired an ugly, hectoring tone.

It wasn't until I got to the bottom drawer that I found the gun—a dull gray Glock 9mm semiautomatic with its distinctive flat composite finish. I picked it up, the composition grip fitting snugly into the palm of my hand. I checked the magazine. It was loaded.

I weighed the pistol in my hand and thought about Beau Rendell sitting where I sat now, filing the threatening letters from the bank. Had he thought about the gun? How could he have not? I opened my hand. The Glock lay across my palm. Perhaps I'd stumbled across another of Beau's plans, the one he hadn't shared with either Harald Feiss or his son, Jeff. I returned the gun to its place in the drawer and realized that I shouldn't have been so surprised. Surely Beau Rendell would not have been the first man who'd contemplated ending his life rather than face public humiliation at the hands of a bank.

CHAPTER

7

Afternoon ground on into evening in the strange cocktail-party torpor that so often follows a death. People arrived to pay their respects, utter platitudes, and console each other in hushed whispers—even as they pressed for details of the tragedy. Jack McWhorter arrived with the second wave of mourners. Gravely handsome and solicitous, he quickly proceeded to fill in for Jeff at Chrissy's side. Chrissy, for her part, seemed grateful for his presence, if only to escape the further well-meaning ministrations of Coach Bennato's wife. It had started to snow, and the front hall quickly filled with boots. Outside the reporters trampled the front lawn into mud.

The phone rang constantly, and I found myself answering it. Reporters called from all over the country wanting to confirm the details of Beau's death and troll for quotes. In between, I spoke to the *Milwaukee Journal Sentinel* about the death notice and obituary, set up an appointment the next day at the funeral home for Chrissy and Jeff, and tried to stay on top of things at my office. Every few minutes someone appeared in the kitchen with a fruit basket or another casserole until the refrigerator was full and the counters overflowing.

By dinnertime the visitors began drifting off, murmuring their farewells, their duty done. Even Harald Feiss, who'd worked the door like a host at a party, finally went home. For better or for worse Jeff slept through all of it. As Chrissy said good-bye to the last of the callers I hung up the phone and turned my attention to the gift baskets, trying to figure out which one contained the most chocolate. By the time I heard the front door slam and Chrissy's exhausted sigh of relief, I had cracked open a box of Godivas and was setting up for a three-course meal—dark, milk, and truffles for dessert.

Chrissy walked into the kitchen, slowly pulling off her earrings. I offered her the box, but she shook her head.

"My feet hurt," she said, pulling up a chair and kicking off her shoes, "and I'm sick of acting sad, and I'm tired of people telling me what a wonderful man my father-in-law was, and I can't wait to get the hell out of this awful house."

"Where's Jack?"

"He left about an hour ago. I asked him to go back to my house and drive the baby-sitter home."

"Are you sure you can trust him with the baby-sitter?" I asked lightly. "He's probably got her parked in some dark alley right now telling her all about big, bad L.A."

"I make it a policy to hire only little old ladies to baby-sit. I mean, Jeff's a lamb, but why put temptation in his way?"

"So who's with the baby now?"

"My housekeeper, Greta."

"Another little old lady?"

"No, a two-hundred-pound German woman. She has arms like a stevedore and a little mustache—"

"I think it's time for you to go home, too." I laughed.

"I have to wait for Jeff. I don't want him to wake up alone in his father's house."

"That's okay. I'll wait. You need to get out of here."

"Are you sure?"

"Absolutely."

"I don't know how to thank you," she said, getting to her feet. "I'll make sure the guest room's all ready for you and I'll even leave a mint on your pillow."

"You don't have to do that," I said. "Actually, I was thinking that I'd just get a hotel room downtown somewhere. You guys don't exactly need company right now."

"You aren't company."

"You know what I mean. I also figured that if it's okay with you and Jeff, I might pay a call on Gus Wallenberg down at First Milwaukee first thing tomorrow morning. I figure that under the circumstances we might be able to get him to work with you on this."

"You mean give us more time?"

"More time, maybe an opportunity to restructure the loan—we'll have to see what I can talk him into. . . ."

"Do you really think he might?" she asked. I found her eagerness almost heartbreaking.

"I don't see why not," I replied. "Beau's death changes everything. But we won't know unless we sit down and talk to him."

"You have no idea how grateful I am that you're willing to try to help us sort out this whole mess," said Chrissy.

"Sorting out these kinds of messes is what I do for a living, my dear. It's a pleasure to do it for a friend for a change."

"I take it you haven't finished with that deal you love so much, the one where you're raising money for those strip clubs."

"Soon, I hope."

"I've heard that before. In the meantime, I don't care what you say. I won't have you staying in some hotel. Your room will be all ready for you by the time you get home. Besides, if you're going to the bank, you're going to need something clean to wear."

"I don't think you have anything in your closet that would fit me. What size are you wearing these days?"

"Four," she answered sheepishly.

"I hate to break it to you, but I don't think I wore a size four when I *was* four."

"Oh, I don't know. Maybe we can let out one of my old maternity dresses. . . ."

"You'd better leave before I hurt you," I exclaimed, preparing to pelt her with a chocolate heart.

"You're sure you don't mind staying here while I go home?"

"Not at all. Who knows when Jeff's going to wake up? Besides, you've had a rough day."

"You have absolutely no idea. You know what the worst part is? It's not just the shock of it—and lord knows that's awful enough. It's how quickly everybody has started jockeying for position."

"You mean because you're the new owners of the Monarchs?"

"You should have heard the people sucking up to me this afternoon. Don't they realize how transparent it is? Do they think that I'm so upset by what's happened that it's made me stupid? I mean, even Coach Bennato—Jesus. Ever since Beau made Jeff general manager, Bennato and Jeff have been at each other's throats. Bennato spent the entire preseason giving interviews saying that Beau had made a terrible mistake, that Jeff didn't have the experience for the job. Now all of a sudden he shows up at the house with tears in his eyes, and he's telling everybody who will listen what a great team he and Jeff are going to make, how together they're going to turn the season around by dedicating the rest of the games to Beau's memory. It makes me want to barf."

"Get used to it," I said. "It's only going to get worse.

From here on in everyone is going to want something from you."

"You mean until they find out we don't have any money."

"Believe me, it's not the money. You know what my mother always says: 'There's nothing more common than money.' "

"Unless you don't happen to have any."

"Lots of people have money," I replied. "You and Jeff have something that's much more desirable. Just think about it, Chrissy. Do you have any idea how many people would kill for an NFL franchise?"

As I waited in the dead man's house I wandered from room to room gathering up empty glasses and dumping out ashtrays. The phone kept ringing, but I was tired of answering it. After a while I turned the ringer off and just let the machine pick up. Then I made one last foray through the food baskets and, armed with an apple, a pear, and a stick of smoked sausage (for protein), I went into the library and made myself comfortable.

A copy of that morning's *Milwaukee Journal Sentinel* lay on the coffee table, and I looked through it while I ate. The morning's headline was about a threatened teachers' strike. There was also an above-the-fold story about a toddler who'd accidentally locked himself in a Porta-John at a flea market over the weekend. On the sports page the articles consisted mostly of a series of scathing postmortems of the Monarchs' defeat at the hands of the Vikings that alternately blamed Bennato and Jeff for the rout. There was also an article about the city's proposed stadium renovation plan. In it Beau was quoted as saying, "I'm very excited about this project." I sighed, thinking of what tomorrow's headlines would bring.

Jeff Rendell came into the room so quietly that I jumped

at the sight of him. His clothes were rumpled, and his eyes were still heavy with sleep behind the tortoiseshell frames of his glasses. The wrinkled bed sheets had left their imprint on his cheek, and his hair stood up at the back of his head in an absurd cowlick.

"Where is everybody?" he asked, his voice still thick with sleep.

"They all left around dinnertime. Chrissy finally went home about an hour ago to be with the baby. She wanted to stay, but she was just exhausted, so I sent her home."

Jeff sank down into an armchair and buried his face in his hands. "I can't believe it," he groaned, shaking his head slowly from side to side. "I can't believe I killed him."

"What?" I demanded. Two things went through my head in rapid succession: that anything he told me would be protected by attorney-client privilege, and why I had decided early on not to go into criminal law. This was the kind of confession I never wanted to hear, especially from my best friend's husband.

"What do you mean when you say you killed him?" I asked, willing myself to keep my expression neutral.

"He'd be alive right now if it weren't for me."

"How do you figure that?"

"You must have heard by now about the big fight I had with him this morning."

"A day didn't go by without your father having a big fight with somebody. You know what your dad was like. He was the kind of guy who would never whisper if he could get away with shouting instead. It was his personality."

"Yeah, but this time it was different."

"Different in what way?"

"He had a heart attack and died afterward," he replied bitterly.

"Is that all?" I demanded, unable to suppress an audible sigh of relief.

"What do you mean, is that all?" repeated Jeff, sounding shocked.

"I thought you were going to tell me something else, that's all," I said quickly. "What did you and your dad fight about?"

"I told him I was quitting."

"Quitting as GM?"

"Quitting the team. I told him I was fed up with losing, sick of being treated like an errand boy, and I wasn't going to hang around and watch him destroy the team that he'd spent his whole life building."

"What made you decide you were going to quit? Why today?"

"I don't really know. I guess things have been coming to a head for a long time. The money, the bank, the fact that Coach Bennato seems to have forgotten how to win football games—suddenly it all seemed impossible. It didn't help that Dad still refused to even discuss the Los Angeles offer. I guess I was just feeling angry and frustrated."

"So that's what you went in there to talk to him about? The fact that you were quitting?"

"No. I wasn't planning anything. He buzzed me to come into his office. He wanted me to run down to the bank and pick up some contracts he wanted from the safe-deposit box."

"What kind of contracts?"

"We keep the player contracts locked up. That's what got me started. I mean, here I am, the general manager of a National Football League team, and I'm still running errands for my dad."

"So is that what the key is for?"

Jeff nodded.

"But why give it to me? Why not hold on to it your-self?" I took the key out of my pocket and went to hand it back to him.

"I think it's better if you keep it, if that's okay."

"Why's that?" I asked.

"I don't want anybody else to get their hands on it."

"Who'd want to?"

"The police. The newspapers."

"Why? What's in it? I thought you said it was just contracts."

"There's some other stuff," he replied, licking his lips nervously.

"Team documents?"

"Personal documents."

"You mean financial stuff?"

"For god's sake, Kate. It's personal. Private. What-ever's in there has nothing to do with anything. It's just that there are things in there that would be really embar-rassing if anybody got hold of them."

"Embarrassing to whom?"

"To Chrissy," he whispered miserably. "It's something she doesn't even know about."

"And you're sure it has absolutely no bearing on your father's death?" I asked, wondering what secret Jeff had that he was so desperate to keep from his wife. Off the top of my head I could think of quite a few possibilities— an unrevealed previous marriage, a child he'd agreed to support . . .

"No," he replied emphatically. "I swear to you, it has absolutely no bearing on anything that's going on with my father or the team."

I hesitated for a moment, turning the key over and over in my hand, torn between the desire to protect Chrissy and fear of taking part in deceiving her.

"In that case I'll hang on to it for you," I said, finally.

"But you have to understand that if the police ask me directly if I have it, I won't lie."

"I wouldn't want you to."

"Good. So tell me, how did you leave things with your father?"

"What do you mean?"

"You said that you had an argument and that you told him you were quitting the team. Then what?"

"Then I stormed out, went into my office, and started throwing stuff into boxes."

"And how did your father seem when you left him?"

"He seemed fine."

"He didn't seem ill or anything?"

"I really didn't notice," answered Jeff unhappily. "I was so upset, I didn't pay much attention. I just wanted to get the hell out of there. I was so angry."

"As angry as you were when they told you that he was dead?"

"What do you mean?"

"Coach Bennato said that you kind of freaked out when you saw your father's body."

"What do you mean?" he inquired, sounding genuinely bewildered.

"He said you pushed the paramedics out of the way so that you could get to your father. . . ."

"What paramedics?" he echoed.

"You don't remember pushing the paramedics out of the way and kneeling over your father's body?" I demanded.

"No," replied Jeff blankly.

He really didn't remember—either that or he was a terrific actor. I knew that trauma often caused memory loss. Accident victims often have no recollection of the events that caused their injuries. Even though I understood that it was a natural mechanism of self-protection, it was still creepy to see. It also wasn't going to do Jeff very much good. By tomorrow there were going to be people falling all over themselves to tell him exactly what he'd done.

"So what happens now?" he continued.

"Well, for one thing we have to decide what, if anything, to tell the police about the team's financial situation."

"Why do we have to tell them anything? What business is any of this to the police?"

"The police investigate every unattended death. As far as they're concerned, your father wasn't just well known, he was also very wealthy. They're going to want to make sure that they do a thorough investigation."

"Of course, but I don't see what the team's finances have to do with how my Dad died."

"You have to realize that there were lots of people at the stadium this morning who must have heard you fighting with your father. The cops are going to want to know what it was all about."

"How much do I have to tell them?" he asked, miserably. "The last thing I want anyone to find out is that we argued about moving the team. Do you have any idea what would happen if word got out that we were discussing an offer from L.A.? It would be all over the papers in a minute."

"I understand all the reasons you don't want that to happen," I explained, "but I also want you to realize that you're playing a dangerous game the minute you start withholding information from the police—no matter how good the reason."

"So what do you think I should tell them?"

"It's up to you. But if you're serious about keeping the L.A. offer under wraps I suggest you tell the cops that you and your father were discussing confidential team business. Period. Then be prepared to have them push you a little."

"Why?"

"Because that's their job," I replied. "Don't worry too much about it. You have other things to deal with."

"Like the bank."

"Exactly. I talked to Chrissy this afternoon while you were sleeping. If it's all right with you I made an appointment to go to the bank and sit down with Gus Wallenberg tomorrow. I'm hoping that in light of what's happened he'll give us a little more time."

"Chrissy always tells me I'm not really good at saying thank you," said Jeff, sheepishly, "but I want you to know how much I appreciate your help."

"You know I would do anything for you guys," I said, meaning it.

"I know it's an awful lot to ask," he began, slowly, "but I was wondering if you'd consider representing the team."

"You mean replace Harald Feiss as attorney for the Monarchs?"

Jeff nodded.

"What about Feiss?"

"What about him?"

"He's not going to be happy about being replaced. Not only that, but he's also in a position to make things difficult. . . ."

"Feiss has *already* made things difficult," was Jeff's reply. "He's half the reason we're in the mess we're in. Not only is he a bad lawyer, but all he ever did was tell my father exactly what he wanted to hear. You know what I always ask Coach Bennato whenever we start talking about a particular player? Can he get the job done? If he can't, then I don't want him. That's how I feel about Feiss. A lawyer who won't tell you the truth can't get the job done."

"Well then, I'm not going to lie to you. I'd be thrilled to represent the Monarchs, but you have to understand that with your father's death, you're in worse shape today than you were yesterday," I said, watching his face carefully to see how he was handling it.

"Worse in what way?"

"The way I understand it, your father bought the team thirty years ago for the then-unheard-of price of $48 million. Since then he's borrowed against absolutely every penny of that. In addition he's mortgaged this house, and from what Chrissy tells me, you've borrowed against your personal property, as well. Not only that, but as a condition of the latest First Milwaukee loan, the *in vivo* trust that would have protected his assets from estate taxes was dissolved."

"Meaning?"

"Meaning that while you don't have a pot to piss in right now, as far as Uncle Sam is concerned, you're sitting on an asset that's worth $300 million. That means that even after you deduct your liabilities and stretch the payments out for as long as the law allows, you're still looking at something like a $100 million tax bill."

CHAPTER

8

Chrissy and Jeff's house was just inside the city limits, a historic landmark mansion erected at the turn of the century by one of Milwaukee's early brewery barons. It was also one of the prettiest houses I'd ever seen. Perched on a high bluff overlooking Lake Michigan, it was set back from the street and flanked on either side by elaborate formal gardens. I parked my car in the circular drive and followed Jeff down the drive that led beneath the porte cochere to the side door that the family used.

Inside, the kitchen was half-timbered and had been decorated by Chrissy in the country French style with hand-painted tile from Provence, glass-fronted cabinets, and an enormous fireplace where tonight logs blazed and crackled. Chrissy, dressed in a quilted velvet bathrobe, sat in an oversize rocker in front of the fire feeding baby Katharine her bottle. There was a glass of wine at her elbow, and another stood empty beside it, no doubt waiting for Jeff.

I knew that there would be very few moments of privacy for the two of them in the days ahead so I did not linger. Pleading exhaustion and promising to talk in the morning, I kissed the top of my namesake's head and made my way up the familiar broad staircase and down the hall to the suite of guest rooms where I always stayed. Chrissy had laid a heavy terry cloth robe across the foot of the bed and a neatly folded Monarchs T-shirt, size XXL, that I could sleep in. True to her word, there was even a mint on the pillow.

Given the amount of sleep I'd gotten over the past few days, I should have been ready to crawl between the sheets, but I was strangely keyed up. In part it was the prospect of having the Monarchs as a new client, but it was also a peculiar brand of jealousy that seemed to strike whenever I found myself under Chrissy's roof. I know it seems unfair. We have always been so different, I tell myself that it's foolish to compare. And yet I see her in the soft light of the fire with her baby in her arms and I can't help but hold my life up against hers and measure.

I kicked off my shoes, stripped down to my underwear, and washed my face. Then I quickly pulled the pins from my hair and took down my French twist, not wanting to linger at the mirror. The office-induced pallor of my skin stood out in stark relief against the mass of my dark hair, giving my face a haggard look I found depressing. I sighed and slipped gratefully into the bathrobe, telling myself that it was going to get worse before it got better. I picked up the telephone from the bedside table and dragged the cord across the room to the overstuffed chaise and dialed my office to pick up my voice mail. There were calls from all of the usual suspects, including a half a dozen messages from one or the other of the Brandts. I was also half expecting a message from Stephen Azorini saying that he was bailing out of our meeting with the decorator that was set for tomorrow, but I was disappointed. Although I'd made enough of an issue out of it for him to be there, this time I actually found myself wishing for one of his hurried excuses on the tape. With everything else that was going on, wallpaper was the absolute farthest thing from my mind.

I hung up the receiver and hugged the telephone to my

chest for a minute before punching in the other number. No matter how many times I told myself that I wasn't doing anything wrong, I still always felt guilty for calling Elliott. I couldn't help it. I'd spent the last three years trying to deny that there was anything more than a professional relationship between us. Of course, now that I had no cases he was working on and we were still on the phone a couple of nights a week, the fiction was getting harder to maintain.

Elliott is the other man in my life, the one that I am not moving in with. He's a former prosecutor and an ex-marine who struck out on his own as a private investigator and has built a thriving business specializing in the investigation of white-collar and financial crimes. In Chicago, a city filled with experts, he is simply the best there is. He has also never made any secret of how he feels about me. I am the one who is confused, who alternately rushes toward him and then pulls away.

"Are you okay?" he asked at the sound of my voice. It was his standard greeting.

"Why do you always assume I'm in some sort of trouble?" I demanded.

"Because you usually are. Where are you? I just called your apartment a couple of minutes ago and got the machine."

"I'm in Milwaukee. Beau Rendell died this afternoon. He was—"

"He was the owner of the Milwaukee Monarchs," cut in Elliott. "I know that because I have a Y chromosome. Is there anybody that you *don't* know?"

"Are we talking domestic or foreign?"

"I'm serious. How do you know the Rendells?"

"My friend Chrissy is married to his son."

"Who is now the new owner of the Monarchs. They're

saying on the news that he died of a heart attack. They just did a piece on him on *SportsCenter*. When's the funeral?"

"I don't know yet. It'll probably be in a couple of days. In the meantime you'll be thrilled to know that you are now speaking to the new attorney for the Milwaukee Monarchs football team."

"Wow. I'm impressed. Can I ask you something?"

"Ask away."

"What the hell do you know about football?"

"What the hell do I know about doing a striptease?" I countered. "That hasn't stopped me from representing Tit-Elations. Business is business."

"Have you had a lot of reporters?" he asked, as if he were inquiring about an infestation of roaches or any other kind of pest.

"Not too bad. Of course, we've gotten a million calls, but we haven't found anybody going through the trash yet."

"You will."

"Why? What have you heard?"

"Nothing. But that's not going to make any difference."

"What do you mean?"

"It's human nature. For some reason people don't seem to be able to accept that famous people die just like everybody else. We expected extraordinary things from them in life, and that's what we want from them in death. Dropping dead from a heart attack is just too ordinary. Americans think that an oversize life calls for an oversize death. Look at Marilyn Monroe. Look at JFK. In this country, when you're famous, you don't just die, you get a conspiracy theory, too."

"Wonderful. And to think that I called you expecting to be cheered up."

"Just be careful, Kate," said Elliott, suddenly turning serious. "The last thing you want is for this to turn into something it isn't."

* * *

I had made arrangements to see Gus Wallenberg at his office at the bank the next morning. When I came downstairs, I found the baby-sitter in the kitchen, bundling up the baby for an outing in her stroller. Jeff and Chrissy, she reported, had both slept badly and had gone back upstairs to rest. I left them a note on the kitchen table and made my way through Milwaukee's sedate rush hour to the First Milwaukee Building on Wisconsin across from the stately old Pfister Hotel.

Wallenberg's office was a cathedral-like space on the top floor of the building and, as such, far removed from the actual commerce of banking that still took place from behind the gilded teller cages on the first floor. Wallenberg came out and ushered me back to his wood-paneled office himself, his wing tips gleaming. He was a tall man with a rigid, parade-ground carriage and an aura of brusque authority. His hair was gray and thinning, dragged tight across his scalp and slicked down with some kind of pomade that smelled vaguely of lavender and reminded me of my grandfather. He was, I guessed, the kind of man who couldn't go ten minutes in conversation without finding some way of telling you just how tough he was.

He waved me into a clubby leather chair with one hand and settled himself behind his massive desk, the kind that seems at the same time imposing and impenetrable, like a mahogany bunker.

"I must confess that I was a little surprised by your call," he announced, getting right to the point. "Up until now I've always dealt with Harald Feiss."

"No doubt that was the case while Beau Rendell was alive."

"And now that he's dead, poor Harald's out on his ass, is that it?" he inquired gruffly.

"I'm sure that Mr. Feiss will continue to play a role during this transitional period," I replied. I knew that in some sense Milwaukee was a very small town, a place where all the power players operated on a first-name basis, which couldn't help but put me at something of a disadvantage. "Nonetheless, Jeff felt that as the new owner of the Monarchs he needed a fresh perspective."

"I hope you don't think me coarse for saying so, but I have to tell you that whichever way you look at it, what Jeffrey Rendell inherited looks like a pile of shit."

"Meaning the Monarchs' current financial situation?"

"Meaning that he's not only going to be the youngest owner of an NFL franchise, but he's also going to be the one who owns it for the shortest amount of time."

"That's what I came to talk to you about."

"So talk."

"Considering his father's sudden and tragic death, I've come to ask you to extend the grace period on the loan agreement for an additional sixty days."

"You don't want much, do you? Maybe you'd prefer it if I'd just agree to forgive the loan, and while I'm at it, maybe you think I should take you downstairs, open up the vault, and let you guys help yourselves?"

"That's awfully generous of you to offer, Mr. Wallenberg," I replied with a smile, "but under the circumstances I think we'd be happy with the additional sixty days."

"You still haven't given me a reason why I should give it to you."

"Because you're a decent man who wants to make sure that Jeff has time to bury his father. Because you want to do the right thing. Because you don't want to be always remembered as the banker who drove the Monarchs out of Milwaukee."

"I've known Jeff since he was a little kid. He doesn't have the balls to move the team."

"If you don't give him the extra time, he won't have a choice," I replied.

"*I'm* the one who doesn't have a choice," declared Wallenberg, from behind his desk, his voice ripe with self-pity. "Do you have any idea how competitive the banking environment is right now? The big boys are all moving in from New York and Chicago, stealing our customers, opening up branches in the grocery stores. We have to stay lean and mean just to survive."

"What about a thirty-day extension?"

"I'm afraid that's not going to be possible either."

"Even if we agreed to make a good-faith payment? Let's say a million dollars by Tuesday in exchange for an additional thirty days," I inquired without the slightest notion of where the Monarchs could come up with that kind of cash.

"This is a bank, Ms. Millholland, not a pawnshop. As far as the Monarchs are concerned, they've already proved that they're a bad credit risk. I suggest you go back to Jeff Rendell and tell him that a deal's a deal. He has until next Tuesday to come up with the money."

As I drove back to Chrissy and Jeff's house I mentally kicked myself for being so stupid. I should have realized what Gus Wallenberg was up to as soon as Harald Feiss told me that the bank had required the revocation of the *in vivo* trust as a condition of the loan. He knew that Beau Rendell was already skating on thin ice, so Wallenberg set up the loan so that if Beau couldn't pay it back, the bank would have a clear shot at the team. Next Tuesday if the Monarchs were still in default, it would be Gus Wallenberg sitting in the owner's box.

Not only that, but I suspected that the Monarchs' bankruptcy would invalidate all of their existing contracts, including the ones that locked the team into millions of dollars of payments to injured or nonperforming players. Getting there might be ugly, but in the end Gus Wallenberg would control an NFL football franchise and be able to run it from a position of strength.

I wondered whether Wallenberg saw this as an act of personal betrayal or whether in his version it was all just business. I was willing to bet that no matter what he'd convinced himself of, if it had been a dairy farm instead of a football team that I'd come to talk to him about this morning, First Milwaukee would have already granted the extension.

As soon as I pulled into Chrissy's driveway, I saw the unmarked Caprice parked in front of the door. Chrissy was waiting for me as well, pacing beneath the porte cochere in a chic black suit and pumps, her agitation making her oblivious to the cold.

"You have to get in there," she said, grabbing me by the arm and practically dragging me into the house.

"What's the matter?" I asked.

"Two cops showed up a little while ago. I told them that we were on our way to the funeral home, but they said it would just take a minute. They insisted on speaking to Jeff."

"Why didn't you stay with him?" I asked as I followed her quickly through the kitchen.

"They wouldn't let me," she replied over her shoulder. "I don't know what's going on." We stopped in front of the door to the living room. "It's so awful," she said in a whisper. "They're acting like he's some kind of criminal."

I pushed open the door and stepped inside. "Good morning, officers," I announced brightly, barging right in, Elliott's warning about the deaths of the famous not far from my mind. It was the same pair of detectives from the day before. I turned my back on them and spoke directly to Jeff, taking his hand, establishing eye contact to reassure him, willing him to calm down. "Chrissy said that you wanted to have your attorney present to advise you while you gave your statement." There was no mistaking the look of relief on Jeff's face. I flashed him a quick wink and then turned back to face the two homicide detectives. "I hope you haven't gone too far without me," I said, making myself comfortable on the couch beside my client.

"Mr. Rendell was just telling us about the last time he saw his father," reported Detective Eiben, less unhappy at the interruption than the fact of my presence.

Jeff looked at me. "And I told them that the last time I saw him he was lying at the bottom of the stairs that lead up to his office."

"I meant to speak to," pursued Eiben.

"The morning he died, then. He and I spoke in his office."

"Just the two of you?" inquired the officer.

"Yes."

"I'm surprised. We took a look at your father's appointment calendar for that morning. He was booked solid with appointments. Coach Bennato, a Mr. Wallenberg, Harald Feiss—they were all scheduled to see him. Your name didn't appear anywhere."

"Our offices were right next to each other. My father and I talked a dozen times a day. I never made an appointment."

"Do you recall what time this conversation with your father took place?"

"No. I didn't notice the time. I was working in my office, and he buzzed to say he wanted to see me."

"What did the two of you discuss?"

"Team business," replied Jeff, catching my eye and looking for my approval.

"Anything in particular?"

"Jeff and his father discussed several items of team business," I cut in.

"I'm afraid we're going to need Mr. Rendell to be more specific," said Detective Eiben.

"And I'm afraid that unless you can offer some kind of compelling reason why you need that information, I'm going to have to advise my client to not answer the question. His discussions with his father involved confidential team business."

"How confidential could it have been if they were screaming at each other at the top of their lungs?" interjected Detective Zellmer, obviously taking the part of the bad cop.

I ignored him and turned to Jeff. "You don't have to answer that," I said.

"Who owns the team now that your father is dead?" asked Eiben, changing tack.

"Jeff and his wife Chrissy are now the owners of the Milwaukee Monarchs franchise," I replied.

"He left it to both of them?" demanded Zellmer, feigning incredulity.

"He left the team to his son," I answered matter-of-factly. "Wisconsin is a community property state."

"So I guess it's safe to say that you're the person who stood to benefit the most from his death?" inquired Zellmer, looking hard at Jeff.

"Children usually are the ones who benefit financially from a parent's death," I pointed out.

From behind his horn rims Jeff's eyes blazed. There was no doubt that the idea that he had been enriched by his father's passing, when indeed the opposite was true, galled him.

"So tell me, how would you characterize your last conversation with your father?" urged Zellmer.

"What do you mean?"

"What was the general tone of the conversation? Amicable? Routine? Angry?"

"I've already told you that we argued."

"Did your father raise his voice?"

"My father always raised his voice."

"And did he on this occasion?"

"Yes."

"Did you?"

"Yes. I already told you that."

"And did this argument turn physical at any time?"

"What do you mean by 'turn physical'?"

"Did you lay your hands on your father at any time during the course of this argument?"

"What kind of question is that?" demanded Jeff, outraged.

"It is actually a very simple question," replied Zellmer with real menace. "Did you or did you not lay your hands on your father?"

"No. Of course not," replied Jeff, looking the homicide detective straight in the eye.

"But if you had, it wouldn't have been the first time you and your father had come to blows," pointed out Detective Eiben affably. "You had struck him before on other occasions."

"That is absolutely not true," protested Jeff.

"Oh, come now, Mr. Rendell. There was even one occasion where it made it into the newspapers as I recall. I believe you punched your father in the face in the parking lot of the stadium after a Steelers game."

"I was fifteen years old, for chrissake! I was just an immature kid!"

"So how would you characterize your behavior yesterday?" demanded Zellmer.

I rose to my feet. "Unless you have any other questions of substance, I'm afraid I'm going to have to put an end to this interview," I announced. "My client lost his father under tragic circumstances yesterday. As far as I know, no crime has been committed and he is not a suspect. I can only assume that it is merely force of habit that has caused you to treat him as one."

Detective Eiben closed his notebook with great cere-mony and put it into his pocket before getting to his feet. "Then we'll just thank you for your cooperation at such a difficult time," he said flatly.

I could sense Jeff relax now that the interview was over. He led the way to the entrance hall, opened the closet door, and, ever the good host, extracted the coats belonging to the two detectives.

"One last question," asked Detective Zellmer, as if it were merely an afterthought instead of the whole point of this carefully choreographed interview. "Do you know anything about a key that was lying on your father's desk the morning he died?"

"A key?" inquired Jeff with a look of such convincing innocence that it completely altered my sense of what he was capable of.

"Yes. A key. It was lying on your father's desk when the photographer from the death investigation unit came through, but by the time we arrived to bag and tag evi-dence, it had disappeared."

"I'm sorry but I can't help you," said Jeff. "I don't know anything about any key."

CHAPTER

9

Once the door had closed behind the detectives I turned to face Jeff.

"You never told me you went back into your father's office," I said, unable to conceal the irritation in my voice.

"I told you that there were things in that box that I wouldn't want anybody to see," countered Jeff, defensively.

"And you swear that they have absolutely nothing to do with your father, or the team. . . ."

"Absolutely nothing. You have my word."

"So where did you find the key?"

"On the desk, just like the police said. Dad took it off his ring and put it there when he asked me to go down to the safe-deposit box, but I forgot all about it after we started arguing."

"So when did you remember it?"

"Afterwards, when the police showed up. I realized that I'd left it there on his desk. I was sitting in my office and I heard Feiss talking to the cops in the hall, so I ducked in there and grabbed it. You've got to believe me, Kate, what's in there has nothing to do with any of this."

I looked at Jeff, his face exhausted and pleading, and decided for the time being not to push it.

"What did they talk to you about before I showed up?" I asked. "Did they say anything about how your father died?"

"No. When I asked them they said they're still waiting for the autopsy results, but I spoke to the funeral director this morning. He said that the body was going to be released sometime this afternoon. The funeral is scheduled for Thursday morning."

Chrissy stuck her head in through the door from the kitchen. "Are they gone yet?" she asked.

"The coast is clear," I replied, doing my best to make light of it.

"What is the deal with them anyway?" she asked, stepping into the room, her arms folded across her chest indignantly. "I thought they were supposed to be public servants. I swear, I've never been treated so rudely in my life!"

"Homicide detectives don't go to charm school," I pointed out. "Their job is to shake the tree and see what falls out. I don't think anybody likes it much."

"The two of them seemed like they were enjoying themselves," pointed out Jeff, ruefully.

"They were just trying to get under your skin," I said. "It's all an act. They'd sing their questions like opera if they thought it would get you to open up and tell them what they wanted."

"Speaking of getting what you want, how did it go at the bank?" asked Chrissy.

"They refuse to budge an inch," I replied. "Gus Wallenberg is determined to be the new owner of the Milwaukee Monarchs. That's probably been at the back of his mind from the very beginning. The day he okayed the loan I'm sure he figured he was giving Beau the rope to hang himself with. That's why he insisted that the trust be revoked. He wanted to be sure that the bank was first in line in case the loan went sour."

"So now what?" asked Jeff.

"Now you go down to the funeral home and make

arrangements for your father. I'm going to head back to Chicago and start digging through the boxes of Monarchs documents in my office. I'm also going to fax you a letter to sign authorizing the transfer of any files and records from Harald Feiss to Callahan Ross's Milwaukee office. They'll make arrangements for someone to go to Feiss's office and pick them up."

"I didn't realize you had an office in Milwaukee," said Chrissy.

"It's relatively small, less than fifty attorneys, but they'll make sure we get what we need from Feiss."

"And then what?" asked Chrissy.

"Then we come up with plan B."

"You realize we only have six days before Wallenberg calls the loan and puts us under," said Jeff.

"Wasn't there some famous coach who said, 'It ain't over till it's over'?"

"That was Yogi Berra," replied Jeff, "and he was talking about baseball."

By the time I got back to Chicago, there were two dark green shopping bags waiting for me on top of my desk. I had wanted to stop at my apartment and change clothes on my way to the office, but when I'd called Cheryl from the car, she'd informed me that the porno brothers had just arrived and were closeted in the conference room with Stuart Eisenstadt, eagerly awaiting my arrival. With a groan I told her to scare up something for me to wear, find me a bag of M&M's, and put on a fresh pot of coffee. It was turning out to be one hell of a day.

Drawn as much by curiosity as the necessity of bringing me coffee, Cheryl followed me into my office to see what the personal shopper had sent over this time. As one of eight children, she'd grown up in a household where anything new was cause for excitement. Besides, most of my emergency purchases ended up in her closet anyway. By the time she graduated, Cheryl was going to be the best dressed first-year associate in the city.

"Stuart just buzzed to say that they're still waiting for you in the north conference room," she said, setting my coffee on the corner of my desk and standing on tiptoe to peer eagerly into the bags. She had a heart-shaped face, a cap of blond hair, and the kind of ferocious intelligence that is prized in any profession. I could not imagine what my life was going to be like without her.

"Have we heard anything from the SEC today?" I asked, pulling a black jacket from the bag and freeing it from a cocoon of tissue.

"I talked to Janice right after I got off the phone with you," she reported. Janice was the secretary of the SEC administrator assigned to Avco, and from the very first, Cheryl had cultivated a phone friendship with her. They spoke three or four times a day. Cheryl knew everything about Janice—about her crazy mother-in-law and her husband who was finishing up a three-year hitch in the navy. She was also able to pick up a stunning amount of information about where Avco stood in the regulatory process at any given moment. "She says they've accepted our latest answer and that it looks like they won't be sending us another comment letter."

"Yessss!" I said, making one of those gestures of victory that we've all learned from watching pro athletes on TV. "Any idea how long it will take to get final approval?"

"It'll be four or five days before everyone who has to has signed off on it."

"When this deal closes, I'm sending you to Bermuda for a week," I said. "You can take Janice with you."

I pulled the skirt out of the bag and held it up to my waist with a frown. The hem hit me somewhere between midthigh and scandal. They say that skirts go up with the stock market—the stronger the market, the shorter the skirts. I thought about sitting down, getting in and out of taxis, and walking outside in the cold and found myself fervently wishing for an economic downturn.

"Oh, good," I observed, "now I'll have something to wear in case I ever have to go to a funeral for a hooker."

"Don't worry," replied my secretary over her shoulder as she headed for the door. "I guarantee you don't have anything the porno brothers haven't seen already."

Most men may lead lives of quiet desperation, but there was certainly nothing quiet about Avery and Colin Brandt. For one thing there were two of them, and while identical twins might be adorable when they're below the age of five, there's something distinctly creepy about two adults who are exact duplicates of each other, especially when they're two middle-aged men who look like Marv Albert clones complete with gold chains and bad toupees. It didn't help that they both had heavy tanning salon habits, so that even in the dead of the Chicago winter they both looked like they'd been dipped in cocoa.

"Ah, finally, the woman we've been waiting for!" declared Avery in his weird pan-Atlantic accent as I pushed open the conference room doors. You couldn't tell them apart until they spoke. Colin, the one who handled the financial side of the business, had the softer voice—also a slight lisp.

"I'm so sorry to have kept you gentlemen waiting," I said, giving the bottom of my skirt a quick tug in the hopes of miraculously making it cover more of me. "I didn't realize that you would be coming in today."

"We were just in the neighborhood, as it were, in a meeting with the investment bankers," said Avery with a toothy grin no doubt meant to be charming. I knew immediately that something was up. Until now both Brandts had treated me like hired help.

"So how's everything with the bank?" I asked.

Grisham & Polk were the underwriters for the deal. They were a shady outfit with a reputation as the hyenas of the financial world, feeding on scraps and making their living from marginal, cast-off deals. Every time I thought of them performing due diligence or maintaining a fiduciary relationship, I got chest pains.

"They say everything's still a go on their end," Avery assured me smoothly. "They're just waiting for SEC approval so that we can close."

"That's what we're all waiting for," I replied, thinking of all the things I should have been doing instead of sitting locked in a conference room restating the obvious.

"So, I guess the $40 million question is when?" demanded Colin anxiously. "According to what Stuart was just saying, we should be hearing practically any minute."

"I'm afraid that the government never moves that fast," I replied, silently wishing Eisenstadt dead. So much of getting a client through the IPO process was just managing their expectations. "Even if they don't hit us with another comment letter, it'll be at least another five or six days before they sign off."

This is not what the Brandt brothers had come to hear. One look at their faces and I knew that Avco must be having cash-flow problems. Not that there was anything unusual about that. As a rule, companies go public because they need to raise money; unfortunately the costs associated with an IPO usually did a pretty good job of depleting whatever cash reserves they might have had. Although Callahan Ross and the investment bankers would take their fees out of the proceeds, there were plenty of upfront costs to be paid. In Avco's case I knew that the bill from the legal printers alone was more than $200,000. No doubt the fact that the SEC had dragged out the process to more than four times its usual length had taken its toll, as well. The Brandts were probably over the same kind of barrel as Jeffrey Rendell and the Monarchs, though I suspected that the Brandts' lender might be the kind who starts breaking legs when his customers defaulted—at least, I secretly hoped so.

"It won't help us to go public if we go bankrupt first," complained Colin miserably.

It occurred to me that this was probably what the SEC had had in mind all along, but I didn't say so.

"Perhaps you should sit down with your investment bankers and see about setting up some kind of short-term bridge loan," I offered, not eager to get into a discussion of Avco's cash-flow problems.

"That's exactly what we've just been discussing," Avery assured me. "But afterward, talking to Stuart here, my brother and I had a little thought. You see, all we really need is a small bridge, somewhere in the neighborhood of a million dollars, just to get rid of some long-running payables and meet our payroll until we close the IPO. Grisham and Polk say that naturally they'd be happy to raise the money, but their fee is fifteen percent right off the top. Do you have any idea how much money that is?"

"A hundred and fifty thousand dollars," I replied, pleased to be offered this opportunity to show off my mastery of simple arithmetic.

"But don't you see? If we're really just a week or ten days away from SEC approval, then we'll end up paying a six-figure fee for a ten-day loan."

"Very few people have the liquidity to write that kind of check," I said. "That's what you're paying for."

"I bet you do," said Avery.

"Pardon?"

"I bet you could write that size check."

For some reason my thoughts immediately turned to the apartment renovation—probably because that's what the plumbing contractor thought about my checkbook, too.

"I'm afraid that I'm not in a position to do that," I said. It was horribly inappropriate for them to even ask, and I was furious that Eisenstadt had let them put me in this position.

"Oh, I'm sure for someone with your background what we're talking about is pocket change," pressed Avery.

I wanted to tell him that no matter what anyone's background was it was still a million dollars. Instead I said, "Perhaps Stuart didn't realize it because he's relatively new to the firm, but Callahan Ross has a policy against attorneys investing in a client's business. It's a clear conflict of interest." I didn't even bother to keep the contempt out of my voice. I was having a hard enough time trying not to sound as if I'd just been slimed.

When I got back to my office, I ripped open the bag of M&M's and had Cheryl hook me up to the telephone headset I used when I had an impossibly long string of calls to return or was feeling too hyper to sit down. Whenever I used it, I felt like a cross between a Hollywood agent and an air traffic controller, but today was definitely one of those days when I knew I'd think better on my feet.

First Milwaukee's refusal to budge on the default deadline had put us on immediate combat footing. There were a million things that all needed to have been done yesterday. Not only that, but I couldn't help but feel handicapped by my incomplete knowledge of Beau Rendell's business dealings. I called Harald Feiss, hoping to get some answers and offer him the professional courtesy of letting him know that he'd be receiving a change-in-representation and transmittal-of-records letter from Jeff Rendell shortly, but his secretary said that he was unavailable to come to the phone. I suspected he'd instructed her to refuse my calls.

I tried to call the Honorable Robert V. Deutsch, the mayor of Milwaukee, but was informed by an aide that hizzoner was attending an international conference of mayors in Beijing of all places. However, he was planning on cutting short his trip in order to return for Beau Rendell's funeral. I explained that I was the new attorney for the Milwaukee Monarchs, and the aide agreed to set up a tentative meeting for me with the mayor the afternoon of the funeral. After I hung up with city hall, I put a call in to Jack McWhorter and left a message for him to get in touch with his people in L.A. It was time for them to come up with a proposed timetable for making a deal.

As I worked, the irony of what I was doing did not escape me. While I was prepared to fight to the death to allow Jeff and Chrissy Rendell to hang on to their football team, the truth is, I don't really much care for football.

Talk of sports lubricates the world of men. It gives them a common language and sets them on common ground. In my office, at Super Bowl time, men who command $500 an hour joke and wager as equals with men who empty their wastebaskets for minimum wage. I can think of nothing else, not even religion, that is such a powerful leveler.

I started reading the sports page when I first came to work at Callahan Ross. I did it for the same reason that a refugee makes the effort to master the language of his adopted country—to assimilate and survive. I have also, in the interests of entertaining clients, gone to see every kind of game that can be played with a ball. Over time I have even learned to appreciate the rough ballet of pro hoops, the indolent poetry played out by the boys of summer, but I have never really developed a taste for football.

There is a reason for this. At its primitive heart football

is a game about knocking people down. It is also monumentally boring. There was even a time when I was foolish enough to tell people this. Whenever I did, they would look at me sadly, start talking slower, and explain that I didn't really understand the game. After seriously weighing the possibility, I have to say that they are wrong.

Last year I handled a transaction involving four telecommunications companies from three different countries. My clients traveled to Chicago from Tokyo, Frankfurt, and Taipei because I'd figured out how to put $2 billion in their pockets in a way that had simply not occurred to anyone else. I refuse to believe that the game of football is beyond my understanding—especially when it is widely assumed that men with beer bellies the size of the moons of Jupiter are able to grasp every nuance of the game.

But that doesn't mean that I don't understand what football means to people, how it lifts them up and binds them together. With Beau's death, the Monarchs might now belong to Jeff and Chrissy Rendell, but they also belonged to the working people of Milwaukee who, year in and year out, put down their hard-earned dollars and went to the stadium to root for the team they'd grown up cheering for.

Of course, I knew that Jack McWhorter would probably disagree. He would argue that football was a business, and when they bought their tickets, the fans got their money's worth. To him the NFL was a brand, entertainment was the product, and the players, albeit overpaid, were as interchangeable as workers on an assembly line. As I worked on through the afternoon, sifting through the possibilities and weighing the alternatives, I found myself wishing that I could subscribe to his point of view.

In the unyielding language of the balance sheet, moving the team to Los Angeles provided the easiest road to salvation. However, given the tax burden placed on the team by Beau's death, the terms that L.A. was offering suddenly seemed less generous. But once you strayed from the realm of the merely black and white, the thought of moving the team was deeply disturbing. It was like contemplating a disfiguring amputation. You knew that you would survive, but you also knew that you would emerge from the experience forever changed.

The other options at this point were much more difficult to pin down. An important chunk of arithmetic depended on how far Beau had gone with his discussions of a stadium renovation deal with the city. Unfortunately, I was going to have to wait until Thursday to find out.

While never much of an option, selling the team was no longer a viable alternative. Whatever the Rendells could get for the team would immediately go to the government for inheritance and capital gains taxes. They'd end up literally with nothing.

What the team needed, I decided, was a white knight. Someone with more money than sense who'd be willing to ride to the rescue of the team. Surely there must be a Milwaukee millionaire who would be willing to spend a chunk of change for a piece of a debt-riddled franchise in exchange for civic sainthood. I started jotting down a list of likely candidates.

In the meantime there were still some ground balls to be run down. I still hadn't received Sherman's memo on likely lease issues, and there were other things I hoped to learn as soon as I received Feiss's records. I felt like I had twenty-seven different facts in front of me; it was at the same time too many and not enough.

Cheryl came in tapping the face of her wristwatch, reminding me that it was time to meet Stephen and the decorator at the new apartment. My mother was also coming just to round out the party.

"You go," I groaned. "I'm prepared to pay you handsomely."

"You couldn't afford what it would cost," replied my secretary, taking my coat from the hanger and holding it for me.

On my way out I bumped into Skip Tillman, the firm's managing partner, who stopped long enough to congratulate me on landing the Monarchs as clients for the firm.

"Norm Halperin in the Milwaukee office just called to give me the news. He was practically beside himself. What a coup! I told him you'd be in touch to coordinate about making sure that you have the manpower you need. Remember, it's big-name clients that make us such a big-name firm," he concluded with a knowing chuckle before moving on.

I breathed a sigh of relief to see him go. As a rule I was much more accustomed to Tillman's censure than his praise, and it made me nervous to suddenly find myself on his good side—especially since the new client he was so delighted with didn't have a dime to pay us.

CHAPTER
10

I hadn't been to the new apartment in more than a week, so I was surprised when I stepped off the elevator to see that after months of hideously expensive structural work—plumbing and electrical repairs that seemed to involve more demolition than restoration—a momentous corner had apparently been turned. The plasterers had been hard at work, and most of the duplex's walls were now crisp, flat, and straight. The floors, sanded but still unvarnished, showed warm promise from beneath a layer of plaster dust.

I found Mother and Mimi, the decorator, already in the solarium, studying wallpaper samples and fabric swatches. Mother was dressed in her most casual clothes—a pair of slate gray Yves Saint Laurent trousers that hung on her slender frame like sculpture, a navy cashmere shell, and a pair of diamond stud earrings only slightly smaller than dimes. Mimi, who'd spent half her career decorating and redecorating Mother's houses, wore a red St. John's suit so old that it sagged in the seat and a pair of scuffed Ferragamo pumps.

"You realize this would be much easier if we could do it in the daylight," complained my mother without bothering to even look up.

"Unfortunately, I work during the day," I said.

Over the years our relationship had acquired a certain

efficiency. We no longer worked our way up to an argument, but instead had them always at the ready and just jumped right in.

"Well, at least you made it. I was beginning to think that your secretary was lying to me again when she said you were on your way. It's amazing how I can come all the way from Lake Forest and still manage to get here on time while all you have to do is travel a few blocks and yet you always keep us waiting."

"Not only do I not have a driver, but traffic is worse in the city," I pointed out. "Besides, I don't see Stephen here yet."

"Oh, I'm afraid he's not going to be able to make it, my dear," cooed Mimi, who adored Stephen with a decorator's passion for what was pleasing to the eye. "He phoned just as I was leaving to say that his flight was delayed in New York. These ambitious young men have to work so hard these days," she declared as if sharing some wondrous insight.

I couldn't believe it. Of all the passive-aggressive bullshit that had been pulled since we'd started in on the apartment, this had to be a new all-time low. It was bad enough that he'd stood me up on the meeting, but the fact that he didn't have the nerve to tell me himself and instead had wimped out and called Mimi was the last straw.

It also didn't help matters any that by the time Mother and Mimi got through with me, I was practically begging for mercy. I felt as though I'd had my brains scrambled. I don't care what anyone says, one Brunschwig & Fils wallpaper looks very much like another, especially once you've already looked at a hundred. It seemed incredible to me that after everything I'd been through over the past couple of days, it took choosing curtains for the downstairs powder room to send me over the edge.

After the decorating mafia had gone, I spent some time

alone in the apartment, wandering through the empty rooms, reacquainting myself with why I loved it, and marveling at how it was all coming together. It was a magnificent place, one of the last apartments designed by the legendary David Adler, and in every room you could feel his genius given physical expression in plaster, wood, and the space they defined. But as the work moved on toward completion I felt something else, as well: the weight of expectations bearing down on me.

Mimi assumed that people who chose light fixtures together must also be in love with each other. My mother assumed that because Stephen and I were moving in together, we would, as a matter of course, get married. I could see it in her eyes every time she crossed the threshold of the apartment. It was like she was mentally filling the place with place cards and bouquets.

My reaction to all of this was visceral and certain. Just thinking about it made me want to run away. Unlike Chrissy, my instincts for rebellion have remained intact from my bad-girl days; now they just play themselves out in different ways. That was the problem. Was it instinct that made me want to run, or was it self-preservation? Was rebellion a habit or a matter of survival? How could I justify saying that I was driven to flee when for three years I have not been bound to Stephen in any way and yet have chosen to stay?

I was surprised when the house phone rang and even more surprised when Danny, the night doorman, informed me that a Mr. Abelman was downstairs to see me. I told him to go ahead and send him up, but as soon as I hung up the phone I was seized by a kind of panic I hadn't experienced since junior high school.

It wasn't so much the prospect of seeing Elliott, but rather the idea of having him see the apartment. As long as I lived in Chicago and didn't change my name, there was no way to hide who I was or where I came from, but up until now Elliott's view of my personal possessions had been limited to my office, which was not technically mine, the apartment I shared with Claudia, which was little more than a student tenement, and my car, which was frankly a disgrace.

This was different. Even in its present, unfinished state, it was like hanging a sign around my neck.

I paced nervously across the foyer waiting for the elevator to deposit him. The apartments in this building were one to a floor. This was the building's only duplex and had been formed by connecting the seventh-floor apartment, which had once belonged to my parents, to the one directly above, where my grandparents had lived, by means of a grand reverse staircase that swung gracefully through the entranceway. Taken together, the two floors made it almost as large as Chrissy and Jeff's house in Milwaukee. Standing there alone it suddenly felt as big as a cathedral.

Elliott stepped off the elevator and slowed his step in order to take it all in. He made his way across the room to the enameled fireplace and ran his hand along the top of the mantel.

"You may be moving uptown," he declared with a wolfish grin, "but I can see that your housekeeping hasn't changed."

"Once a slob, always a slob," I replied, greatly relieved that he hadn't immediately fallen down in shock or decided to hit me up for a loan.

"How did you know I would be here?" I asked, wondering what exactly it was about him that attracted me. Compared with Stephen he was certainly nothing to look at, six foot one with a mop of soft brown hair that fell into his eyes like a schoolboy's. He had dark brown eyes that were flecked with gold and strong hands that felt dry and warm.

He smiled seldom but when he did it was wonder, like the arrival of spring.

"I'm a detective, remember," he admonished, flashing a grin. "I called your secretary and she told me where I could find you." He cast his arm casually around my waist as if this was the most natural thing in the world. "So how about giving me the nickel tour?"

"This whole block of buildings was erected in the early thirties during the heyday of the Beaux Arts period," I began, feeling flustered and starting to prattle. "It's one of the last ones that David Adler designed before his death. Adler was—"

"—an architect justifiably famous for his sense of proportion and eye for detail who specialized in designing city apartments and country houses for the old guard of Chicago society," Elliott cut in. Chicagoans know architecture the same way that the French know cheese; they grow up surrounded by its infinite variety. Even so, I was impressed.

"Adler was a fanatic for detail," I said, beckoning for him to follow me into the library. "Look at the paneling. You can really see it on the doors. There's English paneling on the library side, but it's different on the sides that face the two adjoining rooms. There's French paneling on the bedroom side and a concealed door on the parlor side. Only Adler would have gone to the trouble."

"So is this your favorite room?" he asked, taking in the pin-and-dart moldings and the floor-to-ceiling bookshelves of burled wood.

"No. Come upstairs. I'll show you my absolute favorite place in the world."

We walked side by side up the broad stairway. From the arched window on the landing we could see the headlights glittering at our feet as the last weary commuters headed out of the city for the night. From the jutting peninsula of

Navy Pier the enormous carousel made a slow, luminous circle against the backdrop of the night sky. At the top of the stairs I pushed open the French doors and ushered him into the ballroom.

"It's ridiculous, I know," I said as he just stood there gaping. "It's almost like keeping a horse and carriage, like trying to hold on to another era—one that's never coming back. But I love this room. I remember my parents had parties here when I was a little girl, and my brother Teddy and I would sneak out of bed and hide under the tables and watch them dance. Every time I come in here, I can still remember the swirling skirts and the smell of cigarette smoke mingled with champagne."

"I didn't realize that you'd lived here before."

"Yes. This apartment was a present to my parents from my grandparents for their wedding."

"Gosh. When my sister got married, I think my folks bought her a washer and dryer."

"Yeah, but at least she got to live wherever she wanted. As beautiful as my parents' apartment was, my mother still had to live in the same building as her mother-in-law."

"How old were you when you moved?"

"Six. I was heartbroken when we went to live in Lake Forest. I thought it was the end of the world. It was like being exiled to Gorky. It's funny how much of this apartment I remember. I've always been hopelessly and irrationally in love with it."

"Who says there's anything rational about love?" said Elliott, reaching up and tucking a stray hair that had come down from my French twist back behind my ear. With the simple intimacy of this gesture I suddenly felt as if all the oxygen had been sucked out of the room. The quiet emptiness of the apartment, my growing irritation with Stephen, the unrelenting loneliness of these last months spent pouring myself into the Avco deal all mingled together. I don't remember deciding to kiss him, only that I did.

And then I heard all the other voices, the practical ones that are either women's salvation or their downfall, the one that said that the floor would be hard and that we'd end up covered with plaster dust and feeling ridiculous. I took a step back.

"We have to talk," said Elliott. "Is there someplace where we can sit down?"

I nodded and led the way into the solarium where Mimi had stacked the discarded fabric samples on the deep ledge that formed the long window seat that circled the room. Inside I felt a sense of foreboding, afraid that I was about to be handed a kind of emotional ultimatum.

"What do you want to talk about?" I asked.

"Last night, after you and I got off the phone, I called my friend Marty. He and I were in the corps together. He was originally from some little town in Wisconsin, but he's with the Milwaukee PD now, working vice. Anyway, Marty owes me a favor." Elliott had served three tours of duty as a marine helicopter pilot, years spent plucking the wounded from the battlefield until his luck ran out and he was shot down himself. He came home with a Purple Heart and a long list of guys who owed him favors. "I wanted to know what he was hearing around the department on this Rendell thing."

"And?"

"As you'd expect, it's the talk of the department."

"Why? Just because he owned the Monarchs? Old men drop dead of heart attacks all the time."

"That's true, but this old man didn't."

"What?"

"According to Marty, the medical examiner says he didn't die of a heart attack."

"So it was the fall that killed him?"

"He was already dead when he went down the stairs."

"How do they know that?"

"Postmortem fractures bleed much less than ones sustained before death. Also, bruising that occurs after the victim's blood has stopped circulating has an orangy look, not red like you'd expect if the victim had been alive when they suffered the trauma."

"Then if it wasn't his heart and it wasn't the fall, what killed him?"

"According to Marty, his hyoid bone was fractured."

"Okay. I give up. Where's your hyoid bone, and how did Beau's end up broken?"

"The hyoid is a small bone, very well protected, at the base of the neck," replied Elliott slowly. "In ninety-nine percent of cases where it's been broken, the victim was strangled."

CHAPTER

11

"Are you saying that Beau Rendell might have been strangled?" I demanded in disbelief.

"Not might have, was. Word around the campfire is that the medical examiner has already ruled asphyxia as the cause of death."

"By what means?"

"There were no signs of a ligature or anything mechanical, so my guess is they're thinking it must have been manual strangulation."

"Meaning homicide?"

"It's pretty hard to choke somebody to death with your bare hands by accident—unless you're talking about kinky sex that got out of hand and went too far—"

"I don't think there's any chance of that, not at the stadium in the middle of the day—"

"So then it's homicide."

"I just can't believe it," I said, shaking my head.

"Why not?"

"Why not? Because up until two minutes ago we were all shocked and saddened by the suddenness of his heart attack. Now you're telling me that he was murdered!"

"The cops thought it was natural causes at first, too. You sound surprised that somebody wanted to strangle him."

"Are you kidding? I'm sure there was no shortage of people who'd mentally had their hands around his throat. I had a meeting with him this past Sunday, and *I* wanted to strangle him. No, what surprises me is that somebody apparently went ahead and actually did it."

"You know, everything I've ever heard about Beau Rendell made him out to be a real hard-nosed son of a bitch."

"That may be true, but it still doesn't tell us why somebody strangled him. Who do the police think did it? Do they have any suspects?"

"The cops like Jeff Rendell for the killer. So far he's their number one suspect."

"Of *course* he's their number one suspect. Not only did he argue with his father right before he died, but he also inherits the team. The cops will assume that profit was the motive because that's the easiest thing to think. The only trouble is that they're wrong."

"What makes you say that? I mean other than the fact that he's a friend of yours."

"You have to promise that what I'm going to tell you doesn't go beyond these walls."

"Scout's honor," replied Elliott, summoning up a credible rendition of the traditional two-fingered salute.

I quickly sketched out the Monarchs' financial situation for him. When I was finished, Elliott whistled softly under his breath.

"Do the cops know about any of this?" he asked.

"No."

"Why not?"

"Well, for one thing, if Beau had died of a heart attack—which is what we all thought—there was no reason to tell them."

"They didn't ask what Jeff and his father fought about?"

"They asked, but he didn't tell them."

"So now the cops assume he's hiding something."

"They're right. He is. The only trouble is it's not what they think it is."

"Then you have no choice but to come clean and tell them the whole story—the debt, the bank, the offer from L.A. . . ."

"I'm not sure that would be such a hot idea."

"Why not?"

"For one thing, while we might be taking away one motive we'd just be handing the cops another. Beau made it perfectly clear to us on Sunday that he wouldn't move the team. With him out of the way, Jeff is free to make a deal with L.A.

"Not only that, but the minute we tell the cops, we tell the world. You know that as well as anybody. Think about it. Right now it's bad enough that Jeff and Chrissy are in this mess. They have to go through the funeral and figure out a way to hold on to the team before the bank comes in and takes it away from them. But as soon as word gets out that they're even *considering* moving the team, it will turn into an absolute *nightmare*. The politicians, the media, they'll be out for blood. A reporter from *Dateline* will be waiting for Chrissy behind the lettuce at the grocery store, and the guys from *Hard Copy* will be trying to squeeze through the laundry chute. Unless the cops have something besides the fact that he's the obvious suspect, it's better to keep our mouths shut until we figure out what we're going to do to get the bank off our backs."

"Kate, you don't understand. This isn't a game. As soon as it gets out that this Rendell guy was murdered, the cops are going to be feeling the heat to come up with a killer. They're going to go after your friend Jeff and they're going to go after him hard."

"With what? What have they got?"

"All I know is what Marty told me. I'm sure there's

more. Like I said, when the uniforms first showed up, they thought Beau had fallen down the stairs and either hit his head or broken his neck. From an investigational standpoint, a fall down the stairs is just like a fall from a window. There are two separate scenes—the place where the victim fell or was pushed from, which in this case was the top of the stairs directly off the backdoor of the dead man's office, and then there's the place where the victim landed."

"I don't know if you've ever been to Monarchs Stadium," I said, "but it's a really funky setup. The team offices are in a series of double-wide trailers suspended from the stadium roof and connected end to end like railroad cars. Every thirty feet or so there's a metal staircase that connects the office to the concourse level. The stairs are really steep and narrow, like the gangway on a ship."

"So who else had an office close to Beau's?"

"Jeff's office is on one side and I think Coach Bennato's is on the other, but I'm not sure. There may also be a secretary stuck in there somewhere."

"There is. But Beau's secretary was out sick that morning. They brought a girl from accounting up to answer the phones, but she kept having to run back to her own desk."

"Did she see anything?"

"No, but apparently she heard plenty."

"From what I gather, everyone did."

"But that's not all. The crime lab found drag marks in the carpeting in the dead man's office."

"What kind of drag marks?"

"Parallel heel marks, the kind you'd make if you grabbed hold of someone who was either dead or unconscious by the armpits and dragged them along the ground."

"So let me see if I can get this straight. The cops think that in the heat of an argument Jeff strangled his own father with his bare hands and then dragged him across the office and threw him down the stairs?"

"That's exactly what they think. They figure Jeff must have panicked when he realized what he'd done and decided he'd better toss his old man down the stairs in order to make it look like an accident."

"Oh, come on," I demanded, "don't you think that's a little far-fetched?"

"You've got to remember, Kate. This is the Milwaukee Police Department we're talking about here. They're the same guys who rang Jeffrey Dahmer's doorbell and then took a little peek inside his refrigerator. There's not a whole lot that they're going to think is too far-fetched."

I was already on my way to his apartment when Stephen called me in the car and announced that we needed to talk. I didn't even bother to ask him what it was about. I was still furious with him for the chickenshit way he'd managed to squirm out of the meeting with Mimi. I didn't really want to hear what he had to say. I had something to get off my chest, and I figured it was something he'd had coming to him for a long time.

Our contractor liked to tell stories about other people he had worked for, couples who'd finished building their dream houses just in time to see the divorce papers served. He said it was always the same story: either they ran out of money, or they ran out of love.

With us it was never going to be a question of not being able to foot the bill; our problem was that there'd never been any love there to begin with. Of course, there'd been a lot of other things—loyalty, shared history, not to mention lust in spades. Still, I hoped that the lack of anything deeper might mean that we could manage a bloodless parting. Of course, as a lawyer, the voice inside my head had long ago grown hoarse berating myself about the foolishness of having bought the apartment with Stephen in the first place. Until he brought me to look at it, I had never so much as left a toothbrush at his house. Now, suddenly, we were bound together by contracts, deeds, and a million dollars' worth of real estate. "At least," I told myself as I left my car with the doorman in front of his building, "it won't be for long."

Even so, I felt nervous and uncertain. Unlike Chrissy, I had little experience with the vicissitudes of dating. I'd had too few relationships with men to really have a sense of how to end them. At sixteen Stephen Azorini had been my first boyfriend, and now, more than a decade later, he was still in my life.

He was waiting for me at the door of his apartment, his briefcase and his overnight bag still at his feet where he'd dumped them when he'd walked in from the airport. He'd loosened his tie, but that was as far as he'd gotten. He was still wearing the same dark suit he'd traveled in.

Of course, even rumpled he was still handsome. Six foot five, with broad shoulders that all but filled the doorway, he looked much more like a soap opera star than the CEO of a pharmaceutical company. I thought of all the skin we'd shared and found myself feeling a pang of something very much like regret at giving it up.

"I heard about Beau Rendell on the news this morning," he said, stepping aside to let me pass. We never kissed hello, even under less strained circumstances. "Have you talked to Chrissy?"

"I just got back from Milwaukee this afternoon," I said, slipping out of my coat and laying it carefully over the back of a chair. "I wouldn't have come back at all if we didn't have that meeting scheduled at the apartment with Mimi." I took a deep breath, bracing myself for what I was about to say next.

"That's what I wanted to talk to you about."

"The meeting?" I asked, wondering if he thought he was going to be able to scoot out from under this with some kind of apology.

"No, the apartment."

"What about it?"

In response he went over to the table that held the pile of mail that had accumulated during his absence and picked up a large manila envelope. "Have you gotten one of these yet?" he asked.

"I don't know. I haven't been home since Sunday," I said, my stomach churning at the sight of the familiar return address—Hanrahan & Goldstein, the law firm that handled litigation for Paul Riskoff's real estate empire. "What is it?"

"The bastard is suing us," exploded Stephen angrily.

Completely taken aback, I took the envelope from his hand and made my way into the living room to sit down. I took a few minutes to skim the multicount complaint. While I read, Stephen went over to the bar and poured me a tall Scotch. I took it without looking up.

"I'll say one thing for these guys," I said when I'd finished. "They demonstrate an imaginative interpretation of real estate law. Destruction of private property, theft, violation of the covenant governing the co-op, fraudulent conveyance of title—Riskoff's accusing us of everything but incest."

"But how can he get away with it?" demanded Stephen, plopping down next to me on the couch. "We're just trying to recover our costs for taking his damn playground down before it ended up in our living room. How can he sue us when he knows he's in the wrong?" His voice was filled with a scientist's sense of outrage at the illogic of it all.

"This isn't about right and wrong," I pointed out. "It's about what you can get away with."

"So what can he get away with?"

"Unfortunately, when you're Paul Riskoff, you can get away with an awful lot. He's the most powerful real estate developer in the city. He's also a vindictive asshole. Every judge, every alderman, every building inspector knows that if they cross him, he'll make a career out of making their lives hell."

"Which is exactly what he's got planned for us," observed Stephen, who may be a lot of things, but never slow on the uptake.

"Litigation is a form of war. Riskoff knows that if this ever goes to trial, he won't win, so he's going to make it as painful and expensive as he possibly can for us to get him there. His lawyers will insist on deposing every workman, every carpenter, and every laborer who ever lifted a shovel on the job. He wants us to understand exactly whom we're dealing with. This is just the beginning." I sighed. Suddenly the implications of what I'd just said occurred to me. What would be the point of breaking up with Stephen now that we were going to be inextricably bound together by a tangle of lawsuits that Paul Riskoff was going to make sure dragged out for the next half century?

I laid the complaint on my lap, suddenly feeling completely overwhelmed by it all. Stephen reached down and picked up one of my feet and began slowly massaging it with his enormous hands. Without meaning to, I sighed. Perhaps taking this for encouragement he began kissing my leg, beginning with the inside of my ankle and slowly working his way up. By the time he reached my thigh, I'd completely forgotten what I'd come there to tell him.

What is the worst thing you can say to someone?
The baby was born dead.
The biopsy showed cancer.

Your father was murdered and the police think you killed him.

As I drove up to Milwaukee the next morning, I wondered how anyone ever found the courage to say any of them.

It had turned cold overnight, and the roads were iced over in patches and dangerous. I drank coffee out of a Styrofoam cup and drove slowly, thinking about what whoever had killed Beau had managed to accomplish. The embalmer was probably already laying out his supplies—the gloves, fluids, needles, and implements of stainless steel—that mark our final journey from the is to the isn't. But beyond that I could think of nothing concrete that had been accomplished and certainly nothing that had been gained.

I arrived at Chrissy and Jeff's house, feeling cramped from the drive and even more puzzled than when I'd set out. The domestic tableau that awaited me inside the kitchen made my errand seem all the more difficult. Jeff, dressed in a ripped Monarchs T-shirt and a pair of flannel pajama bottoms, was at the stove frowning at pancakes on the griddle and making tentative stabs at them with a spatula. At the sight of me he raised the utensil in a mock salute. Chrissy was in her rocking chair, the portable phone wedged between her shoulder and her ear, feeding Katharine her bottle.

Over the top of the baby's head Chrissy rolled her eyes to indicate that whoever she was on with wouldn't stop talking, and I pantomimed asking her if I could take the baby. She nodded and I gathered my namesake up in my arms, effecting the transfer without disturbing either baby or bottle. I found a comfortable spot on the other side of the hearth and looked down at the baby, blond like her mother, eyes closed and furiously sucking down the funky-smelling formula, oblivious to everything else. The relaxation in her small body was practically intoxicating.

I waited through a series of Chrissy's yeses and uh-huhs in response to whomever she was talking to on the phone. Jeff poured a cup of coffee and set it at my elbow, returning to the griddle in time to fill a serving plate with overdone and vaguely misshapen pancakes.

Chrissy finally punched the end button with barely disguised relish and ran her fingers through her hair with a sigh. "That was Mr. Massy from the funeral home. He says that we're all set up for visitation this afternoon."

"Does that mean they've already released the body?" I asked.

"I guess so," replied Chrissy, getting up and taking three plates out of the cupboard and laying them on the table. "I don't think many people are going to be willing to make the trip to the funeral home just to pay their respects to us."

"Did he say anything about when the death certificate would be issued?"

"No, he didn't mention it," replied Chrissy.

"What's the big deal about the death certificate?" inquired Jeff, setting the plate of pancakes in the center of the table and rooting in the back of the refrigerator before coming up with a bottle of syrup.

"I talked to a friend of mine who knows a detective in the Milwaukee Police Department," I replied.

"You mean the cute private detective Claudia is always telling me you should dump Stephen for?"

"His name is Elliott," I said, not at all pleased that my friends had apparently been discussing my love life behind my back, "and according to what his friend says, Beau was strangled."

"Strangled?" cried Chrissy, instinctively reaching out for the baby and gathering her back up in her arms. "There must be some kind of mistake. They told us that he'd had a heart attack. Everyone knew he had a bad heart—"

"Are you saying that he was murdered?" asked Jeff, incredulously.

"I'm afraid so."

"Who could have done such a thing?" he inquired, his voice hollow with shock.

"It had to have been someone at the stadium that morning," I replied, taking his question at face value. "Who else was there?"

"Probably a couple of hundred people. The security people could give you a list. What day was it? Monday? The team was there, broken up into specialty teams reviewing Sunday's game films with the coaching staff. The grounds crew was probably getting the field ready for afternoon practice. The front office people were there. The concession guys are always in cleaning up and taking inventory the day after a game. . . . I still can't believe they're saying he was murdered."

"Who was on your father's appointment schedule that morning?" I prodded.

"I don't know. Gus Wallenberg was supposed to have a meeting, so I'm sure Feiss was somewhere around. Dad always sat down with Bennato the morning after a game. But what does any of it matter? Aren't the police in charge of trying to figure out who killed him?"

"Right now the police think it was you," I said softly.

Chrissy and Jeff's response was a stunned silence that was eventually interrupted by the ringing of the telephone. As if in a daze, Chrissy picked up the portable phone.

"Hello?" she asked, sounding unsure whether this was the appropriate greeting. She listened for a few seconds, frowning, then handed the phone to me. "It's for you," she said.

"Who is it?" I whispered, holding my hand over the mouthpiece.

"I have no idea," replied Chrissy with a bewildered shrug of her shoulders. "But whoever he is, he sounds really upset."

CHAPTER

12

It was Sherman Whitehead, who along with Cheryl was supposed to be holding down the fort on the Avco case. He sounding like he was calling from his car phone, but Chrissy was wrong about his state of mind. He wasn't upset. He was hysterical.

"We have a terrible problem," he whimpered through the static.

"What is it?" I shot back, getting to my feet and heading toward the dining room in search of privacy. Unlike a lot of associates, Sherman wasn't an alarmist. If he said we had a terrible problem, then that's exactly what we had.

"I was just out at Avco's offices getting the updated financials like you said. Of course, they didn't have them ready, so I had to sit around and wait for them. After a while I started noticing that there was something going on—you know, people rushing around, whispering, like something big had just happened—but whenever they saw me, they would clam up. When I started asking around, everybody started looking at their shoes. Nobody would tell me what was wrong."

"So did you find out what had happened?"

"I got it out of some girl who works in accounting. She's only been with the company a couple of weeks, and I don't think she realized that I didn't work there."

"So what is it?"

"Avco was served with an EEOC suit this morning."

"You've got to be kidding," I said, suddenly feeling weak-kneed and sick to my stomach. The Equal Employment Opportunity Commission is the federal agency responsible for all suits claiming employment discrimination. "What's the complaint?"

"Four male plaintiffs are alleging that they applied for jobs as food servers at a Tit-Elations in Muncie and were turned down because they're men. They're alleging sex discrimination."

"The only reason is that they didn't look good in pasties and a G-string," I snapped. "I told Eisenstadt that this whole 'they're-only-food-servers' stance would eventually come back and bite us."

Anticipating problems from what he darkly described as "conservative elements," Stuart Eisenstadt had insisted that in all our public filings we characterize Tit-Elation's barely clad female employees as food servers.

"Wait. There's more. Supposedly it's Reverend Marpleson who's behind the whole thing. They think that a lawyer in one of his watchdog groups must have spotted the red herring for the IPO and realized that if they were really food servers, then there was no reason they couldn't be men. The whole thing with the four men applying for jobs was probably a setup."

"What does Eisenstadt have to say about all of this?"

"I don't think you want to hear this."

"Try me."

"Well, as soon as I found out about the EEOC suit, I went straight to Colin Brandt's office and asked him when the hell he was planning on telling us about it. He says he called Eisenstadt first thing this morning—the minute they got it."

"And have you talked to Eisenstadt?"

"I called you first."

"Did you get a copy of the complaint?"

"Yeah. I made one before I left. I've got it with me."

"Good. You head back to the office and wait for my call."

I hit the end button when what I really wanted to do was hit Stuart Eisenstadt. The fact that I'd always feared that something like this would happen, that I'd practically held my nose through the entire IPO process, offered no consolation. Knowing you're going to wind up in shit doesn't make the reality of finding yourself hip deep in it any less unpleasant.

Again and again I'd warned Eisenstadt not to underestimate the ingenuity of the morally righteous. It is always fatal to assume that just because someone holds opposing beliefs—or in this case, any beliefs at all—it makes them unintelligent. I may not have agreed with much of what the Reverend Marpleson stood for, but I also knew that he hadn't become a political force to be reckoned with by being stupid.

And there was no denying that the good reverend had done his homework. Not only had we characterized the dancers as food servers in all of our preliminary offering documents, but in subsequent communications with the SEC we'd argued that the tips they received (and no doubt tucked into their G-strings) were food service gratuities for IRS accounting purposes.

I punched in Eisenstadt's number and paced the floor.

"Kate," said Eisenstadt. "I'm so glad you called. I've been trying to get hold of you."

"How? Using smoke signals? Sherman didn't have any problem finding out how to reach me." I was disappointed. I'd expected him to be a better liar.

"You've already talked to him?" he demanded, uneasily.

"What I want to know is why I haven't talked to you. Why is it that the only way I find out our client has been sued is after an associate accidentally overhears it from an accounting clerk? Were you ever planning on telling me, or were you going to wait until I heard about it on CNN?"

"You have no right to take that tone with me," snapped Eisenstadt, as if he was actually capable of being offended.

"Knock it off, Stuart. Right now we have to figure out whether this is an issue of material disclosure that has to be reported to the SEC."

"Don't you think you're overreacting just a little bit?" he demanded, but there was no mistaking the fear in his voice. "You and I both know that this is a frivolous lawsuit."

"How would I know that, Stuart? I haven't even seen it. But frivolous or not, defending against it is going to rack up some substantial legal expenses for a company that's already having cash-flow problems. That in and of itself is something that has to be considered."

"How can you be talking about telling the SEC when we're this close?" he practically shrieked.

"Panic doesn't become you, Stuart," I replied, sounding exactly like my mother. "Let's not get ahead of ourselves," I continued, softening. "I'm sure you agree with me that it's only prudent to review the complaint before offering an opinion to the client. But I'm telling you right now, if this is a material development, then we have absolutely no choice. We have to disclose it by submitting an updated registration to the SEC. Not only is that the law, but if it is material and we don't reveal it, the SEC will come after us, and the shareholders will be right behind them. If it turns out that the EEOC levels a judgment against them down the road and it adversely affects the company's share price, we'll be defending ourselves in court faster than you can say 'class action suit.' I'm stuck in Milwaukee today so I'm going to have Sherman drive up and bring me copies of all of our filings and correspondence with the SEC along with a copy of the complaint. We'll talk about what to do after I've had a chance to review them."

"Are you out of your mind? The SEC has been looking for an excuse to sink us since day one. Now you're saying that you'd be willing to turn around and give them the gun to shoot us with. I can't believe you'd be willing to torpedo the deal after we've come this far."

"And I can't believe you'd be willing to whore yourself to see it close."

There are plenty of lawyers who get off on being angry. They like the chest-thumping and the adrenaline, the way it invigorates them like a five-mile run without the sweat. Unfortunately, I'm not one of them. When I lose my temper, it's because I'm really angry, and after I've lost it, I feel rotten and guilty. No doubt it has something to do with my childhood.

I spent a few minutes alone in the dining room, looking out the window and willing myself into some kind of internal order. Chrissy and Jeff had enough of their own hysteria to deal with; they didn't need any more from me. By the time I'd calmed down sufficiently to return to the kitchen, Jeff was all alone, looking somber in his black dress suit, carefully knotting his dark tie using the front of the microwave as a mirror.

"Chrissy wants you to go and talk to her upstairs. She's putting on her face. I've got to get down to the funeral home."

"We have to talk," I said.

"Can't it wait?" asked Jeff, frowning with concentration at his reflection in the microwave.

"No. We have to decide what, if anything, to tell the police about what's going on with the team."

"Why do we have to tell them anything?"

"Because the longer they stay in the dark, the longer

they're going to spend running the ball in the wrong direction."

"You mean, thinking that I did it."

"Exactly."

"Listen, Kate," he said, smoothing his tie with the flat of his hand and turning to face me. "I don't like the idea that my father was murdered, and I like the idea of being a murder suspect even less. But I don't want any of this getting out until after the funeral. My father was a big deal in this town. He made a couple of big mistakes, but he made them because he wanted to give the Milwaukee fans a winner, and whatever else you say about him, he should be remembered for the good things, not the bad. He wasn't the world's best father, and lord knows I wasn't a perfect son, but the least I can do is give him that. The funeral is tomorrow morning. Let's wait until after it's over, then let's tell them. Fair enough?" He caught sight of the clock and let loose a groan. "Christ, look at the time. I've got to run."

I stepped up and gave him a quick hug. "Don't worry," I said, suddenly feeling more like a friend than a lawyer. "This is all going to turn out all right in the end."

The look he shot me over his shoulder on his way out the door said, I sure as hell hope you're right.

As soon as the door banged behind him, I went upstairs in search of Chrissy. I found her, as Jeff had indicated, in her bathroom putting on her makeup. The room was roughly the same size as my office, only prettier, with hand-painted porcelain sinks and flattering rose-tinted tile. The vanity was littered with dozens of jars, tubes, compacts, and brushes, including several implements that I had never seen before. I pulled out one of the two pouf stools tucked beneath the counter and took a seat.

"Trouble at the office?" she asked, carefully patting moisturizer around her eyes with her ring finger in the way she'd tried to teach me when we were both in high school—before she gave up trying to make me over.

"Oh, nothing that couldn't be solved with a .45 and a shovel."

"That bad?"

"That bad."

"As bad as what's happening to us?"

I shook my head. "In this case the clients are bad people and they're used to trouble. No matter what happens they'll just disappear under a rock for a while and then ooze back out again after it all sorts itself out."

"Whereas Jeff and I are about to be crushed into the ground and may never recover," observed Chrissy, setting down her brush and turning to look at me.

"I'm not going to lie to you and tell you that you aren't looking a pile of trouble in the face," I said. "But as big as it is, it's nothing that can't be handled. And I promise, I'll be right there next to you every step of the way."

"It's all so surreal," complained Chrissy. "I hold the baby, I look at the house—everything seems exactly the same as it did on Monday morning before any of this happened, only now it seems like it's so fragile that it's made of smoke. One big gust and it will all blow away. . . ."

"The baby isn't going to blow away. Jeff isn't going to blow away—"

"No. They're just going to come and take him away in handcuffs," observed Chrissy bitterly. "And all because they think that he couldn't wait to get his hands on the glorious Milwaukee Monarchs. And you know what the hysterical part of all of this is? While the cops are busy thinking that Jeff killed his father in order to get rich, we don't even have the money to pay for his funeral. That's why Jeff left early. He wanted to be there to talk to Mr. Massy in case our check has already bounced."

"It won't."

"What do you mean?"

"I had Cheryl make arrangements with your bank. Whatever checks you write will be automatically covered."

"We can't take your money, Kate," protested Chrissy.

"You and I have known each other much too long to even be having this conversation," I pointed out brusquely. "So just forget about it. We'll settle up once we've got this whole thing straightened out."

"You mean once we've moved the team to L.A."

"Is that what you and Jeff have decided you want to do?"

"We haven't decided anything. With everything else that's going on we haven't even had a chance to talk about it. On the one hand I know that Jeff doesn't want to be remembered as the guy who took the Monarchs away from Milwaukee."

"And on the other hand?"

"On the other hand I think he'd rather die than see Gus Wallenberg sitting in the owner's box."

By the time that Chrissy and I arrived at the funeral home, the line of mourners was so long that it wrapped all the way around the block. They were friends and acquaintances, funeral buffs and politicians, but mostly they were fans—regular folk who'd come to stand in the cold to wait their turn to pay their last respects and sign the visitors' book as a token of their appreciation of the man who'd brought them thirty years of Monarchs football. Even the Monarchs' court was there, the dozen or so fans who dressed up for every game. They stood near the head of the line, somber in their medieval garb. Beau, ever the showman, would have loved it.

Mr. Massy met us at the door and took Chrissy by the hand, drawing her into the building. He murmured a mixture of condolences and instructions as he led her to her place beside Jeff at the foot of the coffin. Beau, the man who could not have afforded a pauper's pine box, lay in a handsome bronze coffin lined with satin. Dressed in the fine blue suit that Chrissy had selected from his closet, he looked very much as he had in life—cantankerous, demanding, and formidable.

I cast my eyes around the room and eventually found what I was looking for—the two police detectives who'd come to the house to question Jeff, loitering near the service door, conferring quietly. Suddenly the whole thing seemed ridiculous and far-fetched and I was tempted to just walk up and tell them so.

Coach Bennato appeared from nowhere and took up his place beside me, both of us watching the pair of detectives from the distance.

"I see that the police are here," he announced conspiratorially and without preamble. "They were out at practice this morning."

"Really, what were they doing?"

"Asking questions. Snooping around."

"Who did they talk to?"

"Me, the security guard who found Beau, a lot of the front office people. I also heard they went down and talked to Jack McWhorter and some of the concession people to see if they saw anything."

"I'm sure it's all just routine," I replied.

"When my father-in-law dropped dead of a heart attack at the barber shop last year, the cops didn't come around asking questions."

"He didn't own a football team," I pointed out.

"That's true. He also really died of a heart attack."

"What's that supposed to mean?"

"Oh, come on. You don't think that the cops would waste the whole morning trying to pin down Jeff's movements if all they were worried about is what time Beau died of a heart attack, do you?"

"I'm sure they asked other people where they were, too," I said, not feeling happy at all about the direction this conversation was headed.

"Of course, they did," he answered. "But you can be sure they didn't get anything out of me."

"What's that supposed to mean?" I asked, suddenly finding myself looking at the face that had been caricatured on a thousand sports pages: the eyebrows knitted together into a single line, the jutting chin, the flinty eyes narrowed to a slit, giving nothing away.

"I don't know what you think has been going on with this team, but if you think that Beau was the only person who had something to hide, you're sorely mistaken."

The Pfister Hotel is a Milwaukee landmark, a lovingly restored shrine to the Victorian era that sits in the shadow of Monarchs Stadium. I pulled up to the curb, ignored the look of barely concealed disdain the doorman gave my Volvo, and consulted the slip of paper on which I'd written the room number I'd scribbled off my voice mail.

It was the break between afternoon and evening visitation, and I'd left Chrissy and Jeff in the hands of some friends who'd swooped them up and offered to feed them dinner. Lack of courtesy being the partner's prerogative, I didn't bother to call up from the lobby, but instead just made my way to the gilded elevator, took it to the fourth floor, and knocked on the door. I knew that Sherman Whitehead would not be taking a shower or a quick nap or indulging in the illicit pleasures of pay-per-view. What I expected was to find him pacing the floor with a copy of the EEOC complaint in one hand and a Diet Coke in the other. That's why I was so surprised to see Stuart Eisenstadt open the door.

"Hello, Kate," he said. "Come on in."

"Where's Sherman?" I asked, crossing the threshold into the living room of a large suite furnished in hotel Chippendale. The client might be hurting for cash, but that didn't mean that Stuart was cutting corners.

"I thought I'd bring the complaint up myself. That way you and I could just hash things out ourselves."

"Where's the complaint?" I asked, taking off my coat, eager to get this over with and get back to the funeral home.

"Over there on the table."

I sat down and made myself comfortable. Then I read everything through twice, determined to not let Stuart's presence make me feel under the gun.

"So what do you think?" he asked when I finally looked up. "Is that a baseless suit or what?"

"There are a lot of similarities to the Hooters suit," I pointed out. "Some of the language is nearly identical."

Hooters was a privately owned chain of restaurants whose main draw was amply endowed waitresses in skimpy outfits. Got up in short shorts and tight-fitting tops, the female food servers earned all of $2.13 an hour plus tips dispensing food, drinks, and jiggle at over two hundred restaurants around the country. The company had recently settled a class action suit that had been brought against them by seven Chicago men who'd claimed sexual discrimination when the chain had refused to hire them as waiters.

"I thought that thing was settled," protested Eisenstadt, for whom the facts had never been much of a strong suit.

"Yes. For almost $4 million, which was peanuts compared to what the government tried to get them for, which as I recall was damages plus setting up a $22 million fund to assist 'dissuaded' male job applicants. In the end I'm sure the suit cost the company something like $6 million. Besides, you're forgetting, Tit-Elations isn't as classy as Hooters. At Hooters the waitresses not only wear clothes, but they actually serve food."

"Let's not start splitting hairs—"

"If Avco's looking at a potential $6 million settlement, then you and I both know there's no question that this suit will have a material adverse impact on the company's financial performance. That, I remind you, is the issue at hand. Not whether tank tops and pasties are similar articles of clothing."

"And I'm telling you that this kind of frivolous suit is already covered by the routine-litigation-incidental-to-the-conduct-of-business clause in the registration document."

"It's really a question of where you draw the line between what is material and what is incidental. That's a lot of what-ifs. I just wonder whether in your zeal to deliver what you've promised to the client, you're losing sight of your responsibilities in this."

"Our responsibility at this point is to get this deal closed," snapped Stuart.

"By making sure that the letter of the law is satisfied," I shot back. "That's what I have to sign my name to, and I'm telling you right now that I'm not going to do it. I'm not going to risk exposing this firm to shareholder lawsuits down the road based on our failure to make necessary disclosure. Frankly, I don't care enough about whether the world has more topless bars to take the risk."

"I knew it," seethed Eisenstadt. "This has nothing to do with the law. This is about the fact that you're so uptight about a little skin that you can't see straight. If this were some other kind of company, we wouldn't even be having this conversation!"

"If this was a different kind of company, I wouldn't be

worried about how Tillman will look on *Hard Copy*," I pointed out. "You're the one who took us into the gutter in the first place. Don't insult my intelligence by trying to convince me that we're on some mountaintop."

"I always knew you were a prude," said Eisenstadt.

"Right or wrong, that still doesn't change the fact that I'm going to call the client right now and tell them that we need to call the SEC and edit the language in the legal proceedings section before I'll sign off on it."

"I'm going to bring this up with Tillman and the management committee," huffed Eisenstadt.

"Be my guest," I said. "But if you think that I'm a prude, wait until you talk to them."

CHAPTER

13

I'm usually not one of those lawyers who let their clients' problems keep them up at night—those are the guys who make their psychiatrists rich instead of making partner—but that night in Chrissy's guest room I could not sleep. While there is something about a late-night conference call with your client that turns into a screaming match that hardly seems designed to facilitate slumber, it wasn't Avco that was keeping me awake. It was Beau Rendell's murder.

As I tossed and turned in Chrissy's guest room I struggled to put what had happened into some kind of focus, but any sort of rational perspective stubbornly eluded me. I felt as though no matter how hard I tried, I was always either too close to things or too far away to see them clearly. The problem was that when it came to Chrissy and Jeff, I was completely incapable of being objective.

It wasn't just that I had a hard time believing that my friends were involved in anything as sordid as murder, but that I felt torn between the two roles that I was being called upon to play. I had the nagging sensation of always being forced to operate outside of my element—standing with Chrissy at the funeral home when I should have been at my desk figuring out a way to keep the team solvent and rushing off to meetings when I should have been at her side.

I must have finally dozed off because when I woke up, Chrissy was sitting beside me on the bed, shaking me and calling my name. I struggled to sit up, feeling disoriented and surprised to find that it was still dark.

"What is it?" I mumbled, rapidly clawing my way from sleep to panic. "What's happened? Is it the police? Have they come for Jeff?"

"No," whispered Chrissy, her voice sounding shocked and thin, "but you have to see today's paper."

I sat up and scrabbled clumsily at the nightstand, fumbling until I was finally able to switch on the light. Chrissy was dressed in a heavy flannel bathrobe. She smelled of winter and outdoors, and the newspaper that she handed me was still stiff and cold from lying out on the driveway. I was expecting to see a picture of the Reverend Marpleson beside an article accusing Avco of participating in the white slave trade. Instead I was assaulted by a two-inch headline, the size usually reserved for mass murderers and declarations of war: MONARCHS MOVE IN WORKS, it screamed.

At first I couldn't say anything. It took all my energy and concentration to force myself to breathe. Coming as it did so soon upon waking, my sense of internal disorder was so profound that for a fleeting moment I found myself wondering whether I also needed to tell my heart to beat.

I forced myself to read the entire article, whose main thrust appeared to be that Jeff Rendell, without even waiting until his father was decently in the ground, was determined to move the team to L.A. in order to not only enrich himself, but also enjoy the glamorous California lifestyle at the expense of the loyal Milwaukee fans. This was incendiary stuff designed to sell a ton of newspapers. That much of it was untrue seemed practically beside the point.

There was absolutely no mention of the team's financial predicament, only the lurid retelling of Jeff's acrimonious battles with his father and his disagreements with Bennato about how the team was to be run. While Chrissy was outraged by the unfairness of the portrayal of her husband's motives, what troubled me was not what the paper had gotten wrong, but what it had gotten right.

What I found most terrifying were the details—the exact number of luxury boxes that were in the plans for the new Los Angeles stadium and the exact dollar amount that had been offered to help move the team. Whoever had fed the information to the paper had had access to the term sheet that Jack McWhorter had distributed last Sunday morning in Beau Rendell's dining room.

"Has Jeff seen this yet?" I asked.

"No, he's still asleep. I gave him another one of those sleeping pills last night. I didn't have the heart to wake him."

"Let him sleep for now," I said. I needed time to think. From somewhere in the house I could hear the telephone ringing. "Don't get that," I instructed. "It's probably a reporter."

"That's who woke me up this morning. Somebody called. That's why I went out to get the paper."

That made me think of something. "I wonder why no one from the paper called Jeff for confirmation before they ran the story," I mused out loud. "You'd think they would have if only to be able to run a denial or 'no comment.' It doesn't make sense."

"Maybe they tried. Ever since Beau died we've gotten so many calls from reporters, we've been taking the phone off the hook."

"Either that or you're being deliberately sandbagged."

"What do you mean?"

"Maybe whoever leaked the story didn't want you to know that it was being written."

"Who would want that?"

"Maybe the cops."

"How would the cops have found out about the L.A. offer?"

"Maybe somebody fed them the term sheet."

"Beau may have had a copy in his office. Maybe the police found it after he died."

"No. Beau didn't have a sheet. He tore his up at the meeting on Sunday morning. Jack handed out four numbered copies. I still have mine. Assuming that Jeff still has his, that leaves Harald Feiss."

It has been said that there is a shorthand to every crisis, a rhythm to the swells and troughs of catastrophe that, if you are adept enough, can be anticipated and ridden like the surf. John Guttman, the partner I'd been assigned to when I first went to work at Callahan Ross, went a step further and contended that it could be mapped out in code. Like Morse, he favored a binary representation with *B* for big problems and *s* for small. According to Guttman, most crises fell into a BssssBssssBBssss pattern. Even in Avco, the IPO from hell, there were more *s*s than *B*s. But from the morning of the funeral the buzz on the Monarchs was BBBBB!

While Chrissy got dressed and fed the baby, I got on the phone and started waking people up. Poor Sherman, who'd spent most of the night researching case law on sex discrimination, had fallen asleep at his desk. Cheryl, grouchy at having been rousted from her bed at this hour, was nonetheless grateful for the warning. By the time she arrived at the office, everyone from CNN on down would be clamoring for a piece of me. I felt guilty about leaving her on the hot seat, but I had my own problems. When going to a funeral seems the least stressful part of the coming day, you know you're in for one hell of a rough ride.

All things considered, Jeff took the news well. I honestly think he had been so bludgeoned by the events of the past few days that he was beyond all feeling. As he sat at the kitchen table looking at the breakfast that Chrissy had cooked for him, but not eating it, I found myself thinking of my roommate Claudia's patient, the man who'd had his arm amputated while pinned under a truck on Wacker Drive. Looking at Jeff's bloodless face, I found myself wondering whether the wounds that are not physical may be the ones from which it is most difficult to recover.

The doorbell rang and I went to answer it, mentally steeling myself for a horde of reporters. Instead, when I opened the door, I found a single messenger in a black government car delivering an envelope. It was addressed to me. I knew immediately what it was. I opened the envelope and scanned the letter. His Honor Robert Deutsch, the mayor of Milwaukee, felt that under the circumstances it would be inadvisable for us to meet at this time. I realized that this was just politics, the first step in what would no doubt end up being a very complicated dance. Still, I couldn't help but find it disheartening.

Just as I was about to shut the front door, I saw Jack McWhorter pull up in his black Porsche. He stepped out looking handsome and sinister, like a seductive undertaker in a B movie.

"I came straight from the airport," he said, slamming the car door behind him.

"So I take it you've heard," I said.

"Are you kidding? They have huge posters at the newsstands. From the size of them you'd think we'd just invaded China."

"People don't care that much about China," I pointed out, holding the front door open to let him pass.

"Who the fuck leaked it?" he demanded, giving me the evil eye.

"It had to be Feiss."

"Why Feiss?"

"Because he wants to build a stadium in the middle of the cornfields of Wauwatosa. You know. If you build it, they will come. He leaks the news that the team may move and then starts waving the plans for his suburban stadium around and suddenly he's a hero."

"You realize this makes everything much trickier at my end," confided Jack. "I'm not sure my people ever anticipated getting involved in a situation where there would be negative publicity before the fact."

"Then tell them to grow up," I replied. My entire plan for keeping the team in Milwaukee was based on the credible threat of the Monarchs moving to California. The last thing I wanted was Jack and the Greater Los Angeles Stadium Commission folding on me now. "I want you to set up a meeting for Jeff with your people in L.A."

"When?"

"Tomorrow," I answered. The sooner I managed to get Jeff out of town the better. "I'll arrange for someone from Callahan Ross's West Coast office to come in and start hammering out the terms of the deal. It's put-up-or-shut-up time."

It was hardly the send-off Beau would have hoped for. Not only was there no young widow to sob prettily at the graveside, but the son he left behind to follow in his footsteps stood in the shadow of a murder indictment. As stunned as we'd been by that morning's headline, none of us had given much thought to the fact that in addition to the news of Jeff's apostasy, the paper had also published a map of the route the funeral cortege would take.

From the minute our limousine pulled out of Chrissy and Jeff's driveway, the streets were lined with people. They were dressed in Monarchs colors, and many held hand-lettered signs bidding farewell to Beau Rendell. The communications directed at Jeff were significantly less pleasant. We passed more than one sign that read BURY JEFF INSTEAD! From the underpass near the Art Museum someone had dressed a dummy in a Monarchs uniform and hung it from the bridge so that the funeral procession passed directly beneath its dangling feet. There was a knife stuck into its back and a sign around its neck read JEFF DID THIS.

The funeral mass was to be held at the Cathedral of St. John the Evangelist, the seat of the archdiocese of Milwaukee. Like the German settlers who'd erected it, it was a structure more stolid than elegant, stern rather than inspiring. Once the center of a prosperous neighborhood, over the years changing demographics had left it on the fringes of downtown while earnest urban planners had turned an adjacent vacant lot into a small urban park. It was on this swatch of green, aptly named Cathedral Park, that a crowd of several hundred people now milled angrily, ringed by a cordon of mounted police decked out in full riot gear.

I looked out through the smoked glass of the funeral limousine at the church, dark and forbidding under the oppressive ceiling of low clouds that marked the day. Broadcast vans blocked the curb, electrical cables snaking out through their open doors, up the steps and into the vestry of the church. I caught a glimpse of Harald Feiss talking to a leggy woman with network hair, but I couldn't tell whether they were arguing or getting set up for an interview.

As our car edged closer to the crowd Chrissy shifted nervously in her seat, no doubt saying a prayer of thanks that she'd decided to leave the baby at home with the sitter. Jeff, hidden from view by the limo's mirrored windows, craned his neck to get a better look at the crowd. I examined his face expecting to see fear and was surprised to find something else burning in the back of Jeff's eyes, something very much like satisfaction.

At the sight of the hearse the crowd suddenly heaved and surged like a living organism, pulsing until it had built up sufficient momentum to break through the police line. The officers pulled out their nightsticks, wheeled around, and dug their heels into their horses' flanks in pursuit. I don't know which was more terrifying, the screaming mob or the horde of journalists who thundered after them wielding their microphones like clubs.

Sometimes you don't understand the danger until it has already passed. Events move so fast that their significance can't be absorbed as they happen. It is only afterwards that you realize what might have been, what has been so narrowly averted.

I saw it all in snapshots: the half-eaten cheeseburger that struck the window and slid down the glass leaving a trail of mustard and a disk of pickle in its wake. The man with the big nose and flapping jowls, his Monarchs cap askew, lunging for the door handle. Then the look of surprise on his face as a cop on horseback grabbed him by the scruff of the neck and yanked him away.

There was yelling and the sounds of scuffle all punctuated by the ominous thunks of objects hitting the car. We sat frozen, helplessly watching the mayhem of which we were the center. In the front seat, our driver sweated and crossed himself, mumbling something under his breath—whether curses or prayers I could not tell.

Chrissy screamed as the windshield suddenly seemed thick with blood. It took a minute before we realized that it was ketchup. The driver, with a giggle of relief, switched on the windshield wipers, which smeared the thick liquid grotesquely across the glass.

Suddenly we heard the sound of impact as something

heavy landed on the hood. The Jester, the bandy-legged member of the Monarchs' court, dove across the hood of the car, his bug eyes staring at us through the pink streaks of ketchup. He banged his hands against the windshield in a fury, shouting out some piece of demented gibberish. But he disappeared almost as quickly as he'd materialized, pulled back by strong hands and leaving us with the memory of his pockmarked face, gap-toothed and filled with monumental rage.

CHAPTER
14

Sirens heralded the arrival of reinforcements, and slowly the tide began to turn. As soon as the threat of getting a ride downtown seemed credible, demonstrators took off on foot and quickly disappeared down alleys and side streets, leaving a trail of broken glass and garbage in their wake. After what seemed like an eternity, a uniformed officer approached our car, signaled the driver to roll down the window, and assured us that it was now safe to make our way into the church.

The archbishop, looking shaken, emerged from behind the heavy egg-splattered doors and greeted us on the wide, stone steps. Taking Jeff by the hand, he led the Rendells into the dark sanctuary of the cathedral. I made my way behind them followed by the first tentative clusters of funeral-goers.

The interior of the cathedral was damp and narrow like the inside of a tomb. Above, from the ribbed vaults of the ceiling, the vestments of dead clergy hung like flags while thousands of votive candles flickered in the gloomy alcoves that punctuated the transept. From somewhere behind us the deep-throated organ throbbed the first mournful strains of requiem, and the air was thick with incense.

I took my place in the hard pew beside Chrissy and Jeff and focused my attention on the casket that had just been brought to rest before us. In life Beau had always made himself the focus, the epicenter of attention. Why was it that in death I seemed to be always losing sight of him? His murder had put into motion a chain of events that seemingly swamped the event itself. Whenever I found myself even beginning to think about what had precipitated it all, something else popped up to divert my attention yet again.

Coach Bennato appeared on the altar to deliver the eulogy—one old man's farewell to another. I looked around for Harald Feiss and found him seated across the aisle between Gus Wallenberg and a delegation from the mayor's office. This being an election year, the mayor had no doubt decided that there was nothing to be gained by doing anything linking himself to Jeffrey Rendell, who had, with the publication of six column inches of type, found himself Milwaukee's number one leper.

Marie Bennato snuffled noisily throughout her husband's remarks while her daughter did her best to comfort her. Of the hundreds of mourners who had paid their respects, hers were the first tears I saw shed for Beau Rendell. I suspected she cried at funerals as a matter of course.

Bennato's speech covered the distance between barroom reminiscence and locker room oratory. He told of miraculous victories and bitter defeats, of snowstorms and blown plays, of broken limbs and shattered dreams. He spoke without irony of Beau's faith in his players, his love for the game, and his devotion to his community. His words were met with silence save for the scratching of the pencils of the reporters at the back of the church, scribbling it all for the afternoon editions.

At the conclusion of the service we made our way out of the church between police lines three men deep. Chrissy said it made her feel like the wife of an about-to-be-deposed Latin American dictator. Jeff just huddled in his coat, looking shell-shocked and oblivious. Four days earlier he thought he'd reached the end of his rope when he told his father that he was leaving the Monarchs. Now his father was dead, he owned the team, and he was so vilified by the fans that they were pelting him with garbage. If he were a prisoner, I would have had him placed on suicide watch. I made a mental note to speak to Jack about keeping an eye on him when they were in L.A.

At the cemetery it felt like February. Darkness clung stubbornly to the edges of the day while the clouds let loose a steady stream of freezing drizzle. Most of the mourners had not made the trip to River Hills for the burial. A few friends clustered beneath dripping umbrellas. The entire Monarchs team was there, no doubt Bennato's doing. They stood together, silent and gigantic, like a stand of rain-washed sequoias.

Whatever meager semblance of restraint the press had managed at the cathedral was immediately abandoned in the open air of the cemetery. The clicking of camera shutters punctuated the archbishop's final benediction, and at least one cameraman found a perch on an adjacent headstone in order to capture the most affecting shot of Beau Rendell's casket being lowered into the earth. I don't care what the ACLU lawyers say; the framers of the Constitution, when they contemplated freedom of the press, could not have possibly imagined such gall or such intrusion.

When it was done, we went back to Beau's house and braced ourselves for the onslaught of mourners. Instead, we found ourselves barricaded in Beau's house, under siege by the press, and abandoned by most of the people that Chrissy and Jeff had once counted as friends. Under other circumstances it might have been funny. What if you threw a wake and nobody came? But it was all too clear that the news that Jeff might move the team had set into motion the complex phenomenon of shunning.

It was interesting to see who did show up. The Bennatos

came, either out of a sense of loyalty to Beau or because the coach knew full well that the Monarchs were the only team in the NFL that would have him. The others who came were largely out-of-towners, league officials, sports luminaries, and broadcast executives who'd made the trip from places like New York and Los Angeles and were for the most part oblivious to the exigencies of what was going on in a place like Milwaukee.

Of course, the other owners came, not just to pay their respects, but to welcome the newest member to their select fraternity. Taken together they were a strangely geriatric group sporting, in several notable cases, surprisingly bad toupees. There was no question they were men for whom dollars now made do for testosterone, a fact that their female companions seemed to bear out. I thought of the owners' meetings that were held several times a year and felt a sudden pang of sympathy for Chrissy.

As at the cemetery, the team was there to the man, whether out of loyalty to the franchise, the coach, or merely to do what they could to protect their highly paid jobs was hard to say. Seeing them in Beau's living room made me realize that television does not do justice to football players. To really appreciate what sets them apart you need to stand next to them. Even after years with Stephen Azorini, who was six foot five, I found some of the players, especially the offensive linemen, nothing short of astonishing. Standing together near the bar, they seemed almost like a portrait of hugeness in repose—meaty arms that hung from their impossibly broad shoulders like thick-jointed clubs, hands that looked like they could crush coconuts as easily as peanut shells, necks like tree stumps. Collectively they seemed to evoke as many thoughts about the evolution of the species as they did about the evolution of football.

Suddenly the group shifted and Jake Palmer caught my

eye. He was dressed in what looked like a Brooks Brothers suit on steroids, and he had a pair of delicate wire-rimmed glasses on his nose that lent him the air of the world's largest poet. At the sight of me his face broke into a broad, gap-toothed grin and he excused himself from his teammates to come over and talk to me. He shook my hand, and for an instant it seemed to disappear up to the elbow. I was relieved to discover that today he smelled of aftershave, not whiskey, but I was astonished to find that if anything he seemed even bigger sober than he had drunk.

"I just wanted to say thank you for the other night," he said. "You have to tell me what I can do to pay you back for your hospitality and all—you know, tickets, autographs, anything. You just name it."

"How about you just promise to stay out of The Baton for a while," I suggested.

"Are you kidding?" he demanded with a chuckle that seemed to originate deep within his three-hundred-pound frame and slowly rumble to the surface. "There's no way I'm *ever* going back to that nasty-assed place again!"

"Good. Then you've learned your lesson."

"I don't know about that, but you had better believe that those special-team assholes that brought me there have learned a lesson or two, too," he declared ominously. "But, hey, while we're talking, can I ask you something?"

"Sure."

"Jeff Rendell said that you're some kind of big hotshot lawyer."

"Something like that."

"So then what I want to know is what the hell are you doin' living in a place like the one I woke up at?"

"What? You don't like my apartment?" I asked, in mock offense.

"I didn't say that," he replied quickly. "It's just not the kind of crib I'd expect for some high-priced legal talent."

"The apartment belongs to my roommate, who's doing a surgical residency. It's cheap and it's convenient to the hospital."

"So, you're dating a doctor, huh?" He grinned approvingly.

"No." I laughed. "You met my roommate the other night."

"What? You mean that little girl with the smelling salts?"

"You better hope that if they ever pull you out of a car wreck in pieces that 'little girl' is the one they get to put you back together. She's one of the best young trauma surgeons in the country."

"I may not remember that night that well, but I do know one thing, I still owe you big time."

"Please, don't mention it."

"You don't get it," he replied earnestly. "When I was growing up in Alabama, we lived in a one-room house with outdoor plumbing, all seven of us. There's not one single thing I've got in my life that I didn't earn myself. When I make a mistake, I take my lumps, just like when I'm on the field. When somebody does me a good turn, I pay them back."

I thought of what I had been born into, the doors that open at the mere mention of my name, and looked up at the big man before me with a new sense of admiration. "I understand," I said.

"Then don't forget that I owe you one. Jake the Giant always pays up. Just ask those special-team assholes," he added with a chuckle. "In the meantime, you remember, anything you need, anything at all, you just come to me."

I must confess I found his offer touching—especially coming as it did from a man whose thighs were roughly the same diameter as beer kegs.

*   *   *

The police came calling as soon as the last of the mourners had left. Of course, I knew that they'd been watching the house. I just hadn't realized what they'd been waiting for. Jeff was in his father's study, gathering up some papers, so I went with Chrissy to the door. When the two detectives handed Chrissy the warrant, she passed it to me quickly, as if it had burned her hand.

I read quickly, relief flooding through me. "It's a warrant to search this house," I told her, trying to keep my voice neutral. I didn't want to give Eiben and Zellmer the satisfaction of knowing that I'd expected them to come for Jeff. "They also have one for your house." I turned to the two detectives. "Do these have to be carried out right now?" I asked. "The Rendells are exhausted from the funeral."

"They're not going to have to do any heavy lifting," replied Eiben without any trace of humor. "They don't even have to be present if they choose not to. But we aren't leaving without executing both warrants."

"Could you do them simultaneously?" I asked. "I could stay out here, and Chrissy and Jeff could go back to their house. That way, at least, it won't take all night."

"Suit yourself," replied the detective, taking a toothpick from his pocket, examining it critically, and inserting it in the corner of his mouth as I stepped aside to let him pass.

It was a hideous ending to an unspeakable day. It was also a message from the Milwaukee Police Department, one that said, loud and clear, that the gloves were now off. I whispered what few words of encouragement I could to Jeff before he and Chrissy got into the car and headed, leading a line of squad cars, back to their house to watch while men in uniform rifled through their personal possessions.

As soon as they were gone, I slipped back into the house and checked my address book to make sure that I still had my list of Milwaukee criminal attorneys with me. I'd started keeping one after I'd gotten my first late night call from Jeff about a player who'd gotten himself into trouble. I'd never once imagined that I'd have occasion to consult it on behalf of Jeff himself.

I went back into the house to observe the cops as they executed their warrant. Perhaps naively, I was less concerned with the possibility of planted evidence than I was about the cops lifting pieces of Beau's sports memorabilia. I needn't have been concerned. As I watched the cops turning the house inside out, it was obvious that the object of their search was something small and very specific. It was nearly midnight when they finally finished removing and bagging as evidence every single key they could find.

CHAPTER
15

The next morning the mayor launched a public relations jihad against Jeff Rendell and the Milwaukee Monarchs organization. When I came downstairs, all three networks had preempted their regular broadcasts to carry his press conference (which had no doubt been timed for a live national feed and to be picked up by CNN). Mayor Robert V. Deutsch was nobody's fool. A career politician with a reputation for fiery oratory and an unapologetically confrontational style, he was also a man with a grudge.

Beau Rendell had come out and campaigned actively for his opponent in the last election, one that Deutsch had won by the thinnest of margins. If his press conference was any indication, it appeared that this time around Deutsch was determined to improve on that margin of victory at any cost. I had wondered why he'd been so quick to cancel our meeting, but I had been too preoccupied with the funeral to figure it out. Now I knew. Whoever leaked the news of a possible Monarchs move had handed the mayor of Milwaukee an issue he could ride to victory in the next election.

And ride it he did. Clutching the top of the podium, which was jammed with microphones, he vilified Jeffrey Rendell like a revival tent minister bearing witness against the devil. Alleging that the city had been negotiating in good faith with Beau Rendell "right up to the morning of his death," the mayor railed against Jeff's greed and shocking lack of loyalty to the city of his birth. Somehow, he neglected to mention the fact that we'd contacted him immediately after Beau's death and the fact that he'd canceled our meeting. Maybe with so much political hay to make, it just slipped his mind.

Instead he spoke movingly of how the city had already commissioned an architect to remodel the stadium, only to have Jeffrey Rendell, before his father's body had even been committed to the earth, threaten to treat the beloved Monarchs and their long tradition like just another rich man's plaything. Looking directly into the cameras, his voice cracking with emotion, he vowed that he would not rest until Jeff's efforts to move the team were irrevocably thwarted.

As soon as the courthouse opened that morning, the city was planning on filing suit against the Monarchs, alleging that any contemplated move would breach the team's contract with the city and asking for an injunction keeping the team in Milwaukee. This was as good a piece of political theater as I'd seen, and having grown up in Chicago, I'd been raised on the best. But from the Rendells' perspective it was undeniably a nightmare.

Chrissy was as angry as I'd ever seen her, pacing the kitchen and snapping her fingers. Her face was white except for two red spots that burned high on her cheekbones. As far as I could tell, Mayor Deutsch was lucky that he was safely downtown at City Hall. Chrissy might have weighed a hundred pounds soaking wet, but I still wouldn't have given much for his chances if he found himself in Chrissy's kitchen.

Jeff's reaction was more complicated and harder to decipher. His prevailing emotion appeared to be disbelief, as if a part of him was just waiting to wake up and have this whole unpleasant dream be over. On another level he seemed to be trying to shake off the lethargy of the past couple of days. Although he was far from being fully engaged, he was at least willing to go through the motions to do what had to be done. My guess is there just wasn't that much left over for being mad at Deutsch. That was okay. As far as I was concerned, that was my job.

I looked at the clock. Coach Bennato would be arriving soon to talk to Jeff about the upcoming game against Green Bay. Jeff had tried to beg off; he was due to leave with Jack McWhorter for L.A. in less than two hours, but Bennato had insisted. I suspected that Beau had been calling the shots on the field for so long that Bennato had forgotten how to take responsibility for what happened on the field.

"Why don't you turn that thing off," I said to Chrissy, with a nod to the TV. "It's time to circle the wagons and make a plan."

Chrissy nodded and picked up the remote control. The blow-dried anchor vanished in a blink. In the sudden silence the mechanical crank of the baby swing seemed unnaturally loud. I looked over at little Katharine dozing sweetly with her head resting against the pattern of little lambs that decorated her blanket and tried to find some consolation in the fact that however things turned out, at least she'd have no memory of these events.

I poured myself a cup of coffee and pulled up a chair at the kitchen table.

"Okay, first things first," I said. "From here on in we're on combat footing. That means that neither of you talks to the police without an attorney present and you don't talk to the press at all. Understood?"

Chrissy and Jeff both nodded woodenly. Jeff especially seemed anxious and preoccupied, his thoughts elsewhere. It was as if he couldn't quite get his mind around the fact that this was actually happening to him. But then, of course, neither could I.

"Now that the story of the move is out," I continued, "I don't see any reason why we shouldn't fill the police in on what's going on with the team and the bank. Hopefully that'll help take some of the heat off of you."

"Thank God," interjected Chrissy, with feeling. "Then maybe they'll stop harassing us and start looking for who really killed Beau."

Jeff said nothing, but instead shot Chrissy a peculiar, inquiring look. There seemed to be something off kilter with them today, a kind of edginess to their presence together that made me think that perhaps they'd had a quarrel. I couldn't help but wonder whether everything that was going on wasn't putting a terrible strain on their marriage. Of course, it would be a miracle if it weren't.

The phone rang. "Don't answer that," said Chrissy. "After what happened yesterday we don't have any friends left, and there's no one I want to talk to. Let the machine pick it up."

We listened as a woman's voice came on the tape, identifying herself as a TV producer. She wanted Jeff to call her immediately. She wanted to send a crew right over to give him a chance to explain his side of the story. As soon as she hung up, there was another call, this time a radio announcer who explained that he'd slotted Jeff for a rush-hour interview and was just calling to let him know. When the phone rang a third time, Jeff stood up and carefully took the receiver off the hook. Even the mechanical throbbing noise that was meant to get you to return the phone to its cradle was less annoying than the incessant intrusions of the press. Besides, it turned itself off after a minute. Unfortunately, when it came to the media assault that had been launched against the Rendells there was no end in sight.

"As long as we're all agreed," I continued, "I'll get in

contact with the detectives investigating your father's death and fill them in on the team's situation. In the meantime, we have to decide what to do about the team and the bank. Today is Friday. On Tuesday Gus Wallenberg and First Milwaukee are going to call the loan. That gives us five days. So I guess the big question is, what do you guys want to do?"

"You mean, do I want to move the team to L.A.?" Jeff asked.

"That's one way of asking the question. Another way is to ask what's most important to you both as a family? What do the two of you want? Do you want to continue owning a professional football team? Do you want to stay in Milwaukee? Would you be happy in L.A.? I'll try to get you to wherever you want, but I need to know the outcome you're looking for."

Jeff looked at Chrissy and then back at me. "I want things to be the way they were," he said finally.

"Meaning?" I prompted.

"Meaning before my father sold his soul to First Milwaukee, before Jack McWhorter came waving this L.A. thing in my face . . . I want things to be back the way they were."

"So if I could figure out a way that would be financially feasible for you to keep the team in Milwaukee, that would be your first choice?" I asked.

"How would you do that?"

"First of all I'd try to twist Mayor Deutsch's arm to get him to the table. I'd explain that unless certain conditions are met—like the stadium renovation, like renegotiating the lease on more favorable terms—then you're moving, no ifs, ands, or buts. Then, in the meantime I'd try to find a white knight, a partner with deep pockets who'd be willing to come in as the minority owner of the team in exchange for paying off the note to First Milwaukee."

"Do you think that's possible?" asked Jeff, brightening for the first time since his father's death.

"It's possible, but it's still a lot of ifs."

"I still can't believe you'd want to stay after what they did to us yesterday," declared Chrissy. From the level of grievance and exasperation in her voice I guessed this was what she and Jeff had been arguing about. "How can you possibly want to keep the team here after all those things that asshole Bob Deutsch said about you on TV this morning?"

"Dad liked to always say that football is a rough sport," replied Jeff. "If you can't take your licks, you'd better stick to chess. I just try not to take it personally. It's like the guys who knock the shit out of each other on the field. It's all just part of the game."

Coach Bennato arrived at the door with his hair disheveled and his tie askew after he'd gotten into a shoving match with Chip Henderson, the sportscaster from Channel Four, who'd tried to intercept him in the driveway for an interview. From his tone of voice it sounded as though he'd almost enjoyed it. Bennato also had a few choice epithets for Mayor Deutsch, including a couple that I was unfamiliar with. The kind of transaction-based practice I maintained might be considered the locker room of the legal profession, but in football the locker room was really the locker room.

From the kitchen I heard baby Katharine crying. Chrissy excused herself to get the baby out of the swing and take her upstairs to the nursery. Ever since her father-in-law's death her house, her life, no longer were her own. The phone, the door, fruit baskets, condolence callers, and reporters—all not just unwanted, but unasked for.

I wished Coach Bennato good luck against Green Bay, not wanting to linger. He looked exhausted and irritable rubbing his knuckles in the front hall as if still looking for a fight. The sight of him reminded me that Chrissy and Jeff were not the only ones who'd been profoundly affected by recent events. When Beau died Coach Bennato had lost his staunchest supporter. With Jeff at the helm, his future, along with everybody else's, seemed much less secure.

I hurried up the stairs to gather up my things. I was planning on staying only until Jack came to collect Jeff to take him to the airport. Even though my mandate from the Rendells was to find a way to keep the team in Milwaukee, I'd managed to convince Jeff that negotiating aggressively to move the team to Los Angeles was one of the key elements of my plan. To that end I'd arranged for one of the partners from the firm's L.A. office to meet them at the airport. He was one of the attorneys who handled the Raiders' move to Oakland and was more than capable of moving things along in a convincing manner.

As I stood balling up my clothes and dumping them into my overnight bag, I found myself thinking how fortunate it was that Jack's company had its own jet for their trip to the West Coast. After the mayor's TV blitz I doubted Jeff would make it to the gate in the regular terminal alive.

I was just carrying my overnight bag downstairs when the doorbell rang. I went to answer it, checking through the peephole to make sure it wasn't a film crew from *Hard Copy* before I opened the door. As I turned the handle, I concluded that it was actually someone worse. I pulled the door open and confronted Harald Feiss.

"I'm here to speak to Jeff," he announced, trying to muscle his way inside.

"Is he expecting you?" I demanded, arms crossed, deliberately blocking his path.

"I don't give a rat's ass what he expects," puffed Feiss, treating me to a whiff of last night's gin. "He can either talk to me here or in court."

"Are you sure you still know the way to court?" I inquired. "I understand it's been a long time."

"I don't need to take this shit from you," he fumed. "If Jeff won't see me, I'm going straight down to the courthouse and filing a minority shareholder suit."

"Alleging what?" I demanded. Feiss owned something like 2 percent of the team, which Beau had convinced him to take in lieu of payment when money got tight.

"That, among other things, the Monarchs Corporation has failed to hold regular board meetings and has excluded the minority shareholders from key business decisions."

"You can't possibly be serious," I exclaimed. "You and Beau went out drinking together every night. What did he need to call meetings for?"

"Are you going to let me in or not?" huffed Feiss.

"Let him in," said Jeff from behind me.

He and Bennato had just emerged from their meeting in the dining room. From the look on Bennato's face I could tell he was surprised to see Feiss here.

"We missed you at the house after the funeral," continued Jeff quietly. His voice had a dangerous edge to it that I'd not heard before. I wondered whether sitting down with Bennato had finally brought home the reality that he was now the owner of the Monarchs. "I guess by the time you were done giving interviews about what an ingrate I am, it was too late for you to stop by and pay your respects."

"I was your father's best friend. His death hit me hard," he said. "I know this hasn't been an easy time for you, but it's been tough for me, too."

"Is that what you came to tell me?" demanded Jeff, with more authority than I'd expected. Even Bennato looked surprised.

"No. I came to bring you something," answered Feiss,

producing a large manila envelope and holding it out to
Jeff, who made no move to receive it.

"I already heard. You're suing me. Go ahead, but you'd
better hurry. I hear there's a long line down at the courthouse. Apparently this town is full of guys who think I'm
a pansy and just can't wait to fuck me over," he added
bitterly.

"It's not a lawsuit."

"Then what is it?"

"It's a letter of intent and a check from the Wauwatosa
Stadium Development Corporation."

Jeff reached over and took the offered envelope and
passed it wordlessly to me.

"Aren't you even going to open it?" demanded Feiss in
disbelief. "Don't you even want to know how much it's
for?"

"I'll have to have my attorney review it and get back to
you," replied Jeff coldly.

"What do you mean get back to me? I'm a goddamned
minority shareholder. I have a right to have a voice in
this." He looked at Bennato and gestured to include him.
"We both do."

"Then I guess you should be the first one to know I've
decided to move the team to L.A.," he announced savagely. "I'm leaving for California within the hour to work
out the details."

I had to admire Jeff. I couldn't think of a better way to
make credible the threat of moving the team than convincing Feiss. Obviously Jeff had decided that he wasn't playing chess.

"But your father and I had a deal," protested Harald.
"He *wanted* to move the team to a new stadium in the suburbs. He gave me his word!"

"I have news for you, Harald," declared Jeff. "My father was a shitty businessman who got into a shitload of

trouble by listening to you. Whatever promises he made died with him. From here on in you're dealing with me."

We've learned so much of how to behave from the movies and TV. Actors have set the standards for seduction; the Kennedy widows have shown us how to grieve . . . but in the process it has also crippled us, left us lost and stammering whenever we stray too far from the script. Chrissy knew how to play the supportive wife of an unfairly accused and embattled husband; what she didn't know was what to do once he'd slid into the back of the car that would whisk him to the airport. There was no script for how to be a prisoner in your own home in a town that has overnight made up its mind to despise you.

Reluctantly I realized that there was no way I could just leave her alone and head back to Chicago. I felt worse than torn. It wasn't even a matter of choosing between Avco and the Monarchs. The day of the funeral I'd instructed Cheryl to insert the language that I'd dictated into the revised registration document that had been transmitted to the SEC. There was nothing to be done until we heard back.

The problem was how best to take care of Chrissy. Which did she need more? Someone to stick with her in her terrible isolation or someone to fight to save the team from the jaws of the bank? Before she came downstairs from putting the baby down for her nap, I considered just coming out and asking her, but one look at her face, ashen and exhausted behind her makeup, gave me all the answer I needed.

"Where shall we sit?" I asked. "How about the living room? Why don't you get comfortable and I'll bring you a cup of tea?"

Chrissy nodded and drifted wearily toward the front of the house while I quickly stuck two tea bags into mugs and doused them with scalding water from the instant-hot-water faucet. The limits of my culinary skill thus tested, I followed Chrissy into the living room. I found her curled up on one end of the couch, staring off into space.

"Do you think he could have killed him?" she asked softly as I set down her mug.

"What?" I asked. "Do I think who could have killed whom?"

"Jeff. Do you think that Jeff could have killed his father?"

"Could or did?"

"Did."

"What makes you ask?" I countered, ever the lawyer.

"He was so strange just now. He didn't even really say good-bye. . . ."

"He has a lot on his mind," I replied. "You and I both need to be careful not to read too much into things. Let's just try and take it one step at a time."

"I don't know if I can do that," replied Chrissy. "I mean, sometimes I can force myself. Like when I'm taking care of Katharine or physically doing something. I actually tell myself, 'Now I'm doing the dishes,' 'Now I'm changing a diaper.' It's almost as if I'm trying to convince myself that even though my entire life has been turned upside down, there are some things that are still normal. And then there are other times when I just go off the emotional deep end, when I want to scream or tear my hair or just run away. I couldn't sleep last night. I just lay there in bed looking at Jeff and wondering whether I was lying next to a murderer."

The sound of breaking glass kept me from responding. For a second, maybe two, I wondered whether a picture had fallen from the wall or dishes had shifted in the rack, but I immediately dismissed it. I'd lived in the city long enough to distinguish between broken crockery and a broken windowpane.

"Quick," I whispered. "You run upstairs and call the police, then lock yourself in the baby's room. Go!"

CHAPTER
16

I stood in the living room, listening to the sounds of breaking glass punctuated by garbled shouts of what sounded like profanity coming from the kitchen. I wondered what kind of burglar cared so little about getting caught that he would make that much noise. Then I realized that it wasn't a burglar. It was a fan.

The Jester, looking worse for the wear since yesterday's brief appearance on the hood of the funeral limousine, staggered into Chrissy's living room. He was dressed in torn purple tights and a grimy harlequin vest that looked like it had once been purple and gold, before it had been dragged through the dirt and smeared with what looked like ketchup.

I couldn't tell how old he was, but I could tell that he was drunk. I also knew that he was dangerous. His eyes were red-rimmed from lack of sleep and had the unsteady gaze of a man who'd stared into the bottom of too many bottles and seen only his own sense of grievance. His face was pitted and disfigured by old acne scars, and for a minute I thought that he was wearing makeup, but then I realized that it wasn't eyeliner, but the shadow of an incipient shiner. Apparently this member of the Monarchs' court, instead of spreading merriment and good cheer, had been fighting. Judging from the length of lead pipe he clutched in one hand, my guess was that so far he'd managed to come out on top.

"Where the fuck is he?" he shouted, running the words together. It was hard to understand him over the steam-engine gasps of my own panicked breathing.

"Who?" I demanded, startled by the sound of my own voice, which was thin and tremulous with fear.

"Who the fuck do you think I came here to see, you dumb cunt, King Kong? Your husband!" He started looking under the couches and behind the furniture, singing, "Come out, come out, wherever you are so I can smash your face in—" He staggered suddenly, as if the floor had lurched unexpectedly beneath him, then regained his balance and straightened up with elaborate care. Under other circumstances the whole thing might have been comical—for example if I happened to have an Uzi in my purse. But today there was nothing harmless about his inebriation.

"Jeff's not here right now," I said like some demented secretary. "He's just stepped out. Perhaps you'd like to have a seat and wait for him?"

"Where the fuck did he go?" he demanded belligerently, turning around to take in the room. "Did he have to stop at the bank and count his money? Did he run out to pick up some more fucking caviar?"

"I expect him back soon. May I get you a drink while you're waiting?" I inquired in my new role as lady of the house.

"Sure, whadyagot?" he asked, wandering the room unsteadily, picking up objects and setting them back down at random. I wished desperately that he'd just put down the pipe. I also wished the police would hurry. Fear had robbed me of my sense of time. I had no idea whether it had been ten seconds or ten minutes since we'd first heard the sound of breaking glass.

"What would you like? We have beer, wine, or perhaps

you'd prefer something harder?" I asked, trying frantically to remember where Chrissy and Jeff kept their liquor.

"What, no champagne?" he demanded unpleasantly, as he wheeled around, arms extended, taking in the room. Without even noticing he knocked a pair of Herend rabbits from an end table with his lead pipe and just went on talking, seemingly oblivious to the fact that he'd broken anything. "A place like this—I'd a thought champagne'd come out when you turned on the goddamned faucet."

"Let me go see," I offered, I hoped casually. "Perhaps there's a bottle in the back of the fridge."

Stepping gingerly over the shards of shattered china, I began making my way into the kitchen. Three more steps and I would have been home free, but the Jester grabbed me just short of the door, jerked me roughly by the arm, and pulled me violently toward him. In his other hand was a silver-framed photograph he'd picked up from among the dozen or so clustered on a console table. It was a wedding picture of Chrissy and Jeff. He held it up, adjusting its distance to his face as he struggled to get his eyes to focus on the picture. Then he held the photograph up to my face before he let it drop to the floor.

I made a move to get away, but he yanked me closer. "Who the fuck are you?" he demanded in an ugly voice.

"What do you mean?" I asked stupidly.

"Don't you play games with me!" he shouted, shaking me. I tried to break free, but his grip was too tight and the silk of my blouse was too sturdy to tear. "Who the fuck are you?"

"My name's Kate," I said. "I'm house-sitting for the Rendells while they're out of town."

"Bullshit!" he spat. "That is complete and utter *bullshit*!" His eyes darted around the room, taking in the pair of tea cups Chrissy and I had left on the coffee table for the first time. On his face I saw the flickering realization that he and I were not alone. "Get your ass down here, now!" he shouted to the house at large. "Get your ass down here now before I beat the crap out of her."

"I told you, there's no one here but me," I protested in as loud a voice as I dared, praying that Chrissy could hear the warning in my voice and stay where she was. Even if he decided to get rough, I figured I could hold out until the cops showed up. I must have been watching too many movies.

The first blow hit me on the shoulder and sent me to my knees, the whole world instantly turning red with pain. Then he picked me up by the front of my blouse and hurled me against the wall. A picture clattered down from the wall, smashing against the floor, but the impact knocked the wind out of me and I went down like a sack of flour, oblivious to everything except the desperate struggle to suck down air.

"You better come on down before I smash her skull in!" he bellowed gleefully, warming to the task.

Instinctively I rolled up into a ball, trying to protect myself from the blows that began to rain down on me from the pipe. I had completely lost my ability to process any thought more complicated than basic survival. My entire world had been instantly distilled to two objects—my body and the pipe. I was vaguely aware of someone sobbing and realized, somewhat belatedly, that it was me.

The blows stopped as abruptly as they'd begun, but it took me longer than it should have to grasp the significance of this. I rolled pitifully onto my side, my mouth rapidly filling with blood, just in time to see Chrissy enter the room.

"Well, lookee here," exclaimed the Jester. "If it isn't the queen of the Monarchs' court. Where's your chickenshit husband?"

"He's on his way to L.A.," replied Chrissy in a terrified voice. Her eyes flickered involuntarily toward the stairs that led up to the nursery as the Jester beckoned to her to come closer. As soon as she was within reach he grabbed her by her hair, yanked her to his side, and pushed her to her knees like a recalcitrant dog being taught to heel.

The Jester looked around the room as if trying to decide what to do next. I swallowed blood and probed for loosened teeth with my tongue, silently cursing the inefficiency of the Milwaukee Police Department even as I strained, hoping to catch the first faint sound of their approaching sirens. The only thing I heard was the sound of my own ragged breathing punctuated by Chrissy's terrified whimpers.

Abruptly the Jester dragged Chrissy up by the hair, bringing her to her feet. Using his arm to put her in a chokehold he jammed the pipe into the waistband of his pants as he eased his other hand down her blouse, running his tongue across his lips greedily. Chrissy's face was a frozen mask of revulsion.

"Stop it!" I shouted helplessly. "The police are on their way. If you don't touch her it will be easier for you."

For a moment I was heartened as he stopped his groping, but it was only long enough to reach his hand back under his tunic. But instead of the pipe he pulled out a gun, a pitiful little snub-nosed thing, the kind that you can pick up anywhere for fifty bucks, but deadly at close range. He jammed it into Chrissy's neck.

"Please don't hurt me," Chrissy pleaded. It was practically a whisper.

"Shut up," he snapped. "I guess if we can't get your spineless husband to pay for his crimes, we'll have to make do with you! Come on. We're going for a ride."

"Where are you taking her?" I managed to croak.

"Don't you worry, honey, we're going to have a good

time," he whispered into Chrissy's ear. The look on her face was desperate, pleading. "I bet you have a real fancy car, too," he continued almost to himself. He reached down, grabbed the bottom of her shirt, and pulled it up over her head as he dragged her blindly kicking through the door.

I struggled to my feet, still gasping for oxygen like a beached fish and trying desperately to fight back the dark edge of unconsciousness that threatened to overtake me. My fear for Chrissy overrode everything else. As soon as the Jester had her out of the house, he could take her anywhere, do anything to her. I remembered the terror on her face and I thought of all the bodies of dead women that turn up in ditches every day. I was determined that Chrissy was not going to be one of them.

I practically clawed my way to the library and reached for the telephone to call the police, praying to hear the message that they were on their way. The line was dead. Suddenly, I remembered Jeff taking it off the hook in the kitchen earlier that morning and sobbed in frustration and disbelief as all hope of being rescued by the police evaporated. From the garage I heard the rumble of Chrissy's Suburban as the engine sprang to life. Desperately forcing down waves of panic, I realized that I still had one chance to stop them.

I raced to the front hall where I'd left my briefcase and my purse and scrabbled frantically for my car keys. Then I peeled out the front door, my heart pounding in my chest, terrified that I was already too late.

The garage was at the back of the house, at the end of the driveway, accessible only by passing under the porte cochere that was set just beyond the circular drive at the front of the house where my ancient Volvo was now parked. I leapt behind the wheel, knowing that if I could somehow block their passage up the driveway, I could at least prevent him from hitting the open road with Chrissy.

I turned on the ignition and debated waiting until the car phone flickered on, flipped over to roam, and located its signal, but decided against it. I didn't have enough time. Instead, I waited just long enough to hear the approaching engine of Chrissy's Suburban. Then I slammed my foot on the gas.

I bought my Volvo station wagon while I was a third-year law student, shortly after Russell and I became engaged. We chose it because, in the days before air bags, it was considered one of the safest cars on the road. Now, of course, it was on its way to becoming a rusted-out junker. On the other hand, Chrissy's Suburban was the largest and most modern sports utility vehicle on the market. Equipped with antilock brakes and dual air bags, it also weighed close to six tons, a fact that I was strangely cognizant of as I slammed my foot on the brake, bringing my car to a stop sideways directly in front of hers.

I braced myself for impact as Chrissy T-boned me with her Suburban. I heard the crumpling of metal and felt the Volvo shudder and give way under the impact. The windshield cracked and disintegrated into a cascade of pebbly glass. My chest hit the steering wheel and my horn sounded in protest. I heard the pop of Chrissy's air bags, and I was out the door in an instant, propelled by adrenaline and thoughts of the gun.

I pulled open the passenger door of the Suburban as the Jester cursed and struggled against the air bag. I grabbed him by the leg, the first appendage I was able to get hold of, and pulled him out of the car. I wrestled him to the ground without knowing where the gun was. Whether consciously or by blind instinct, Chrissy managed to shove the lead pipe along the seat so that it fell out with a clang and rolled toward me along the driveway.

The rest happened quickly, actions taken without thinking and only processed later. I remembered the cold of the asphalt beneath my knees, how small rocks dug into my skin, the way the front of the Jester's vest was stiff with dried ketchup that was suddenly mixed with blood as I took the pipe and hit him across the face with it.

The aftermath of crisis is a fertile ground for farce. Chrissy wrestled with her air bag like a character in a cartoon, desperate to be free of the car and to reassure herself that the baby was all right. As she raced into the house I shouted at her to put the phone back on the hook and telephone the police. The Jester lay crumpled and unconscious at my feet, now rendered pathetic and ridiculous. The gun lay beside him on the driveway. I gave it a tentative kick with my foot to make sure that it was out of reach should he come to and was appalled to discover that it was a toy.

I paced the driveway, still tasting the adrenaline in my throat and unable to be still. After a while my injuries began to declare themselves and I realized that I was getting cold. Chrissy came out and brought me a jacket, reporting that the baby was only now just beginning to wake up from her nap, having thankfully slept through all the excitement. Time passed and the Jester started to stir, so Chrissy and I dragged him back into the house and trussed him up using a roll of duct tape that she took from a drawer in the kitchen.

Police or no police, the baby needed to be fed, so Chrissy stepped over the now squirming body of the Jester to get her bottle from the refrigerator and warm it in a pan on the stove. I found a bag of frozen peas, which I applied to the nasty bump that was developing at the back of my head. The peas had defrosted and the baby'd been fed, burped, and diapered before the police finally deigned to show up.

They were two beefy officers in starched uniform shirts and wearing wedding bands. One of them had a thick mustache I suspected of being perpetually wet on the bottom from his lower lip. The other had a weight lifter's build and a blond crewcut that taken together made him look like a poster child for the master race.

They were so completely unapologetic about the delay that I was immediately convinced that it had been deliberate. Obviously the mayor was not the only city employee who was out to punish the Rendells. A week ago the police would have raced to Chrissy's house if she'd called to say her kitten was up a tree. Today it took forty-five minutes, a call that there was an armed intruder in the house, and even then when they finally arrived, they were barely able to conceal their contempt.

"Nice place you've got here," said the one with the mustache, looking around. His name tag said Grubb. His partner's name was Schumacher. "Bet you had to sell a lot of football tickets to pay for it," he said, swaggering up to Chrissy and peering over her shoulder into the house.

"So," said Schumacher, casually plucking a toothpick from his breast pocket and inserting it into the corner of his mouth. "I understand you claim to be having some sort of problem."

"A deranged fan broke into the house and held us at gunpoint," reported Chrissy.

"Now why would a Monarchs fan want to come to *this* house?" demanded Schumacher insolently from beneath his crewcut.

"Why don't you ask him yourself?" I suggested.

"You mean he's here?"

"Tied up in the kitchen."

"Well then, he couldn't have been particularly *dangerous* if all it took was two *women* to overpower him," his partner observed condescendingly.

"You'd better believe I'm tough enough to cause you plenty of trouble if you don't knock it off and start doing your job," I snapped, mentally drafting my complaint against the Milwaukee Police Department. Deutsch wasn't the only person who could file a lawsuit in this town.

Grubb walked up to me until he was so close that his chest brushed against mine and I could feel his nightstick against my thigh. I never realized how much easier it was to act tough when you were wearing a badge and carrying a gun.

"What's your name?" he asked, stretching himself up to his full height in order to better look down at me. I could see the pores in his skin and smell the onions on his breath from lunch.

"My name is Kate Millholland," I said. "I'm the attorney for the Milwaukee Monarchs. Normally my opinion is very expensive, but I have some advice for you that I'm offering for free."

"What's that?" sneered Grubb.

"Go and take a look at your prisoner. We tied him up and took away his gun, but if he croaks at the scene while you're standing here treating us to the tough-guy routine, it's going to be your ass, not mine."

"I'll take you to him," said Chrissy. She was still shaken and had no stomach for games.

Grubb spent a couple more seconds exuding testosterone before he decided he'd made his point. I suppressed a yawn. Then we all trooped into the kitchen.

The two officers took one look at the Jester and immediately radioed for the paramedics. I had to admit that he didn't look very good, though I guessed I didn't either. A quick peek at myself in the door of the microwave revealed the portrait of a lawyer who looked like she'd just crawled out of a Dumpster. Chrissy, on the other hand, looked infuriatingly perfect. Not only did her new role of damsel in distress suit her perfectly, but she must have found time to put on fresh lipstick while I was busy icing down my bruises.

Of course, the paramedics were there in two minutes flat. While they ministered to the Jester, Detective Schumacher made a desultory attempt at taking down our statements. They say that a lack of outrage is an outrage in itself. For Chrissy, his lack of interest, much less sympathy at what she'd been through in her own home, must have felt like a second violation. It certainly didn't help that we could hear the EMTs tenderly ministering to our assailant, lifting him onto a stretcher, and assuring him that they would take good care of him.

When they were finished, Detective Grubb came looking for me. He found me in the living room pacing back and forth while Chrissy sucked up the pieces of Herend into the Dustbuster.

"I thought you might like to know that I've advised Mr. Koharski that he may want to press charges for assault."

"Who is Mr. Koharski?" I demanded.

"The gentleman you assaulted with your vehicle, savagely beat, and then tied up."

"You and I both know that's ridiculous," I countered, seething inside. "We're talking about a man who broke into a private residence and committed felony trespass and assault."

"That may be your version," he replied. "But right now it's your word against his."

It took under a half an hour for Chrissy and me to pack up everything she and the baby needed and load it all into the back of her Suburban, less if you didn't count the time

I spent stuffing the blown air bags back into their compartments and taping them into place with duct tape. The decision had been reached with almost no discussion. The police had sent their message. Chrissy was not going to spend another hour, much less another night, in that house.

Chrissy called and left a brief message at the Regent Beverly Wilshire for Jeff, strapped the baby into her car seat, and climbed into the seat that had most recently been occupied by the Jester. She confessed that she was still much too shaken to drive, and my car was not just undrivable, but I suspected a total loss.

As I pulled Chrissy's car out of her own driveway, I saw her turn in her seat to catch one last glimpse of her house and realized that she had no idea when, if ever, she'd be coming back. What Beau had most feared had now come to pass. The Rendells were being run out of town. I wondered if he was in a position to appreciate the irony of it; in the end he was the only one who was going to get to stay.

There was also the issue of where to go. As we passed the cheese shops and the outlet malls on our way to Chicago, I called and made reservations for her at the Four Seasons. It wasn't until I saw the exit for Lake Forest that I got a better idea. As I hit the off-ramp and turned onto Sheridan Road, I called my mother.

Mother adores being magnanimous, especially when the appearance of generosity can be accomplished with a minimum of effort on her part. She and my father were about to leave for the airport to spend two weeks with friends in St. Bart, so I wasn't surprised that she expressed herself as delighted to open up the guest wing for Chrissy and the baby. In fact, I knew that she was delighted at the idea.

Mother hated that she had to pay her staff when she and my father were away. Having Chrissy at the house appealed to her perverse sense of thrift. Chrissy would have a cook and hot and cold running maids to help her with the baby while Mother would be spared the anguish of knowing that her servants were slacking off while she was yachting in the Caribbean.

It was a strange homecoming nonetheless, greeted by Mrs. Mason, the same cook who'd fed us grilled cheese sandwiches and her own peculiar brand of Baptist spiritualism as children. I left Chrissy and the baby in her hands to be cooed and fussed over and went upstairs to do what I could to make myself presentable. I washed my face as gently as I could and gingerly brushed the dried blood out of my hair, leaving it down to cover the rapidly spreading bruises on my neck. I took off my blouse and examined myself in the mirror. I couldn't tell where the Jester's handiwork ended and the damage from my stunt with the car began. Not that it really mattered.

I found a high-collared blouse in my Mother's closet and paired it with her favorite red Ralph Lauren suit, taking another minute to try my best to camouflage my swollen lower lip with concealer. Fortunately, the worst of the damage to my mouth seemed to be on the inside. Then I threw my dirty and bloodstained clothes into the trash and headed downtown to my office.

When I arrived back at the firm, the receptionist's subdued greeting tipped me off that a war party was waiting for me. Whatever had happened was big and I was being blamed.

Walking down the dark paneled corridors to my office, I knew exactly how Jeff Rendell would feel if he took a walk down the street in Milwaukee. It was almost funny—the way the secretaries ducked down into their cubicles to avoid meeting my eye. I had been gone for less than forty-eight hours—long enough to turn into a pariah.

When I opened the door into my office, I found Skip

Tillman's formidable secretary, Doris, sitting at Cheryl's desk, loading Avco files into a cardboard document box.

"Hello, Doris," I said. "What's going on? Is Cheryl sick?"

"She's been reassigned to the word processing pool effective immediately," Doris informed me, "and Mr. Tillman is waiting to see you in his office."

"Are you going to tell me what I did to earn this trip to the woodshed, Doris?" I asked.

"You'd better hurry," she said kindly. "You know he doesn't like to be kept waiting when he's in a bad mood."

I nodded as she got up and left. Then I took off my coat, hung it carefully in the closet, pausing briefly in front of the full-length mirror that hung inside the door. With my hair down and dressed in her clothes, the resemblance was unmistakable.

"Oh my god," I thought. "I'm turning into my mother." Somehow the thought of that was much scarier than the prospect of what was about to happen to me.

CHAPTER
17

Of course, I wasn't about to make it easy for them. Instead of going straight to Tillman's office I ducked into the library and slunk down the circular staircase that, hidden in the back of the stacks, connects the forty-second to the forty-first floor. Used exclusively by associates and other lowly library dwellers, I knew that by taking it I insured that I wouldn't bump into Tillman or any other person of importance.

I braved the furtive glances of the secretaries in the tax department and made my way into the firm's equivalent of the boiler room—the word processing pool—where Cheryl now toiled in newfound exile.

I walked slowly past the temporary workstation where she labored under a set of headphones, typing the turgid memos of green associates. I was careful not to slow my stride as I passed, but instead merely caught her eye and silently mouthed the words *ladies' room* as I continued on my way. The entire exchange was as quick and slick as a drug deal and every bit as subversive.

Only support staff used the lavatory at this end of the forty-first floor, and it reeked of illicit cigarettes and strawberry disinfectant. There was an old tweed sofa in a particularly rancid shade of green with burn marks on the arms and a stack of dog-eared *Cosmopolitan*s on the scarred plastic table next to it. It was the favored refuge of sobbing typists who'd been yelled at by their short-tempered bosses.

I paced until Cheryl arrived. She looked rattled.

"What happened?" I whispered, pulling her into the handicapped stall.

"Do you want the long version or the short?"

"Short first."

"You're going to get canned."

"Okay. Now what's the long version?"

"This morning Stuart Eisenstadt came looking for you," whispered Cheryl furtively. "Oh, it must have been around ten-thirty. He was so upset, I immediately knew that something was up, but of course, he wouldn't tell me what it was. He just said that I should get hold of you like yesterday. I tried you up at Chrissy's house, but the line was always busy and you weren't answering in your car. I also tried the firm's Milwaukee office and down at Monarchs Stadium, but no one knew where you were—"

"I was at Chrissy's. Jeff took the phone off the hook because they were getting so many calls from the media—"

"Well, the shit was hitting the fan here, too. About a half an hour later Skip Tillman and John Guttman came looking for you—the same lynching party that did the deed when they fired Rick Cooper."

I had no idea who Rick Cooper was, but then, of course, I was as ignorant of the nuances of firm politics as the Jester probably was of portfolio management. Cheryl, on the other hand, kept up. She liked to say it was her favorite spectator sport.

"Naturally, when I told them I hadn't been able to reach you, Guttman jumped all over me, that asshole. He accused me of lying about where you were to protect you."

"You were lucky he didn't break out the brass knuckles and the rubber hoses."

"I think that's what they used on Sherman. Poor baby, he's going to be in therapy for at least the next decade."

"So what's with being reassigned to word processing?"

"My punishment for conspiring with you, I guess."

"So any idea why heads are going to roll, specifically mine?"

"Only that it's got to have something to do with Avco and it's big. After they sent me down here, they told me that if I so much as thought about picking up the phone and calling you that it would mean my job."

"I'm glad you didn't. You wouldn't have been able to reach me anyway. Some psychopath broke into Chrissy's house and tried to abduct her at gunpoint." I unbuttoned my blouse and craned my neck to show her the rapidly intensifying bruise that spread from collarbone to shoulder where the Jester had gotten me with the pipe.

"Hey. If I were you, I'd just take off my blouse for Tillman. Not only is the bruise impressive, but the sight of your lacy brassiere will send him into cardiac arrest—problem solved."

"It's that kind of thinking that's going to take you far in the legal profession," I assured her.

"So what are you going to do?"

"I don't know. I'll think of something. In the meantime I have two things I need you to do for me."

"What?"

"First off, I need you to get me a car."

"You can use mine."

"No, no. I need a car. Mine's totaled."

"The Volvo? How did that happen?"

"It's a long story. Anyway, I need a new car."

"What kind? You know this isn't exactly like sending out to Marshall Field's for a change of clothes."

"I trust your judgment. Pick something. Call Rob

Geller at my bank when you know how much it's going to be, and he'll see that it gets paid for."

"Gotcha. What's the second thing?"

"Promise me you won't let them force you into quitting. I need you too much to have you fold on me now. If they cut your pay, I'll make up the difference. Just promise me you'll hang tough until I've got this worked out."

"Sure, but only under one condition," replied my secretary.

"What's that?"

"That you won't let them intimidate you into quitting either. You are ten times the lawyer of anyone else in this firm, and if they don't know that, then they're even stupider than I thought."

Making my way to Skip Tillman's office, I had the all too familiar feeling of being summoned to the headmaster's office. Even so, Cheryl's pep talk had helped, and the closer I got, the more determined I became to not let myself get lynched. I had already faced down one ugly, angry man and walked away relatively unscathed. I wasn't going to let Tillman get the better of me either.

Doris was back at her post. She punched the intercom button and announced my arrival in the hushed tones appropriate in the presence of the condemned. Tillman rose to his feet from behind his personal acre of polished mahogany, and she closed the door quietly upon us.

He did not smile. His face was pinched and puritanical. He had always fancied himself a father figure, and his disappointment therefore carried with it something of a paternal air. He shook his head sadly in a small gesture of shock and disbelief. He cast his eyes at me as if to say that what was coming would be all the worse on account of his deep affection for me.

I knew it was all bullshit.

"Where have you been? We've been looking all over for you," he demanded, sounding like my father on prom night—actually, prom morning to be more accurate—after I'd wandered in sometime after breakfast, hung over and reeking of dope.

"Milwaukee," I replied without elaboration.

"I figured as much. Ned Bergstrom called and woke me up this morning. As you can imagine, he and the rest of the partners in Milwaukee are extremely upset."

"Why? Because they'll lose their seats on the fifty-yard line if the Monarchs move to Los Angeles?"

"Don't take that tone with me, young lady," he snapped. "You don't think the fact that our firm name is now linked to the most heinous incidence of civic treason in Milwaukee history is an issue of legitimate concern? Ned said he's afraid to go to lunch at his club for fear of what people will say to him! Not only that, but he had to read about it in the newspaper. I can't believe that you would knowingly involve this firm in a controversy of national proportions without consulting anybody. May I remind you that no matter what you seem to think, this firm is not your private fiefdom—"

"Is that what this is about?" I cut in incredulously. "Ned Bergstrom being too ashamed to have lunch at his club?"

"I know it seems hard to believe that you could be the cause of an even more serious problem than the Monarchs' mess, but apparently your reputation for being a lightning rod for trouble is nothing if not well deserved." He paused to emit another sigh, steepling his fingers together and laying them on the desk in front of him in a schoolmasterly gesture.

"Well, are you going to tell me what I'm supposed to have done," I demanded, "or do I have to ask the secretaries?"

"Avco has fired us for cause. We received written notification this morning that they are actively seeking representation elsewhere."

For a minute the earth actually moved and Tillman's patrician office seemed to rock beneath my feet. Under the terms of our agreement with Avco, if they fired us for cause, then they were no longer bound to pay us. Providing that they had a valid reason, the firm would lose in excess of a quarter of a million dollars in fees for work already performed.

"Of course, with a matter of this magnitude I have no choice but to bring it formally before the management committee," continued Tillman. "Gil Hendrickson is in New York and not due back until late tonight, that's why I've scheduled it for ten o'clock tomorrow morning. Naturally, you will be given an opportunity to present your explanation of events at that time."

Stunned, I stood there for a fraction of a second before willing myself to make my way toward the door. There was a rushing sound in my ears, like surf, that drowned out everything else. It took me a minute to identify it, but when I did I realized that what I was hearing was the death rattle of my career.

I would be lying if I said that one of the attractions of what I do isn't the risk, the fact that there's nothing like standing on the high wire to keep you focused, to prevent your mind from straying into the messy gray areas of your personal life. Of course, the downside is that sometimes you fall.

The trouble was that what was happening both with Avco and the Monarchs was no longer just happening to the client. It was happening to me. It would be as if Claudia, who gets her kicks from her heroic feats of surgical legerdemain, suddenly felt herself being pulled from the wreckage and about to go under the knife.

I went back to my office and thought briefly about storming out, or feeling sorry for myself, or calling Stephen and seeing if I could lose myself in sweaty sex. But I've never had much appetite for self-pity, and when I called Stephen, all I got was this year's assistant telling me that he was in a meeting that was expected to last for the rest of the afternoon.

After that I did what I always do. I sat down at my desk and got to work. I did not call the Brandt brothers and beg them to take us back, though I had no doubt that's what Skip wanted me to do. Frankly the only consolation in the whole mess was that I'd never have to speak to them again. I didn't call Stuart Eisenstadt either. His strategy of building himself up with the clients by tearing me down had backfired when—surprise, surprise—they showed no compunction about screwing us both. What I did do was call Paul Riskoff. He seemed surprised to hear from me, no doubt since we were busy suing each other, but as far as I was concerned, this was my day to deal with the thugs in my life. I figured I might as well get it all over with in one lump.

That done I pulled out my disc player, slipped on my headphones, and tackled the ramparts of work that now obscured every square inch of surface on my desk. I was determined that with Avco, however ignominiously, out of the way, the time had come to get the Monarchs' troubles sorted out. As Matchbox 20 sang about shame, I read through every scrap of material I'd been given about the Monarchs. Then I wrote a letter to Mayor Deutsch setting out what I saw as his alternatives, and explaining exactly why I was the only person on the planet in a position to make him a hero.

It was a sign of how far from normal things had strayed that Elliott Abelman sidled into my office unannounced. I was so absorbed in what I was doing that when he finally moved into my field of vision, I leapt from my chair like a cartoon housewife who's just seen a mouse. I think I may have actually said "eek."

"I didn't mean to startle you," he said, sliding into the visitor's chair. It scared me how glad I was to see him. "But Cheryl said it would be okay if I dropped by."

"When did you talk to Cheryl?"

"She called me a little while ago. I asked her to let me know when you got back into town. She also happened to mention that you're experiencing something of a career crisis."

"Is that why you came?"

"You mean to make sure that you weren't standing on the ledge outside your office window?" His face lit up with a sudden smile. "No. I swear as I walked over I didn't even look up." He paused for a minute, adjusting the shoulder holster under his jacket against the chair. "You want to talk about it?"

"Absolutely not," I replied.

"It's not that you're feeling overcome with remorse or anything for screwing the Milwaukee fans out of their football team, because, hey, if you are, I'll personally lend you my gun so that you can do the right thing."

"You don't think you're being a little bit harsh?" I asked. Even Skip Tillman hadn't gone so far as to suggest that I kill myself.

"How would you feel if you woke up one morning to find out that some millionaire's kid had decided to move the Art Institute to Poland, or that the Eiffel Tower was going to be relocated to Texas?"

"Believe me, we're doing everything humanly possible to keep the team where it is. But unfortunately Jeff owes the bank a small matter of something like $18 million."

"There's also a small matter of whether the new owner is going to be watching the games from behind bars."

"What have you heard from the cops?" I demanded.

"Only that they're close to swearing out a warrant for your friend Jeff. I guess a check of the phone records the day that Beau was killed showed a 911 call placed from the dead man's office right around the time of the murder."

"Aren't all 911 calls recorded automatically?" I asked.

"They are. Unfortunately, whoever called never said anything. Not a word. The call runs twenty-six seconds and all you can hear is breathing."

There was no reason to think that Jeff Rendell had not strangled his father and every reason to think he had. Indeed, I'd closed my eyes to fact after fact in order to indulge in my naive and self-serving belief in his innocence. He'd fought with his father the morning of his death. They couldn't find him to tell him what had happened to his father. His bizarre behavior—pushing the paramedics out of the way in order to assault the body of a dead or dying man—was hardly what you'd expect from a bereaved son. Now the phone call from his father's office that seemed to indicate that whoever killed Beau had, at least initially, meant to do the right thing and call for help. It wasn't until he'd had some time to contemplate the repercussions of what he'd done—twenty-six seconds to be exact—that he'd elected to move on to plan B.

Any cop will tell you that all kinds of people try to make a death into something that it's not. Somebody has too good a time at a party where there are drugs, and his buddies take him for a ride and dump his body in the country. Grandpa dies surrounded by girlie magazines with his pants around his ankles, and the family gets him dressed before the police show up. An argument gets out of hand,

and a son's hands end up around his father's throat. Appalled by what he's done, the son throws the body down the stairs, hoping the death will be put down to the fall.

And then, of course, there was the business of the key. I couldn't believe I'd been stupid enough to allow myself to become an accessory to murder. I made a silent vow to hand it over to the police the very first chance I got.

I did not go to the new apartment intending to end things with Stephen Azorini. In a way it's frightening to realize that if it had been any other day, we probably would have just continued on our old, familiar path. But the tightness in my chest should have warned me that there was too much in my life that was beyond my control. That instinct would propel me to change what I could, if only to conserve the resources I would need to deal with what I could not.

I started out with the best of intentions. A check of the past day's voice mail messages revealed a rambling communication from Mimi letting me know that the fabric that we had ordered to cover the panels in the dining room had finally cleared customs and been delivered to the apartment. Anxious that it might be inadvertently dirtied or damaged by one of the workmen, she suggested that Stephen or I take it home for safekeeping until we were ready to use it. I hopped a cab and told the driver to wait for me while I darted upstairs to grab it. I was surprised when Danny, the night doorman, told me that Stephen had just gone up himself.

I found him standing in the kitchen, examining the newly laid tile backsplash, his aquiline nose no more than two inches from the ceramic surface. "I don't think these are perfectly straight," he said, without looking up.

Of course, there were many possible responses to this. "Nothing is ever perfect" certainly springs to mind. Or,

"You'll never notice because it's going to have a stove parked in front of it." In a million years I wouldn't have predicted what actually came out of my mouth, which was "I can't live here with you."

"What did you say?" inquired Stephen, straightening up and turning to face me, a look of surprise on his face.

"I said I can't live with you," I replied, feeling a kind of preternatural certainty flowing through me. I wasn't at all sure of what I was doing, but I knew in my bones that I had no choice but to go ahead and do it. "The whole thing was a mistake."

"You've chosen quite a time to come to this realization," remarked Stephen, obviously taken aback.

"I guess you can't always choose when enlightenment is going to strike," I said. Then, to cover the awkward silence I added, "I realize that this is going to be inconvenient."

"Inconvenient?" echoed Stephen incredulously. "What is wrong with you? Have you gone off the deep end? Both our names are on the deed. We've been jointly named in a lawsuit. It's not going to be inconvenient, it's going to be a *nightmare*."

"I'll buy back your share of the apartment and pay you for everything you've spent on the renovation to date," I replied, with the strange sensation of being outside of myself looking in. "The real estate department at Callahan Ross will take care of the conveyance of the deed and make sure that your name is removed as a defendant in any pending suits."

"Are you going to give me a reason for this remarkable decision?" asked Stephen in a puzzled voice.

"I don't want you to think that it's because I'm afraid," I said slowly. "Actually, it's just the opposite. Moving in here with you would be the coward's way out. And some things happened to me today to make me realize that no matter what, I'm not a coward."

CHAPTER
18

The management committee met in the largest of the firm's nine conference rooms, a formidable quintet of Callahan's most senior partners arrayed somberly around the massive table. They were dressed in suits and ties—unusual for a Saturday—and no doubt meant to signal the serious nature of these proceedings. Skip Tillman sat at the head of the table, and you could tell that even after all these years it still gave him a secret thrill.

It didn't help that I felt like roadkill. Muscles in my neck and back that I'd never even given a thought to now screamed out for my attention. The bruise on my shoulder where the Jester caught me with the pipe now extended halfway to my waist and was complemented by a perfectly round imprint, in deep purple, of the circumference of my defunct Volvo's steering wheel that now graced the center of my chest.

Overnight, I found that I'd developed a newfound appreciation for the work of personal injury attorneys. If Callahan Ross gave me the boot, maybe I would be able to find gainful employment in that field. Too bad there was nobody to sue in my accident. In my life the worst damage has always had a way of turning out to be self-inflicted.

My discomfort was not entirely physical. I'd been up half the night contemplating my life and wondering what had ever possessed me to say what I had to Stephen. I'd spent the other half of the night wondering why he hadn't said a single thing to try to get me to change my mind.

Aching and unable to sleep, I'd finally gotten out of bed, wrapped myself in an old flannel bathrobe that had once belonged to my husband, and sat on the glassed-in porch of the apartment that I shared with Claudia. From there I was able to watch Hyde Park street life as it played itself out on the busy corner outside my window. If I'd been hoping for an epiphany, I was disappointed. I saw dope deals, arguments, tired people coming home from work on the bus, but no answers.

And yet what I saw beyond my window made me realize something important. In the years since Russell died, I'd spent my waking hours in the five city blocks that surround my office, blocks crammed with granite, avarice, and old men. I'd let my world grow much too small. If I was willing to allow the phlegmy old men of Callahan Ross, who now sat frowning above the wattles of their chins at me, to be my judges and declare my worth, then I'd allowed my soul to be narrowed hopelessly, as well.

All this went through my mind as I stood and faced them. As painful as it was to find myself taken to the woodshed by such an experienced and vindictive bunch, I told myself there wasn't much they could do to me without my consent. Partners are not subject to summary dismissal, and right now the most they could do was try to shame me into quitting.

Not that they couldn't make life difficult for me. No one wants to belong to a club where the other members were determined to make life as unpleasant for you as possible. Now that my secretary had been demoted to the word processing pool, I fully expected to come in on Monday and find that I'd been reassigned to an office in the supply closet and my name deliberately misspelled on the firm's letterhead.

Skip Tillman cleared his throat. "We've called you here this morning to give you an opportunity to give your own account of events leading up to this firm's being dismissed as counsel from Avco Enterprises."

From his tone of voice it was clear that I was being called on the carpet. The words might express the intention to be fair, but everything else about the exchange indicated that the outcome was a foregone conclusion.

"No," I said.

"Pardon me?"

"No. I do not wish to explain. Everyone in this room knows what happened yesterday. I see no reason to go into it."

"Kate," said Tillman sadly, "I don't think you fully understand the gravity of the situation."

Rumor had it that all of his political brownnosing had finally landed him on the short list for appointments to the federal bench. It sounded to me like he'd already started practicing his delivery.

"Skip, if you don't think I'm smart enough to understand what's going on, then you should never have made me a partner in the first place. As you know, I have been retained to represent the Milwaukee Monarchs football team, which is in desperate need of our services. I was in Milwaukee on that matter yesterday when I was regrettably detained." I was not about to regale them with tales of the break-in at Chrissy's house. Not only did it sound too much like the dog-ate-my-homework excuse, but also they'd never believe it anyway.

"Even if you were out of town on another matter," broke in Myron Schap, the brindle-haired partner who was widely held to be both Tillman's Iago and his successor, "you were not only out of town but unreachable."

"Accept my explanation or ask for my resignation, but never, *never,* call me a liar—especially to my face."

"You realize that Avco has categorically refused to pay one penny of our fee," sputtered Edwin Margolis, the head of the tax department.

"Avery and Colin Brandt, who are the principals in Avco, are complete scumbags. If you recall, I believe that those were the exact words I used when Stuart Eisenstadt first suggested that we represent them in this matter. As far as I'm concerned, there was never any guarantee that they were going to pay us in any event. Besides, they won't be the first client that we've had to sue in order to collect and I guarantee that they won't be the last."

"It's easy enough for you to be flip about a quarter of a million dollars," snorted Gus Rolle hypocritically. His wife was a dog food heiress and if her family's company weren't one of the firm's biggest clients, Callahan Ross wouldn't have even hired him as a paralegal.

"Oh, I think I have an idea of how many zeros we're talking about," I assured him. "What I don't know is what all of you want. Is this conversation enough for you? Would you feel better if I broke down and cried?" I looked around the table and felt every inch the bratty teenager. "Because what you see is what you get. This is all the satisfaction I'm prepared to offer. If it's not enough, you can try to fire me."

I looked around the table, standing my ground. In the background the grandfather clock could be heard ticking ominously. "In that case I'm going back to my office," I announced. "I have work to do."

Then I marched out of the room and smiled to myself. No matter what else, I'd reduced five lawyers to complete speechlessness, which, when all was said and done, was no small feat.

By the time I got back to my office, my breathing had returned to something very close to normal. As I turned the corner I was pleased to see Sherman Whitehead waiting for me. He was wearing a light blue golf shirt buttoned all the way up to the neck and a pair of plaid high-water pants.

"How did it go this morning?" he asked.

"I remain bloody but unbowed," I reported.

"Gregson said that they were going to try to can you."

Tim Gregson made partner the same year I did. He was a money-hungry deal lawyer with the face of a choirboy and the ethics of a crack dealer. I had no doubt he'd be managing partner someday.

"It's early in the day yet, but so far I'm still here."

"Then do you have a minute?"

"As long as it doesn't have anything to do with Avco. I am officially off the case."

"No. It's about the Monarchs. I stayed up last night going over their balance sheet."

"Pretty scary. No wonder you couldn't sleep."

"The bank is trying to force them to go under, aren't they?"

"Wouldn't you if you were in their shoes? Not only will they get the franchise for ten cents on the dollar, but now that some asshole's leaked the possibility of the team moving to L.A., instead of being the heartless bankers that took the Monarchs away from the Rendells, they're going to be the heroes that keep the team in Milwaukee."

"I take it you think they were the ones who leaked it to the press."

"First they had to know it to be able to leak it. My guess is that either Harald Feiss told them or he leaked it himself."

"Why would the minority owner want to do that?"

"I don't know, maybe he's cooked up some kind of side deal with the bank. He claims that Beau was planning on making a deal to move the team out to the suburbs to anchor a planned sports/entertainment/retail complex."

"Where?"

"Someplace out in the boonies called Wauwatosa."

"That's what I came to talk to you about. Last night, going through the financials, I came upon a hefty line item for real estate taxes for an unidentified parcel of land. I looked up the plat numbers this morning and it's all in Wauwatosa—an enormous tract, at least a couple of hundred acres. The real estate taxes alone are something like seventy grand a year."

"Are they delinquent on the taxes?"

"Nope. They're current."

"Are you sure?" I asked, my interest piqued. Going through Beau Rendell's papers I had found no account that was less than sixty days overdue, including the property taxes on his house. If he was up-to-date on the taxes for this parcel, that in itself was noteworthy.

"I'm sure. I checked with the County Recorders office on-line. But that's not what I wanted to talk to you about. I can't find any record of the purchase or the deed in the records you gave me. I mean, if they're laying out for the real estate taxes, you'd expect them to hold the deed."

"Maybe it's kept under lock and key somewhere," I suggested, my thoughts turning to the safe-deposit box.

"I looked it up. The Rendells don't own the land, and it's not deeded to any of the holding companies associated with the team. Instead, it appears to belong to a corporation called Debmar, Incorporated."

"Who the hell is Debmar?"

"From what I can gather, it's a holding company. I traced it through two other shells to another holding company in the Caymans."

"In the Caymans? It sounds like somebody is hiding something."

"Do you want me to keep looking?"

"Yeah. Do that. Of course, if there's any hands-on investigating that needs to be done in the Caribbean, I think it's better if I handle it personally. After all, I may be in the doghouse, but partnership still has its privileges."

Late that afternoon a messenger delivered an envelope to my office. Inside was a key. The accompanying note may have been unsigned, but I had no trouble recognizing Cheryl's handwriting. All it said was *It's downstairs in your parking space*.

I'd completely forgotten that I'd asked her to get me some new wheels. Even barred from communicating with me, she'd managed to do what I'd asked. Propelled by curiosity, I packed up my briefcase, picked up the key, and took the elevator down to the parking garage. There, in my space, was a sleek new forest green Jaguar sedan with chrome Cragar wheels.

I walked around it once, peering in through the windows, looking for what, I don't know. Then I unlocked the door and slid behind the wheel. With its leather seats the interior smelled like the inside of a glove. The burled wood of the dashboard gleamed. I put the key in the ignition, and the deep-throated engine purred to life.

"Not bad," I thought to myself as I pulled out of my spot and headed down the ramp toward the exit. It wasn't until I was heading east on Balbo toward Lake Shore Drive that I realized there was no way I could take this car home to Hyde Park. In the alley behind my building a car like this would have a half-life of something like six minutes. I might as well cruise the parking lot where the drug deals went down and hand the keys to the first dealer that I met.

I fumbled around looking for where the British engineers had hidden the car phone. I eventually located it in the console between the seats, but only after I'd switched on the lights, the windshield wipers, and launched myself into cruise control somewhere in the vicinity of Soldier

Field. First I called Cheryl and left a message saying thank you on her answering machine and promising her a test drive. Then I called Chrissy at my parents' house and asked her if she minded having company for the night. She sounded pleased at the prospect of not being alone, but also preoccupied. When she mentioned that she'd just gotten off the phone with Jeff I figured that was probably the reason and decided not to pursue it, at least not over the phone. Instead I told her to put a bottle of wine on ice and save a glass for me.

After I hung up with Chrissy I dialed the mobile operator and asked to be connected to the Regent Beverly Wilshire only to be told by the hotel operator that Mr. Rendell's room wasn't answering. Frustrated at just having missed him, I left a message for him to call me just as I pulled into the alley behind my building.

I rolled down the window and offered a kid on a bicycle twenty bucks if he watched my car for ten minutes. Eager for the twenty—hopefully not the hubcaps—he agreed, and I pelted into the apartment and grabbed a change of clothes. I also stopped long enough to listen to the answering machine messages. There was one from my bank confirming the transfer of funds to pay for the Jaguar and another from Cheryl reminding me that I had seventy-two hours to switch my insurance coverage from the Volvo. Then the machine clicked and I stood there listening to the whir of the tape as it rewound, feeling confused by my sense of disappointment. After all, I was the one who'd done the deed, made the break, put an end to things. Then why on earth had I been hoping that Stephen Azorini would have called?

CHAPTER
19

That night Chrissy and I stayed up late in the twin beds of my old room talking about boys. Drinking wine and staring up at the eyelet canopies above us I told her about Stephen and how, without ever consciously deciding to do so, I'd ended the relationship we'd shared for almost half my life. Chrissy, in turn, talked about her marriage, confessing that under the twin burdens of a new baby and the Monarchs' financial woes, it had suffered under the strain.

She also confided that even before his father's death, Jeff's behavior had begun to alarm her. At times preoccupied, jealous, paranoid, and withdrawn, his moods were unpredictable and his anger always just beneath the surface. In recent months she'd felt herself walking on eggshells, trying as hard to avoid his temper as she did to be supportive.

Sometimes the bonds of friendship feel like chains around your heart. More often it is just the opposite. There is comfort in being heard and freedom in being understood. Even though we fell asleep with nothing solved, we both felt better for having shared what was bothering us. The same as in seventh grade.

The next morning I left for the office while Chrissy was still asleep, arriving downtown while the penitent were still in church and the sinners still in bed. I found a copy of the draft Memorandum of Agreement between the Greater Los Angeles Stadium Commission and the Milwaukee Monarchs there waiting for me. Ken Gunther, the partner from our L.A. office, had faxed it to me late the night before.

With the two-hour time difference it was still much too early to call the coast. Besides, Ken's cover sheet indicated that he and Jeff were heading out for a round of golf with the governor bright and early. He said he'd call me when this important networking had been concluded to go through any concerns I might have about the deal.

I turned my attention to the fax. Despite its bulk—the twenty-eight-page agreement had more than thirty pages of exhibits and side letters—it represented only the bare bones of the agreement. Even so, it was evident after wading through it that the terms were as good as any sports team owner was going to get. In order to bring football back to La-La Land the State of California was prepared to spend over $250 million. The Memorandum called for the construction of a seventy-thousand-seat, open-air stadium dedicated solely to football, the acquisition of land for a practice facility, a new training complex, and a lump sum payment to defray the costs of relocation and litigation.

It was less than the team would have netted if Beau were still alive, but it was still preferable to playing in the rusted-out hulk of a stadium where they played now or next to a shopping mall in Wauwatosa. Right now, it was the best answer to Jeff's problems—provided he didn't find himself on trial for his father's murder first.

I was surprised when the switchboard put a call through for me. Usually Sundays were a respite from that kind of interruption. Besides, few people knew the firm's weekend number. I suddenly found my heart beating fast in the absurd hope that it was Stephen. Needless to say I was disappointed to find Detective Eiben of the Milwaukee Police Department on the other end of the line.

"Where's your client?" he asked after the most perfunctory exchange of greetings.

"Which one?" I countered disingenuously.

"Don't even think about playing games with me. You fucking well know which one I mean. Jeffrey Rendell. We've been calling his house and there's no answer."

"Why are you looking for him?" I asked. There was something about his tone that put my hackles up.

"Because I have a warrant for his arrest."

"Really?" I replied, trying to sound nonchalant. "For what crime?"

"Shoplifting," he snorted. "What the hell do you think? We want him for the murder of his father."

"Don't you think you're rushing into this?" I inquired, less than pleased by this new development and thinking fast. "After all, you're going to look pretty stupid if it turns out that he didn't do it."

"Why don't you let me worry about how I'm going to look and you just tell me where he is?"

"He's in Los Angeles on business."

"What about his wife? Is she with him?"

"No. She's in Chicago with me. She and I are spending the weekend at my parents' house."

"When the cat's away, the mice will play, is that it?"

"What's that supposed to mean?"

"You know, you're not doing yourself any favors by hustling the husband out of town. No judge is going to grant him bail after he knowingly attempted to flee the state."

"Oh, come on," I shot back. "No matter what you think he did or did not do, Jeffrey Rendell is not some crackhead that you're trying to make for a back-alley shooting. He's the owner of a National Football League franchise, and he's in L.A. on team business."

"Is he coming back, or am I going to have to get an extradition order?"

Suddenly I'd had enough of his tough-guy routine. My whole body still ached from my encounter with the Jester, and I was in no mood to put up with this kind of bullshit.

"You'd better go ahead and get an extradition order," I said, hoping that when I hired a criminal attorney for Jeff he wouldn't skin me alive when he found out what I'd done. "My client was originally scheduled to return to Milwaukee tomorrow, but I'm afraid that under the circumstances I'm going to have to advise him to remain out of state."

"I don't care who you think you are," spat the detective angrily. "If you're helping your client avoid arrest, I will have you behind bars faster than—"

"I don't want him coming back to Milwaukee because your department can't or won't protect him," I interjected. "Or didn't you hear about the little hostage drama that got played out at the Rendells' house on Friday?"

"Yeah. I heard about that. A bunch of us went down to the lock-up to get the guy's autograph. You know, that Jester guy is really funny."

"I know. I still have bruises from laughing so hard," I said, right before I slammed down the phone.

Paul Riskoff's apartment was only two floors below the one that I'd been foolish enough to buy with Stephen, but as soon as you stepped off the elevator it felt as if you'd landed on a different planet. In the entrance hall a crystal chandelier as big as the Macy's Christmas tree hung above an erupting fountain, and you had to squint against the glare of all the mirrors.

Riskoff, looking bemused, was waiting for me himself. He was wearing a navy blue blazer with a gold crest on the pocket, gray pants, Gucci loafers, and no socks. Every strand of the dry pompadour with its telltale absence of gray was exactly where he wanted it to be.

"Welcome, neighbor," he said without irony, extending his hand.

"Thank you for agreeing to see me," I said. "I know that your time is very much in demand."

"Shhh," he replied with a conspiratorial wink, "or my wife, Tiffany, will hear us and think we're up to something. The woman has the ears of a bat."

I wanted to add, "and the IQ, too," but under the circumstances it seemed mean-spirited. Tiffany Riskoff was the real estate developer's second wife, and she was nothing if not a tabloid cartoon of the Other Woman, a blond bombshell you could throw the cliché manual at. We'd ridden the elevator together once, I in my jeans and sweatshirt on my way to check up on the construction, she on her way back from shopping in a hot pink Escada suit. She had a Versace bag in one hand and a yappy, useless, powder puff of a dog in the other. I remember what really got to me was that the dog's toenails were painted exactly the same shade as Tiffany's.

Without prompting, Riskoff led me into the apartment and gave me the tour, pointing out the highlights—the onyx columns that had come from a castle in Italy, the neo-Romantic frescoes in the guest room, the semi-pornographic carved ivory frieze in the dining room. The ivory was a bit of a no-no, he admitted, sounding like a man who's used to being forgiven.

He ushered me into a room that looked like it had been decorated from a fire sale at Buckingham Palace. Everything was overstuffed, draped, tasseled, swagged, and smothered with throw pillows. There was a Renoir on one wall and a view of the lake from the window.

"This is my favorite view," he said, gesturing toward the window, "but then, of course, you're already familiar with it."

"Yes. We have the same one upstairs."

"Is that what you've come to see me about? Because if it is, I'm glad for a chance to sit down and settle this thing face-to-face—no bullshit."

"Actually, I've come to talk about something else."

"What?"

"A business proposition."

"Oh, I hope you aren't trying to get me to invest in a limited partnership or buy stock in some hot high-tech company. I have people who do that kind of thing for me—"

"No," I said. "I've come to ask you whether you're a football fan."

I worked the phone the whole way back to Lake Forest. First I called the top criminal attorney on my list who showed absolutely no surprise at being asked to represent Jeffrey Rendell—indeed, he acted almost as if he'd been expecting the call. Of course, when I told him that Jeff was in L.A., I thought he was going to have a stroke. I figured I'd let Eiben tell him the rest.

That done I put a call in to Jeff and ended up leaving another message. Let him enjoy his golf, I thought to myself. Who knows when he'll get to play again? After that I checked my voice mail at home and back at the office. Someone from the mayor's office had left word at Callahan Ross that he was willing to sit down and meet with me early Tuesday. Whatever ended up happening, we were going to be cutting it close.

After I finished listening, I transferred over to Sherman

Whitehead's line and found him, as usual, at his desk. I told him to draw up a power of attorney transferring control of the Monarchs from Jeff to Chrissy and to hold on to it. I figured that if Eiben made good on his threat to put Jeff behind bars, we'd better have someone on the outside who was empowered to make decisions for the team, but I didn't want Sherman faxing it out to California until I had a chance to explain to Jeff what was going on. The way I figured it, he was already in for enough nasty surprises.

For the rest of the drive, I gave myself over to the not inconsiderable pleasures of driving the Jaguar. It wasn't so much the big things as the luxury of the simple ones; the fact that it still had a radio that worked or that every encounter with a pothole didn't cost me another piece of the undercarriage. I remember thinking that I could get used to this.

When I got back to my parents' house, I found Chrissy curled up on the couch in my father's study, the room in the house that constituted his only sanctuary from my mother. It was the place where he came to drink, smoke cigars, and scratch himself where it itched.

Chrissy was nursing a bottle of Evian water and watching the NFL pregame show on TV. She had the same look on her face that you see on onlookers at a four-car pileup.

"Where's the baby?" I asked, opening up the armoire that hid the bar and pulling out a cold can of Coors from the little refrigerator that was concealed there.

"She's sleeping," she replied distractedly, her eyes glued to the tube. "Mrs. Mason's up there with her in case she wakes up."

"Have you heard from Jeff?"

"No, and I hope to god he's still out on the golf course."

"Why?"

"Because I don't want him to see this."

"What is it?"

"They're showing the demonstrations outside the stadium in Milwaukee. Mayor Deutsch is there. He made a campaign appearance eating turkey legs with the King and his fucking court," continued Chrissy, her voice trembling with anger. "The Jester was there."

"They let him out already?"

"Apparently. But that's not even the worst part. There are all these guys holding up homemade stop signs that say 'Stop Jeff.' Oh, and look," she continued, pointing to the TV, "they're showing the electric chair again."

I came over and sat down beside Chrissy. On the screen there was indeed a mock-up of an electric chair. In it was strapped a dummy with horn-rimmed glasses, meant to be Jeff.

"Turn it off," I said. "I have to talk to you." Chrissy picked up the remote and pushed the button. "The police called me at the office this morning. They have a warrant to arrest Jeff."

"Oh my god!" she sobbed with a sharp intake of breath. Other than that, her body was immobile, like the split second after you've been hit in the face and you still can't believe you've actually been struck.

There was a discreet knock on the study door.

"Come in," I called out, reaching across to Chrissy and giving her hand a quick squeeze. One of the maids apologized for disturbing us. "There are two policemen at the front door who say that they have to see Mrs. Rendell."

Chrissy said nothing, but her eyes were as round as saucers.

"Don't worry," I said, suddenly wishing that my breath didn't smell like beer. "You stay here. I'll take care of this."

I made my way quickly to the front of the house where

two uniformed Lake Forest police officers waited respectfully, hat in hand.

"Mrs. Rendell?" one of them asked.

"No. I'm Kate Millholland. I'm Mrs. Rendell's attorney. What can I do for you officers?"

"We have some news for Mrs. Rendell. Is she here? May we speak to her?"

"What kind of news?" asked Chrissy softly, appearing at my side.

"Are you Christine Rendell?" he asked, stepping forward.

"Yes," she whispered.

He consulted the small notebook he carried in his hand. "Are you married to a Jeffrey Rendell of 1783 Lake Drive, Milwaukee, Wisconsin?"

"Yes," she whispered, this time so softly you had to strain to hear her.

"I'm sorry to have to tell you this, ma'am, but there's been an accident."

"What kind of accident?" I cut in.

"Mr. Rendell has been shot."

"Shot?" demanded Chrissy, her voice rising in hysteria. "Shot dead?"

"No, ma'am. He's not dead as far as we know. But apparently he's been badly wounded. That's why the Milwaukee police requested our assistance in contacting you."

"Where was he shot?" I demanded.

"I don't exactly know. From what they told us he might have been hit in a couple of places. He's in surgery last we heard."

"No," I protested. "Where did it happen? Was he in his hotel? In the car?"

The officer consulted his notebook before replying. "They found him at the home of a Mr. Beauregard Rendell in a town called River Hills. The local authorities think that he must have surprised a burglar."

"His father's house?" demanded Chrissy. "That's not possible. My husband's in L.A.!"

CHAPTER
20

Even in the Jaguar the drive was an agony—a kind of interstate Le Mans filled with near misses of triple-trailer semis and close encounters with terrified old people who pulled over onto the shoulder and clutched their steering wheels as we screamed past. I don't think I dropped below ninety except to pay tolls and even then it was very definitely a drive-by kind of thing.

Chrissy seemed oblivious to the danger. With the baby safe in Mrs. Mason's care back in Lake Forest, her mind was free to imagine the very worst. She alternated between crying and calling the hospital every few minutes, but the news was always the same. Jeff was still in surgery. For Chrissy this was reassuring, but I knew better. If Jeff had died on the operating table, it's the last thing they would have told Chrissy over the phone. Jeff might still be in surgery, but if he'd already stopped breathing, the surgeons who worked on him were probably drawing straws to decide who would get the unpleasant task of breaking the news to the family.

In between calls to the hospital Chrissy finally managed to get hold of a police spokesman who was willing to take a break from briefing the media and tell the victim's wife what was going on. What the Lake Forest patrolmen had told us was true as far as it went. Apparently Jeffrey Rendell had surprised a burglar who had broken into

Beau's house assuming that he would find it empty and unattended during the Monarchs-Packers game. Somehow in the confrontation both men had been shot, but so far neither had died. It was not known who had called 911 or whether there was one gun involved or two.

No one knew what Jeff was doing in Milwaukee when he was supposed to be in California. All they could tell us was that the officers who arrived at the scene found both men unconscious. I couldn't help thinking about how long Chrissy and I had waited for the Milwaukee PD to show up and wondered how long Jeff had lain there bleeding before the cops finally decided to make an appearance.

Just as I feared, the press had beaten us to the hospital, taking up their positions outside the entrance to the St. Mary's trauma center, which was located in a futuristic six-story circular building that didn't so much resemble a place of healing as a wedding cake on LSD. I stopped the car and circled back, figuring that at the very least the Jaguar entitled me to park in the doctors' lot with impunity.

I fished the cashmere scarf out of the pocket of my coat and told Chrissy to use it to cover her blond hair. Then I took off my jacket, rolled it in a ball, and had Chrissy tuck it into the waistband of her leggings under her coat. Then, operating under the assumption that nothing attracts attention more quickly than someone trying to hide, we walked brazenly down the street and into the entrance marked MATERNITY.

Once we were safely inside it took us a few minutes to convince the admitting staff that no one was expecting a baby anytime soon. I was eventually able to find a sympathetic orderly who, in exchange for a twenty, was willing to lead us through the series of underground passages that linked the laundry, the cafeteria, and the morgue to the trauma center.

We took the elevator to the sixth floor, where we had no trouble locating the surgical family waiting area, a space cruelly lacking in both comfort and privacy. It consisted of little more than a group of vinyl chairs bolted to the floor strategically located between a bank of busy elevators and the double doors to the surgical suites.

Signs directed us to check in with the volunteer at the desk, a disapproving woman with starched hair who took our names, pointed to the alcove where the coffeepot was set up, and handed us a map to the cafeteria. Throughout the entire exchange her demeanor eloquently communicated the fact that while she might not know the exact details of Chrissy's distress, it was to her mind certainly no less than Chrissy deserved.

I got Chrissy settled and went to pour us each a cup of coffee. It was too terrible to actually drink, but there was comfort in just being able to wrap our hands around the familiar warmth of the Styrofoam cups. In the corner, mounted high up on the wall so that the volume control and channel changer were out of reach, the TV blared the third quarter of the Monarchs game. Milwaukee was leading Green Bay 27 to 10.

Time wore on. People came and went. When we first arrived, there had been a young black woman sitting alone, huddled in the corner crying quietly. She was gradually joined by several other members of her family whose family resemblance now extended to the similar expressions of shell-shocked disbelief.

There was another group that was the center of attention. They were congregated around a middle-aged man dressed as a mechanic in a set of blue overalls that said "Ed" in curly script above the pocket. He had the same kind of impenetrable face as Coach Bennato, hardened by what it had seen. He was with three women, any one of whom might have been his wife, and a gaggle of scraggy teenagers with bad skin and worse teeth. They were all dressed in tight jeans and T-shirts emblazoned with the names of their favorite headbanger bands.

I was pouring myself a cup of fresh coffee, still trying to keep myself occupied by trying to figure out how the mechanic and the other people were connected, when the double doors of the surgical suite banged open. Two surgeons walked out and scanned the room. We all waited, terrified, collectively holding our breaths, wondering whether they were coming for us.

"McGyver?" the older of the two surgeons called out wearily. Chrissy and I relaxed.

The mechanic answered "here" as if responding to roll call at school. The surgeons pulled off their caps and squatted down in front of the family, introducing themselves and launching into a rapid-fire explanation of what was being done for their loved one. When one of them got to "I don't know what he was despondent about, but from the wound it looks like he must have put the barrel of the gun directly to his chest before pulling the trigger," Chrissy got up and fled to the most distant corner of the waiting area.

A few seconds later the double doors burst open again, and this time a trio of surgeons emerged, the V necks of their scrubs ringed with sweat. They did not call out a name but made a beeline for Chrissy. They introduced themselves so fast that there was no way I could catch a name. One, like my roommate Claudia, was apparently the trauma surgeon who'd been on call in the emergency room when they'd brought in Jeff. The other was a vascular surgeon and the third a thoracic specialist. Together they had just spent six hours trying to save Jeffrey Rendell's life.

"How is he?" Chrissy blurted desperately.

"The next twenty-four hours will be critical," replied the trauma surgeon, drawing us aside and speaking for the others. "He was shot two times. One bullet went through his neck, nicking his trachea before exiting his body. The other bullet entered his chest, ricocheted through his lung, and lodged in his abdomen. Normally, with this kind of injury you'd expect the victim to bleed to death pretty quickly, but apparently the way he fell exerted pressure on the exit wound and slowed the bleeding. Still, by the time he got here, he was in full cardiac arrest and his heart had stopped beating."

Chrissy made a sound; it was less a sob than a kind of primal mewing. I put my arm around her shoulder and immediately felt the futility of the gesture.

The mechanic at my garage gives me the news more kindly when he tells me how much a new transmission will cost. Knowing Claudia for as long as I have, I understand that the qualities that are prized in a surgeon—concentration, a fanaticism about perfecting technical skill, self-confidence, and risk-taking ability in the face of pressure—do not necessarily a compassionate person make. But then, of course, a compassionate person would find it too soul destroying to deliver this kind of news day in and day out.

"We did our best under the circumstances," he continued, trying to reassure us. "But even so, we had to remove most of his spleen, and it's too early to tell whether or not one of his kidneys might need to be repaired. We'll be watching your husband very carefully for signs of kidney failure over the next few days. Like I said, the next twenty-four hours will be critical."

"Will he live?" asked Chrissy softly.

This, when all was said and done, was the only question that mattered. To her, everything else—the bullets, their

trajectories, the damage they had done as they'd ricocheted through his body—was all secondary to whether he
was ever going to go home again with Chrissy, with
whether he was going to be there to see baby Katharine
grow up.

"Unfortunately there are no promises," replied the
trauma surgeon, not unkindly. "The best we were able to
do in the operating room was give him a chance. I'm
afraid now we can only wait and see."

"Can I see him?" breathed Chrissy.

"He's in recovery right now. As soon as he's stable
enough we'll try moving him over to intensive care. You'll
be able to stay with him there. However, bear in mind that
he'll still be unconscious and intubated. It will be a while
before we'll know whether he'll be able to breathe on his
own."

"Ever?" inquired Chrissy, her voice high with fear.

"Right now I think it's best if we just take things one
step at a time."

There is absolutely nothing subtle about the press. They
move in like a herd of hyenas and tear at their victim's
flesh until their hunger for a sound bite or a story is satisfied. Then they move on. While what had happened to Jeffrey Rendell was unspeakably tragic, it was also a good
story and for that reason had rendered Chrissy a target. In
the if-it-bleeds-it-leads school of journalism, the burglar
who had tried to kill her husband had turned her into page-
one news.

Fortunately a media spokesperson from the hospital arrived close on the heels of the surgical team and carefully
explained the arrangements that the hospital had made to
safeguard the Rendells' privacy. It all went by Chrissy
completely. Even though she looked the young woman
from the hospital in the eye and made the appropriate

noises of polite gratitude, I knew that it was all just a matter of instinct.

The only time that she was able to really get through to Chrissy was when she asked her for permission to have the surgeons who'd operated on her husband give a press conference.

A flicker of something like shock passed across Chrissy's face, but I urged her to say yes. I actually saw the hospital's request as the first good sign we'd had. As crass as it might sound, I figured they'd be less likely to trot out the docs if they thought that Jeff was going to die. Besides, journalists are usually as lazy as they are venal. Why else would they spend so much time interviewing each other and trying to pass it off as news? I figured that whatever we could spoon-feed them would make them less rabid about coming after Chrissy.

What followed was the kind of negotiation no one should ever have to enter into, hammering out what could be said about Jeffrey Rendell as we stood in the corridor outside the surgical suite where he still hovered between life and death. Fortunately, the hospital spokeswoman was too inexperienced to object to the guidelines I set down. Either that or she was being careful not to queer the hospital's chance at future donations. I had just finished outlining what kind of information could be released when a nurse appeared to take Chrissy to see her husband. As soon as Chrissy was gone, I took the opportunity to do what every lawyer does in a crisis; I asked for a telephone.

The hospital spokeswoman offered me a desk in an empty office. As soon as I got there I set about dialing the world. As far as I was concerned, the first order of business was to find out what the hell Jeff Rendell was doing in Milwaukee when he was supposed to be in L.A. I tried the number I had for Jack McWhorter at his apartment, but all I got was an answering machine. I fared no better with

Ken, who I caught at home watching the postgame wrap-up of the Monarchs' game on TV.

He almost had a heart attack when I told him what had happened. Jeff had called Ken early that morning and begged off golf, explaining that he'd woken up with the flu. Ken wasn't surprised that with all the stress Jeff had been under he'd picked up some kind of virus. Ken had offered to call a doctor, but Jeff had been adamant that he just needed to sleep. After that Ken obliged by rescheduling the day's appointments and then had taken the opportunity to catch up on his dictation. Until that moment he'd assumed that Jeff was sound asleep in his hotel room.

What was Jeff Rendell doing in Milwaukee? Why had he lied to Ken? Why the obvious deception? I racked my brain but could come up with no plausible explanation. Frustrated, I called Elliott Abelman. He picked up on the first ring.

"Are you okay?" he asked as soon as he heard that it was me.

"I'm fine."

"I heard about what happened. Where are you?"

"I'm in Milwaukee at the hospital with Chrissy. Jeff just got out of surgery. They're moving him to intensive care."

"Is he going to make it?"

"Unfortunately I think it's just wait-and-see time."

"That bad?"

"It's bad."

"I thought you said he was going to L.A."

"He did. He went to L.A. on Friday. This morning he told the partner who's out there with him that he had the flu and was going to bed. Obviously between the time he hung out his Do Not Disturb sign and the time he surprised a burglar in his father's house in River Hills, he hopped a plane back to Wisconsin."

"Why?"

"That's what I want to know."

"Any idea who the burglar is?"

"No, but now that you mention it, I wonder whether it might not have been the Jester."

"You mean the guy who roughed up you and Chrissy?"

"Yeah, only this time he decided to bring a real gun with him. I can't believe they actually let him out of jail."

"Oh, that's not the best part," offered Elliott. "You'll never guess who the lawyer was who paid his bail."

"Who?"

"Your friend, Harald Feiss."

I went off in search of a ladies' room and found the woman from the hospital PR office standing at the mirror carefully lining her lips with a pencil and then filling them in with a brush, getting ready to face the cameras. Chrissy put hers on the same way. I found myself wondering whether I was the only woman in America who just slapped her lipstick on straight out of the tube.

"Can you show me the way to the ICU?" I asked.

"I can take you up to the family lounge on the fifth floor. I'm afraid they allow only one family member into the intensive care unit at one time."

"No exceptions?" I inquired. I've never been any good at wringing extra privileges out of people, especially under these circumstances.

"I'm afraid not," she replied. "It's not an arbitrary rule. There's so much equipment in the ICU and so many personnel that space is very tight."

"Just promise me that Mr. Rendell's doctors are as conscientious about his care as they will be answering the press's questions."

"They're very good, especially with a VIP patient. They'll tell you every time they take his temperature if that's what the family wants."

"And what about your less important patients?" I demanded irritably. My experience with Russell had left me with a long list of issues I still needed to work out about how medical care is delivered.

"Our hospital policy is to give the same level of high quality care to every single patient without regard to their circumstance or ability to pay," she replied promptly, spouting the corporate line. "I guarantee you that the man who shot Mr. Rendell is getting the very same level of care that he is."

"The man who shot him is here?" I demanded incredulously. "He's here? In this hospital?"

"We're the only level-three trauma center between Madison and Chicago. I understand he was very seriously injured. There's no place else they could have taken him."

"And he was shot?"

"Yes. Three times. I believe once in the head. As far as I know he's still in surgery."

"What's his name? Who is he?"

"Oh, I don't know if I can give out that information—" she sputtered.

"It's a matter of public record," I declared, taking a step toward her. "I bet you've already told the media."

"His name is Darius Fredericks," she said quickly.

"The wide receiver?"

She nodded while I grappled with my disbelief.

Until the day he'd nearly killed a call girl in a hotel room after a game, Darius Fredericks had played football for the Milwaukee Monarchs.

CHAPTER

21

Football is a game of violence; a sport where the players hit hard and they hit first, where knocking an opponent unconscious is a badge of honor and breaking bones a treat. Violence isn't just part of the game. It is the game. I once read an interview with an offensive lineman with the Chicago Bears who calmly explained that he liked to play mad. "Not mad at anyone in particular," he was quoted as saying, "but mad at the world."

But there are some players who can't distinguish the violence of the game from real life, players who are mad at the world, not just for the three hours they are on the field, but all day long. Couple that kind of rage with the sense of entitlement that comes from being a twenty-three-year-old millionaire sports celebrity and you get Darius Fredericks.

By the time Darius Fredericks reached the NFL, he was already no stranger to the law, and Amber Cunningham was by no means the first young woman the 220-pound professional athlete had used as a punching bag. However, she was the first one that I ever saw, and let's just say it left an impression.

I couldn't get to the hospital until the early hours of the morning. I'd had to first arrange for representation for Fredericks and then issue a statement to the press. All I really wanted to do was go home. But Jeffrey Rendell had begged me to go and see her. To his credit he was not just terrified of the publicity, but genuinely concerned that whatever could be done for Amber Cunningham and her family be done.

When I got upstairs to her room the nurse spoke softly, as if the girl already lay dead. She explained that Cunningham was nineteen and, according to her driver's license photo, very pretty. But there was no way to tell any of that from the mangled lump of flesh in the hospital bed. There were dozens of tubes and lines running in and out of her body, and her face was the color and consistency of raw hamburger.

Her mother was at her bedside, furious and weeping. When I told her who I was and why I'd come, she'd vented her anger—a cold and hissing stream of hate. I stayed until she was done, asked her if there was anything that she needed, and got out of there as fast as I could, feeling sick at heart and thoroughly ashamed of myself. When I got home I took a shower, but I knew that no amount of water would wash off what it was that clung to me.

In the weeks that followed, Amber Cunningham did not die. Indeed, according to the truncated metric of the medical world, she got better. Eventually the bruises faded and the fractures healed. The lines were removed and she was sent home. However, she would never again be pretty. Or walk. Or have children.

For his punishment a jury of twelve sentenced Darius Fredericks to two years in prison. In a separate civil suit Cunningham was also awarded $9 million. From that day on the Monarchs started sending Fredericks's paychecks to his victim. Amber's parents would never be able to heal their daughter or erase the reality of what had happened to her, but they were at least able to return Darius Fredericks to the poverty from which he'd started. I never had a chance to ask them whether they considered this enough.

I remembered seeing that he was out. He'd served something like eleven months and had been released for good behavior or whatever other administrative excuse they use to make room for the influx of fresh felons that keeps pumping through the criminal justice system. His release was a one-day story, covered by the networks and collectively forgotten. The cameras showed Fredericks emerging from the prison downstate, sporting a buff, prison-yard physique and announcing that he was readier than ever to go back and play in the NFL.

Who knows, perhaps he would have. There were already coaches making noises that Fredericks had paid his debt to society. Besides, isn't sports all about second chances? But no one counted on Amber's mother.

Enraged at the thought of her daughter's assailant once again playing before a crowd of adoring fans, and committed to preventing what had been done to her daughter from happening to anyone else, Mrs. Cunningham began taking her daughter on the tabloid news shows. After *Dateline* ran the story contrasting Fredericks, fit and transparently unrepentant, to Amber, drooling and disfigured in her wheelchair, all talk of Fredericks returning to the NFL evaporated.

I thought about the cascade of tragedy that had swept through the Rendells and threatened to destroy them. I also remembered the question I'd asked myself earlier in connection with Harald Feiss. What happens when you take away what matters most to a man? What happens is you make him dangerous.

I went off in search of Chrissy and found her in the family lounge adjacent to the ICU. She was sitting in one of the institutional stacking chairs facing Detectives Eiben and Zellmer. Her posture could be best described as finishing-school upright—ankles crossed, hands folded demurely in her lap. On her face was the same ice-queen look that was so familiar from my mother. She was so still, she might have been sitting for a portrait, one titled *I'm furious and I think you're lower than dirt*.

"And when was the last time you saw your husband, Mrs. Rendell?" inquired Detective Eiben, loosening his tie and making himself comfortable, no stranger to this part of the hospital.

"I was just with him when you arrived."

"No, I meant to speak to."

"Yesterday, we spoke briefly on the phone."

"Why only briefly?"

"Because he was in Los Angeles on business and he was leaving for a meeting."

"And how did he sound to you?"

"I'm sure he sounded like a man whose father had died recently," I interjected. "I'm afraid I don't understand the point of this line of questioning. What does Jeffrey Rendell's state of mind have to do with anything? It certainly doesn't sound as though he was attempting suicide."

"This is not an adversarial proceeding," Detective Zellmer assured me. "We just throw out questions and hope that some of the answers lead somewhere."

Personally I hoped that homicide investigations were a bit less random than that, but I didn't say anything. I think under normal circumstances I wouldn't have felt so snippy, but I was tired and feeling emotionally beaten up, and it wasn't even my husband who was lying in the next room hooked to enough equipment to launch the space shuttle. I was desperate to protect Chrissy. I'd promised her that everything would be all right and look where we were sitting.

"Did your husband mention anything about returning to Milwaukee today?"

"No," replied Chrissy. "When the officers came to the

door this afternoon to tell us what had happened, I was so surprised. I had no idea."

"Any idea what he was doing at his father's house?"

"Absolutely none."

"Do you think it could have had anything to do with your decision to flee Milwaukee?"

"Oh come on," I countered, "she didn't flee. She left. And her husband knew exactly where she was."

"And you planned to remain with Ms. Millholland in Lake Forest the rest of the day."

"I don't know. I didn't really have a plan; originally I hadn't even planned to leave Milwaukee. I just . . . I mean . . . after what happened I couldn't stay in my house anymore."

"I'm surprised you didn't ask Jack McWhorter to come and stay with you. After all, the two of you are close. Wouldn't it have made you feel more secure to have a man in the house?"

"Jack is in L.A. with my husband."

"No he's not. We just spoke with him at the stadium. He flew back to Milwaukee late last night. Apparently there was a fire in one of the concession areas. He said he flew back into town last night to make sure everything was ready for today's game. I'm surprised he didn't call you."

"He may have," replied Chrissy, "but I was already in Lake Forest."

"And you didn't perhaps call home and retrieve the messages from your answering machine?"

"What, and listen to all the reporters and TV producers urging me to tell my side of the story? No thank you."

"And where were you earlier in the day?"

"I was at the Millhollands' house in Lake Forest."

"You didn't leave?"

"I went for a walk and had coffee earlier that morning. The baby was napping, and one of the maids said that she would be happy to listen for her if I wanted to do anything. I was feeling restless so I went out for a while."

"How long?"

"I don't know. As you can imagine, the past couple of days have been very stressful. I went into the village, took a walk, stopped at Starbucks, and read the paper."

"Did you see anyone you knew?"

"No."

"Anyone recognize you?"

"No."

"And what time did you return?"

"I'm not sure. When I got back, Katharine had been fed and was down for another nap. The pregame show was just starting. . . ."

Detective Eiben reached inside his jacket and pulled out a Ziploc plastic bag. Inside it was a single sheet of paper that had once been folded into a square but now was smoothed flat. One edge of the page appeared to be covered with brown stains. After a closer look I realized that it was blood.

Chrissy took the offered page and read it, carefully holding the edges of the bag, her hands trembling. I scanned it over her shoulder. It was obviously a fax. According to the routing information that appeared at the top of the page, it had been received at the Regent Beverly Wilshire at nine-forty the preceding evening. I did not recognize the number of the transmitting fax, but it had a Milwaukee exchange. I made a mental note of it.

The message itself was simple. One line, hand-printed in block letters: *If you want to catch them at it, try your father's house tomorrow at 2:00.* It was not signed.

"Do you have any idea what this fax might be referring to, Mrs. Rendell?"

"No," replied Chrissy, "I have absolutely no idea."

"So it wouldn't happen to have been you that had a meeting or an assignation at two o'clock today?"

"Absolutely not!" retorted Chrissy indignantly.

"So you deny that you were having an affair with Jack McWhorter?"

Chrissy rose to her feet, her mouth open in an expression of speechless disbelief. I confess I was pretty surprised at this latest development myself.

"Are you now or have you in the past had an affair with Jack McWhorter?" demanded Detective Zellmer again slowly.

Chrissy wheeled around to face the other detective, obviously in the throes of a mixture of strong emotions. "Let me explain something to you," she said passionately. "Before I met my husband, I ran with a very fast crowd. I did lots of things I would never want my daughter to do. My parents were dead, I was alone in the world, and I went out with a lot of different men. I did a lot of experimenting.

"But when I married Jeff, that ended. Not only did I settle down, but also I understood that there was a certain responsibility that went along with being Jeff's wife because of his association with the team. I accepted that I would have to be like Caesar's wife, absolutely above reproach, and I took that obligation very seriously. So, to answer your question, I am not having an affair with Jack McWhorter or anyone else. And I challenge you to offer me one scintilla of evidence that indicates otherwise."

CHAPTER

22

A hospital cafeteria at 3 A.M. is hardly the best place to get any kind of thinking done, but I didn't have a lot of alternatives. It was either there or in the patient lounge where the mechanic whose son had tried to kill himself lay slumped across two chairs, snoring noisily. Besides, I was starving. It was a good thing, too. Because only someone truly desperate for nourishment would even think about consuming what lingered on the steam tables at that hour.

Only one counter was open, serving gray and congealing Salisbury steak, mashed potatoes, and hamburgers that looked like they'd been sitting out since lunch. I bravely asked for the steak, helped myself to a mug of coffee, and gave my money to the woman with a cumulus of red hair who managed to tear herself away from her copy of the *National Enquirer* long enough to make change.

I made my way into the nearly deserted cafeteria and set my tray down on the nearest table. In an effort to save money they'd turned off most of the lights. In some sections the chairs had been set upside down on top of the tables. Somewhere in the gloom I could make out a bored janitor swinging a desultory mop.

As I ate I did my best to take stock of the situation. Jeffrey Rendell had been lured to his father's house by the fax to his hotel. Had he known who'd sent it? Who did he expect to catch? Obviously the police thought it was Chrissy and Jack McWhorter, but all my instincts told me they were wrong. That Jack had eyes for Chrissy was obvious, but I'd never once seen her return his interest.

For a moment I contemplated the possibility of some kind of a relationship between Chrissy and Fredericks, but immediately dismissed it as being too farfetched. Indeed, the whole thing was ridiculous. I'd been with Chrissy off and on all weekend and she certainly hadn't acted like someone who'd been planning to sneak off to meet a lover.

I tried to set aside conjecture and instead focus on what was known for certain. With less than forty-eight hours left before the default deadline with the bank, two members of the Rendell family had met with violence. Surely there was something more at work here than the freakish cruelty of coincidence, but what?

On a practical level Jeff's having been shot inserted an enormous question mark into a situation already fraught with uncertainty. Normally I would have expected the bank to grant us an extension, if only on humanitarian grounds. However, Gus Wallenberg had shown no such inclination after Beau Rendell's death, and I could see no reason why Jeff's incapacity would move him further. After Thursday's leak to the press regarding the possibility of the team's moving to Los Angeles, there was very little public relations downside to screwing the Monarchs' new owner even as he lay fighting for his life in intensive care. I cursed myself for not having had Jeff turn over power of attorney to Chrissy earlier.

I was startled from these and other dark thoughts by the sound of a chair scraping against the floor. I looked up and saw a young black woman carrying a cafeteria tray.

"Do you mind if I join you?" she asked.

I looked quickly around at the dozens of empty tables

surrounding us. "Be my guest," I replied, not quite knowing what else to say.

As she set down her tray and sat down, I was able to take a closer look at her. She was closer to twenty than thirty and was dressed in a Miami Dolphins sweatshirt over jeans. Her hair was shiny with brilliantine and swept into an elaborate conch on top of her head. I wondered if she worked for a personal injury firm, making the rounds of hospitals in the middle of the night, chatting up the families of car-crash victims—an illegal but nonetheless widespread practice.

"I don't know if you remember me from the trial," she said quietly. "I'm Renee Fredericks."

"You're Darius's sister," I said as the information clicked into place.

She'd come to the courtroom every day her brother was on trial. My mother always liked to say that good manners prepare you for the unexpected, but even I was unprepared for a conversation with the sister of the person who'd just shot my client.

"I'm one of his sisters, anyway," she said, managing a shy smile. "The one who still talks to him, at any rate."

A great deal had been made of Fredericks's childhood during the trial. We'd learned how he'd grown up in the slums of south central Los Angeles, one of the six children his mother had had with six different men. We'd heard about his ninth birthday spent in the Venice Beach homeless shelter and of the year and a half he and three of his sisters had lived in the back of an abandoned Chevy.

"How is your brother doing?" I asked.

"The doctors have done all they could for him in the operating room," she said. "They say he's still got a bullet lodged in the front of his brain. They're afraid if they take it out, the surgery will kill him."

"And if they don't?"

"I'm a nurse, Ms. Millholland. I moved to Milwaukee when my brother signed with the Monarchs. I work downstairs in peds. I've seen enough to know that it's better if he doesn't live. Darius isn't coming back, not the Darius we used to know. I hope God sees fit to take him. How is Mr. Rendell?"

"The bullets did a lot of damage. Right now we can only wait and see." I actually suspected that the surgeons, with their experience with hundreds of patients who'd been as seriously wounded as Jeff, probably had a good idea of what the outcome was going to be. However, their job was sewing people up, not making predictions. "I hope you don't mind me asking," I continued, "but do you have any idea what your brother was doing at Beau Rendell's house?"

"The detective I talked to says they think he broke in to rob the place. They say he was after all of the sports memorabilia that Beau Rendell kept there. I told them they were crazy. Darius had more trophies and signed footballs than he knew what to do with. What would he want with more?"

"Perhaps he intended to sell them," I offered gently. "Was he strapped for cash?"

"Darius was *always* strapped for cash, even when he was playing in the NFL. He ran through money like water. Listen, I'm not saying that Darius is perfect. He has his problems, but stealing has never been one of them."

"So what do you think he was doing at Beau Rendell's house?" I asked.

"I think Jeff Rendell set it up."

"What for?"

"I got a call from Darius yesterday. He was all excited. He told me that he had this secret, something big."

"Do you know what it was?"

"Oh, yeah, Darius never could keep anything from me, especially when he was happy."

"He was happy?"

"Of course, he was happy. He was going back to play for the Monarchs."

It was four o'clock in the morning when Jeffrey Rendell died. The reporters had long ago gone home. Chrissy was with him at the end, sitting in the molded plastic chair at his bedside, when the monitors bleated out their flat alarms. She was shoved out of the way when the crash team sprang into action and went through their heroic but ultimately unsuccessful efforts to resuscitate him.

I dozed through all of it in an armchair just outside the double doors. What finally woke me was the screaming, the shrill sounds of the nurses crying out for security, and the sounds of crashing as medical equipment was knocked to the floor.

I stumbled to my feet, propelled by instinct as much as anything else and followed the sounds of shouting. Under the harsh fluorescent lights I got there just in time to see Chrissy Rendell, in her Prada pants and designer sweater, being pulled off the body of Darius Fredericks. In the few seconds that she'd had she'd pulled out every tube and line she could get her hands on, so that sounds of her curses mingled not only with the horrified voices of the nurses, but the sound of the various alarms of the devices that had been monitoring Fredericks's vital systems.

By the time I reached her, Chrissy's hair was disheveled, her eyes wild, and the perfect alabaster of her skin was speckled with the blood of the man that she believed had murdered her husband.

CHAPTER
23

We act out what we can't put into words. Perhaps that is the real explanation of madness, at least the kind that had taken hold of Chrissy. Certainly it was something that Renee Fredericks seemed to understand. Perhaps it was having seen the violence that spilled out of her brother or maybe it was just plain kindness, but in the end it was Darius's sister who convinced them not to call the cops. No harm, she pointed out, had been done and her status as a nurse in the same hospital also carried considerable weight. For the time being the incident was allowed to go unreported, at least until one of the half a dozen or so witnesses discovered that there was money to be made from selling the story.

I honestly don't think Chrissy cared what happened to herself. Her rage spent, she now seemed hollowed out and near shock. I put my arm around her thin shoulders and half lifted her out of the chair in order to propel her toward the door.

As we left Renee Fredericks alone with the rasping of the ventilators I said a silent prayer that her wish would be granted and her brother would be taken.

We walked through the deserted parking lot to the car unmolested. The hospital had promised to give us a half an hour head start before releasing the news of Jeff's death. However, pulling into Chrissy's drive I noticed a car parked on the other side of Lake Drive. It probably belonged to one of the more tenacious reporters, but there was nothing I could do about it.

Chrissy was so devastated by grief that even the simple act of retrieving her house key from her purse was beyond her. I had to root through her shoulder bag until I found the ring and then fumbled in the dark until I was finally able to unlock the door. Groping for the light switch, I led her inside and steered her into the rocking chair while I quickly made my way through the house drawing curtains and closing blinds against the intrusions of the outside world.

By the time I got back to the kitchen she was crying—a good sign. I took her upstairs and helped her get undressed and into bed as if she was an invalid. I went into the bathroom and found the envelope of sleeping pills in the medicine cabinet, intending to offer her one.

We had only the smallest window of relative calm before the news broke of Jeff's death. She needed to get whatever rest she could, but when I returned to her bedroom she was already asleep. I was glad. As bad as today had been, tomorrow was going to be worse.

Elliott Abelman arrived within an hour of my call. I had never been so happy to see anyone in my life. I hugged him as soon as he was through the door, lingering longer in his arms than I ought to have, grateful for the momentary respite from the horrors of the day. I'd put on a pot of coffee while I waited for him, and I poured him out a cup. We sat and drank it at the kitchen table while I filled him in on that night's events, especially what I'd learned about Fredericks.

"So I take it you think the whole thing was a setup?"

"Absolutely. Somebody made a deal with Fredericks. Shoot Jeff and you can come back and play in the NFL."

"If that's really the case, then it limits the suspects to

people who could credibly make the offer. So who does that leave us?"

"Harald Feiss. He's a minority owner of the team, and he called the shots with Beau while he was alive. With Jeff out of the way I'm sure he's convinced he'll be able to get Chrissy to do what he wants. The coach could also make a credible contract offer, though I'm not sure why he'd want to. I don't really know who else. It's got to be Feiss."

"What about Jeff?"

"What do you mean?"

"Do you think he could have engineered the whole thing himself?"

"That's absurd. Why would he want to do such a thing?"

"You said yourself he was in financial trouble. Maybe he took out a big fat life insurance policy and then arranged to have himself killed."

"I don't think so," I replied. "If Jeff was really desperate to get out from under financially, all he had to do was agree to move the team to L.A."

"What if it wasn't the money?"

"You mean what if he murdered his father."

"Exactly."

"In that case I'd expect to find him with a gunshot wound to the head and a suicide note, not wrestling with an intruder in his father's house. The whole thing doesn't make any sense."

"What about Chrissy?"

"Chrissy? You can't be serious."

"Come on. With her husband out of the way she owns the team. Not only that, but word around the campfire was that she was cheating on her husband."

"I know that's what the cops think," I said, "but I don't buy it. They showed up at the hospital and flat out accused Chrissy of having an affair with Jack McWhorter."

"And?"

"She categorically denied it."

"And it doesn't bother you that McWhorter also flew back to Milwaukee on Saturday night?"

"I heard there was a fire in one of the concession kitchens at the stadium."

"He could have had it set."

"You've been watching too many cop shows on TV. If he'd wanted to come back to Milwaukee, there were ten different excuses he could have come up with, none of which involved arson. Besides, I told you, Chrissy denies having an affair with Jack."

"And naturally you believe her."

"Listen. Chrissy is not an angel. We are talking about a girl who used to get around. I mean *really* get *around*. But the operative term is *used to*. She could have had any one of a dozen rich millionaires who wanted her for a trophy wife. She married Jeff because she loved him."

"Yeah, but did she decide to have him killed when she found out he didn't have any more money?"

Coach Bennato arrived practically at first light. He showed up at the door in his boxy black coat, hat in hand as grave as a visiting priest. If he was surprised to find the front door answered by Elliott Abelman, he did not show it. Indeed he looked like a man who was beyond noticing anything. I wasn't even sure whether he remembered who I was and suspected that he accepted my presence the way you expect to see strangers in a house of bereavement.

"I heard about what happened on the news this morning," he said as I took his coat. "I came as soon as I could."

I caught sight of Elliott out of the corner of my eye. He looked like a star struck little boy in the presence of the legendary football coach. Suddenly I realized that my impression of Bennato had always been skewed by Jeff's dissatisfaction with his performance in recent years. Now, what I was seeing in Elliott's eyes was the other side of the coin.

I effected an introduction and watched with amusement as Elliott seemed to grow a foot taller on the spot. To his credit, he didn't make anything further of it, excusing himself quickly to continue his rounds of the property, making sure that all was secure. As he'd been careful to point out, two members of the Rendell family had recently fallen prey to violence. This wasn't the time to be taking chances.

"How is Chrissy?" Bennato asked. "It breaks my heart to think of her and that beautiful little baby. My wife Marie says to tell her that she would be happy to come and watch the baby if that would help."

"Little Katharine is back in Chicago," I said. "Chrissy had to leave her there yesterday when she got the news about Jeff."

"Is Chrissy up to seeing people? I'd like to talk to her for a minute, if that's possible."

"I don't know. Let me go upstairs and see if she's awake." I found my friend in her bedroom already dressed and putting the finishing touches on her makeup.

"I couldn't sleep anymore," she said. "I kept on hoping that I'd wake up and it would all have been a bad dream, but I guess it's not."

"No. I'm sorry. Coach Bennato is downstairs to see you. What do you want me to tell him?"

"I'll come down and talk to him," she said. "I'm not going to be able to hide in my bedroom forever. I might as well go downstairs and get it over with." As we walked down the stairs she asked, "Are there a lot of reporters?"

"Elliott hired a couple of security guards. They're keeping them off the property. They'll get tired of staking the house out once they realize they're not going to get anything.

"I called Mrs. Mason this morning. She said that Elliott's sent armed guards to your parents' house to make sure that the baby stays safe. I was worried about the baby but she says she seems to be doing just fine."

"Mrs. Mason is a rock."

"That's a good thing," said Chrissy, swallowing hard and doing her best to blink back the tears. "Somebody has to be."

At the bottom of the stairs Bennato enveloped Chrissy in a warm embrace. "I'm so sorry," he said.

"Thank you."

"I only wish that when the judge locked up that animal, he'd thrown away the key."

"You mean Fredericks?" I asked.

"Of course I mean Fredericks. I can't believe they let him out after what he did to that girl. That judge called and asked me what I thought of him before he sentenced him and I told him exactly what I thought of him. I said that Fredericks was a complete sociopath, that he was capable of anything. If only the judge had listened!"

"Kate talked to his sister yesterday and she said that he thought he was coming back to play in the NFL."

"Darius Fredericks thought he was Jesus, Allah, and Muhammad Ali all rolled into one," replied Bennato with barely disguised contempt. "That doesn't make it true. But let's not talk about him. I don't want to intrude, but I just wanted to know if there was anything I could do."

"That's very kind, Tony," said Chrissy, taking his hand and giving it a squeeze, "but right now I can't think of a thing. I'll let you know as soon as we have the funeral arrangements made. We're going to do something quiet, just family and a few close friends. I hope you'll be there."

"Of course," he said, with a bow of his head.

"Now if you'll excuse me," she said.

Chrissy withdrew into the front of the house, and I retrieved Coach Bennato's coat from the front hall closet. "What's going to happen now?" he asked me in a much more businesslike tone.

"You mean with the team?"

"Yeah."

"It's up to Chrissy. She's the new owner."

"So what's she gonna do?"

"I don't know," I said. "But I have to say that if I were in her situation, I'd move it." I looked around the room where we stood. "There are a lot of painful memories for her here. You really couldn't blame her if she decided that what she wanted was a fresh start."

CHAPTER
24

I knew that Elliott couldn't stay. He had other cases to attend to, not to mention a business to run, but that didn't make it any easier to see him go. But once he'd made sure that Chrissy and I were okay and there was no one lurking in the bushes there was no real reason for him to remain. For the time being at least, the press seemed willing to keep their distance. I'm sure it helped that Harald Feiss had been doing nothing but giving back-to-back interviews since the news of Jeff's death first broke. I confess I felt safer knowing where Feiss was.

I grabbed a sweater of Chrissy's off the hook near the back door and wrapped it around my shoulders as I walked Elliott back out to his car.

"What happened to the Volvo?" he asked as we passed the crushed carapace of what had once been my car. "It looks like you parked it in a Tyrannosaurus rex crossing."

"Something like that," I replied, explaining how my attempt to foil the Jester had netted me not just an assortment of nasty bruises, but a new Jaguar.

"And you say this guy's back out on the street?"

"Yeah. But, hey, if he'd actually raped and abducted either of us, I'm sure they would have kept him in for another five or six hours."

"Just promise me you'll keep the doors locked and won't let anyone in you don't know."

"I promise," I said as we stopped beside his car.

"You know, I'm wondering why the whole thing went down at Beau's house," mused Elliott. "I mean, if it was a setup, why not here?"

"Because whoever set it up didn't know that Chrissy wouldn't be here. The whole thing with the Jester just came up out of the blue. No one could have known that Chrissy would feel so unsafe in her own home that she'd leave town."

"You know what else I'm wondering?"

"What?"

"What about the gun? I mean, I assume that Darius showed up packing, but what about Jeff? How did he end up doing some of the shooting?"

"There was a gun at Beau's house," I said, feeling a wave of remorse and wondering if things would have turned out differently if I hadn't left the gun where I'd found it in Beau's bottom drawer. "It was in the study. A 9mm Glock in the bottom drawer of his desk. Jeff probably knew it was there, and when he saw Fredericks, he went for it."

"Now you're making it sound like an interrupted burglary again. Would you please make up your mind?"

Elliott fixed me with a long, appraising look, and I suddenly realized I must look like hell. As if reading my mind he reached out and gently tucked a loose strand of hair behind my ear.

"I broke up with Stephen," I said, without meaning to. It just sort of slipped out.

"Did you?" he asked quietly, unable to completely suppress his slowly spreading grin. I knew he was going to kiss me and I did not move away.

"We have a crummy sense of timing," he said, finally pulling away.

I pressed my lips together. "I know," I sighed. "Funerals keep getting in the way."

"When will you be back in Chicago?"

"Not until after Jeff's funeral. Besides, I have a meeting with the bank and another one with the city."

"And then?"

"And then I'm going to go back home and see if I can't make sense out of my life."

"That sounds like an awfully big job. Maybe you'd like some help."

"We'll see," I replied shyly.

"In the meantime I brought you a present."

"What is it?"

Elliott opened up his trunk and pulled out a thick file. "This is a copy of the police file on the Beau Rendell murder investigation. If anyone finds out you have it, you have to promise to take your cyanide pill before you tell them where you got it."

"Scout's honor," I said. "So what's happening with the cops?"

"They think that Jeff killed his father, and now Jeff is dead. They know that it was Fredericks who shot Jeff—whether it was a setup or in self-defense, who cares? If Fredericks lives, he's going to be a human eggplant. Case closed."

"You mean they're going to stop investigating? Even though there are so many unanswered questions? I mean, who sent the fax to Jeff in L.A.? Who did he think he was going to catch in his father's house? I mean, come on!"

"Cops are supposed to close murder investigations, Kate—not look for reasons to keep them open. You should know that."

"Great. Now every time Chrissy sees her name in the paper it will say, 'Mrs. Rendell, who became the owner of the Monarchs after her husband allegedly murdered his father.' All Beau wanted was to pass the team down to his grandchildren, keep it in the family. Now Chrissy's baby is going to grow up with everyone whispering that her father was a killer."

"Maybe he was."

"And maybe he wasn't," I shot back, frowning. "But if the cops drop the investigation, we'll never know, will we?"

Elliott leaned forward and kissed me again, this time chastely on the forehead. "The police are responsible for a lot of things, Kate Millholland. Providing happy childhoods for millionaires is not one of them."

I went back in the house and found Chrissy methodically emptying her kitchen cupboards. I didn't need to ask her what she was doing. I indulged in similar behavior after Russell died. Sorting, cleaning, and rearranging. Your inner life is in turmoil so you seek to impose physical order on the objects around you.

I pulled up a chair. "Do you mind if we talk while you do this?" I asked.

"Not at all," she replied, separating the wooden spoons and spatulas into different piles.

"I have to know what you want to do about the team," I said.

"I know."

"Well?"

"I just got off the phone with Jack. He said that L.A. is prepared to fax me a commitment letter to take to the bank."

"So you want to move the team?"

"No," she said, looking up. "Until a few minutes ago I thought I did. But being home, seeing this house, all my things, this is really where I belong, and more importantly this is where the team belongs. I've been trying to think of what Jeff would have wanted, what he would have considered to be the right thing, and I'm pretty sure that this is it. Even the idea of taking on a partner, which I know bothered Jeff, actually seems like a good idea now. That way I won't be making all the decisions alone."

"Then let me go ahead and see if I can work out a deal," I said. "But until I do, you have to promise me you won't tell anyone about your decision. Right now my best lever is the notion that you can't decide what to do. As soon as you make a decision it substantially weakens my bargaining position."

"I understand."

"I especially don't want you discussing this with Jack. I know you view him as a friend, but believe me, he's an interested party in this and you need to keep him in the dark just like everyone else."

"What do you mean by interested party? Do you think that I'm having an affair with him, too?" she asked in an aggrieved voice.

"Not unless you tell me you are," I answered truthfully. "But I have no idea what kind of finder's fee or deal he may have struck with the people in L.A."

"Do you think that there's really a chance that someone would be willing to make a deal for part of the team?"

"We'll know today. I mean, it's one thing to think about what fun it would be to own a football team. It's another when you start getting the lawyers involved and it's time to start writing the check. Personality is an issue, too. When you take on a partner, you have to give some real thought to what it's going to be like dealing with them day in and day out, year after year."

"I understand," replied Chrissy, "but you also have to understand that right now I'd make a deal with the devil just to be able to put all of this behind me."

*   *   *

I left Chrissy with the spoons and spatulas and went to call my office.

"Congratulations on your promotion from word processing," I told my secretary after she'd picked up the phone.

"No thanks to you," she replied. "I went to the secretarial administrator and told her that I was going to sue the firm for discrimination if they didn't reinstate me."

"And it worked?"

"Apparently. I have been thinking of changing the way I answer the phone to 'Good morning, Pariahs R Us.' It's catchy and it pretty much sums things up when it comes to your career."

"Is it that bad?"

"I'm sure they'll eventually stop blaming you for losing the firm a quarter of a million dollars."

"What's going on in the rest of my life?"

"I don't know. You tell me. Stephen called this morning and started asking me all these weird questions. What's going on with you two?"

"We kind of broke up."

"So I gathered. Congratulations. It's about time."

"Is that what you told Stephen?"

"I didn't tell him anything. I just played dumb. I mean, you can't expect me to do *everything* for you. I take it you like the car?"

"I do, but it's a big change from the Volvo."

"Well, if you decide that it's too nice for you, you can always pass it along to me. I'm sure if I look hard enough, I could find some decrepit old heap to replace the Volvo."

"I'll keep that in mind," I replied. "Now, if there are no more areas of my life you desire to make over, can you get Paul Riskoff on the phone for me?"

* * *

That night Chrissy went to bed early. She'd spent the day alternately weeping, cleaning, and obsessively calling Mrs. Mason every fifteen minutes to reassure herself that the baby was safe. By nightfall she was exhausted. I was glad. Talks had gone well with our possible white knight, and after a few false starts, I felt that I had finally been able to craft an agreement that was acceptable to both parties.

However, even someone of tremendous wealth doesn't keep their millions in their checking account. Even if they were willing to accept our proposal and transmit a letter of intent and a credit letter from their bank by close of business that day, it would take seventy-two hours for the funds to actually transfer—not in time to cure the default with First Milwaukee. Still, I had not come this far to have it not work. I told myself that I would think of something.

I made myself a peanut butter sandwich and checked the doors and windows to make sure that the house was secure. Then I switched on the security system. Thus reassured, I grabbed a Diet Coke from the refrigerator and took my plate upstairs to the guest room. There on the bed, I made myself comfortable and set about going through the accordion file of documents that Elliott had left with me that morning.

The first thing I pulled out were glossy eight by tens of Beau's body lying face down at the bottom of the stairs. I gave a little scream of surprise. I don't know what I was expecting—a little warning perhaps—or maybe it was just that my nerves were getting as frayed as Chrissy's. I quickly turned them over facedown on the quilt, saving them for later.

I read through the witness reports. The first consisted of an interview with a woman named Rebecca Galen, the young woman from accounting who was filling in for Beau's secretary. She reported that she'd taken in a pile of checks for Beau's signature around nine forty-five and found his office empty. There was another statement from a man who worked in media relations. He said that he'd come up to ask Beau about doing an interview with *Sports Illustrated* at—he thought—sometime around ten-twenty, but had turned away halfway to the owner's door when he heard the sounds of voices raised in argument.

Coach Bennato had also given a statement. He reported that he'd come up to see Beau at ten-thirty for their usual postmortem on the Vikings game, but when he arrived, he found the owner's door closed. Even though the police had pressed him, he'd refused to offer an opinion about who might have been arguing with Beau. However, another statement, this time given by an accounting clerk, indicated that when she was heading down to Beau's office, she ran into Bennato, who told her it would probably be best if she came back later, seeing as Jeff and his father were behind closed doors and did not wish to be disturbed.

I found Bennato's loyalty both touching and infuriating. No doubt he thought he was acting in Jeff's best interest by refusing to cooperate fully with the police, not realizing how his stubbornness had ended up having the opposite effect of casting suspicion upon him.

The next reports I came to were from hair and fiber. Apparently fibers matching the carpet in the dead man's office were found on his clothing, not just on his shoes and the bottom of his pants, but also on the back of his jacket and in his hair. The report concluded that this was consistent with his body having lain for some time on the floor of his office. Moreover, the direction of the fibers seemed to indicate that the body had, at some point, most likely been dragged along the carpeting, as well.

The medical examiner had found no evidence of defensive wounds on the dead man's body—no bruising on his arms and no evidence of skin having been trapped under his fingernails, which one would expect if he'd made an effort to fight off his attacker.

There was a lot of techno jargon—notice taken of the compromised state of the dead man's cardiovascular system, not to mention the sorry state of his liver after a lifetime love affair with the whiskey bottle. Much was also made of the fracture of the hyoid bone, which was offered as conclusive evidence of strangulation. Other fractures and contusions noted on the body were all apparently made postmortem, either to disguise the strangulation or in consequence of the fall down the stairs.

There was a lot of other stuff about lividity, morbidity, and internal body temperature, and the weights and condition of all of his internal organs were also noted. His last meal, apparently, had been an Egg McMuffin with cheese.

I took a deep breath and steeled myself to look at the photographs. I flipped through the autopsy shots as quickly as possible and set them aside. It wasn't just squeamishness. I honestly had no idea what I could possibly learn by examining a close-up of Beau Rendell's liver. Instead, I turned to the crime scene photos and carefully laid them out. As Elliott had indicated, there were two separate crime scenes and therefore two separate sets of photos—one of Beau's body at the bottom of the stairs, which I turned to first, and the second set, showing his office, the place from which he had presumably fallen.

Beau's body lay in shadow in a crumpled heap on the concrete floor of the stadium. His body was folded up on itself, making him look much smaller than I remembered. In death, he looked more like a pile of old clothes dumped in a dark corner than the difficult and mercurial owner of an NFL team.

There were also at least a half a dozen shots taken of Beau's office, including one that showed the safe-deposit key on the far side of the desk as if Beau had slid it across toward whoever sat opposite him. I cursed myself silently for having forgotten my promise to myself to go to the bank and look at the contents of the box. Without Cheryl to hold my hand I really was completely hopeless.

Then something else caught my eye. Glancing through the photos, I was struck by something incongruous, not on the desk, but on the floor. I flipped through the glossies until I found the shot that presented the best view, including the stretch of carpeting on the opposite side of the desk where a visitor might have stood.

It was a newspaper. Nothing particularly sinister. Just a copy of the *Milwaukee Journal Sentinel* lying on the carpet as if it had just been dropped by someone who'd then forgotten to pick it up. I flopped back onto the pillows of the bed, thinking.

No matter who had dropped it, its presence was significant. Not because of what it said necessarily, but merely because it was there. Beau Rendell was a man with white carpeting in his house and who balanced his checkbook even though he had no money. In short, a neat freak. I was absolutely certain there was no way that he would have tolerated a dropped newspaper on the floor of his office for even one second while he was still alive.

CHAPTER
25

The last thing I expected to be doing was rooting through old newspapers in the middle of the night—certainly not in Chrissy Rendell's freezing cold garage. But there was no way I was going to be able to sleep without knowing what, if anything, was in that newspaper. Somehow I was certain that it was important. It didn't help that I was plagued by a vague sense of uneasiness, a feeling of not exactly déjà vu, but of having covered the same ground before and having missed the significance the first time.

From the time I was a little girl my mother used to tell me that I had a one-track mind. She did not intend it as a compliment, but she was right. As a lawyer, my greatest strength is my willingness to give myself over to a case wholeheartedly and without reservation. Perhaps, I thought ruefully to myself, dragging the recycling bin over to the spot left vacant by the absence of Chrissy's Suburban, that's why Avco blew up in my face.

I had no doubt that was also why understanding Beau's murder had always seemed out of focus and just beyond my grasp. A firefighter will tell you the hardest kind of blaze to battle is the kind that rages on two fronts. From the very first, from that day I drove up to Milwaukee to listen to Jack McWhorter deliver L.A.'s proposal, I had been dividing my attention and my energies—with disastrous results.

259

I emptied the bin onto the floor of Chrissy's preternaturally clean garage and began going through the papers, carefully pulling out the *Wall Street Journal*s and putting them in a separate pile. From the crime scene photos it had been clear from the configuration of the masthead that the newspaper in question had been the *Milwaukee Journal Sentinel*.

Thanking my lucky stars for Chrissy's tidy-mindedness, I assembled the papers for the week preceding Beau's murder, even though I was pretty sure that what I wanted was the edition from the day of his death. Then I carefully cleaned up, turned off the lights, and went back upstairs to examine my find.

Comparing the papers to the one in the photographs, it was easy to see that I'd been right. The newspaper in question was indeed the edition that had been published the last day of the team owner's life. More than that, I knew that I'd seen it before. I remembered quite clearly having read the article about the two-year-old who'd passed the night forgotten and locked in a Porta-John at the flea market. There had been a copy at Beau's house that I had read while waiting for Jeff to wake up from his pharmacologically induced slumber.

While I pondered the significance of this, I read the entire paper from cover to cover, beginning with the headline about the threatened teachers' strike and ending with the final classified for a cottage for rent at White Bear Lake. I went back to the articles about the Monarchs, beginning with the front-page article about the proposal for renovating the downtown stadium.

And then I felt it click, that feeling somewhere between *eureka!* and *oh my* that tells you from deep in your gut that you finally understand. I sat up in bed and set the newspapers aside, feeling my face drawn wide in what was no doubt a ridiculous expression of amazement.

The police had been right from the very beginning. Not about who, of course, but about how. Beau may have been strangled, but he had not been deliberately murdered. He had been killed in the heat of an argument by a killer who'd almost instantly come to regret what he'd done.

I'd wasted all my time mentally running in the wrong direction because I'd started from the assumption that whoever killed Beau had done so in order to profit from his death. Beau's murderer had never intended to kill him; indeed, he'd had the most to lose from his best friend's death.

From the beginning Harald Feiss had insisted that Beau had intended to move the Monarchs to the suburbs. But Beau had been playing every end against the middle, not even willing to confide in his son what his plans really were. I could only imagine how furious and betrayed Harald must have felt when he'd woken up and read in the newspaper that Beau and the city had reached "an agreement in principle" to renovate the downtown stadium. Especially after Harald, despite being nearly as strapped for cash as his friend, had been making the payment on an enormous tract of empty land in Wauwatosa month after month, waiting for his big payoff.

Of course, he'd been playing the police from day one, from the day he'd stayed down at the stadium feeding them lies while he sent Jeff home with Bennato with instructions to dope him up to keep him quiet. Who better to convince the cops that Chrissy had been having an affair with McWhorter, and what better way to try to sour the deal with L.A. than to try to convince Jeff that his wife had an ulterior motive for wanting to be in L.A.? But Jeff had been reluctant to believe that Chrissy had been unfaithful, and then what? He'd demanded proof. That's where Darius Fredericks came in, Darius and the fax luring Jeff back into his father's house.

Perhaps Fredericks really had been a burglar—either that or Feiss had set him up to take the fall. I didn't really care which one of them had been the shooter. As far as I was concerned I knew who had been behind the crime irrespective of who had actually pulled the trigger. I looked at the clock and decided that it was too late to call Elliott. I'd let him sleep and dazzle him with my powers of deduction in the morning.

I got up early the next morning, showered, and dressed almost as carefully as Chrissy. The house was quiet and I decided to let Chrissy sleep. We'd turned the ringer off the phone the day before, plagued by unwanted phone calls from the press, and I figured it was best to maintain the status quo for now. Before I left I checked all the windows and the doors, making sure that they were still locked. At the end of the driveway I stopped and spoke to the uniformed security officer, who was busy keeping warm in the front seat of his car. I described Harald Feiss to him and explained that under no circumstances was he to set foot on the property.

From the car I dialed my secretary, joining the pitiful trickle of cars that masquerades as rush hour in Milwaukee.

"You must be very important," announced my loyal secretary who was already at her desk. "The mayor of Milwaukee has agreed to meet with you, but he wants to keep things hush-hush."

"Oh, yippee. What does he want to do? Meet in the churchyard at midnight? Smuggle me into his office disguised as a policeman?"

"Close. He's faxing me directions for where you're going to rendezvous with his security people. I guess you're going in through the backdoor. He actually managed to use the word *covert* about six times. The man sounds like an asshole."

"That's probably because he is one. Anybody else call that I should know about?"

"Jake Palmer called. He seems anxious to speak to you. He says he has some information you might want about Darius Fredericks."

"Did he leave you a number?"

"No. He said to tell you that he can't be reached this morning, but if you wanted, you could meet him at a restaurant called Mader's at one o'clock. I have the address."

"I think I know where it is," I said, "but let me take it down anyway." I reached over toward the passenger seat and was rewarded only by the feeling of rich leather. "Do me a favor—make a note that I want a dozen legal pads put in the car and a bunch of pencils."

"So, do you still like your new car?"

"It needs some breaking in. Anybody else call?"

"Just Stephen. He says he thinks you two need to sit down and talk."

"Call him back and tell him that I have a funeral to go to," I replied, "and all things considered, he's lucky that it's not his."

"Everything go okay last night?" inquired Elliott when I got him on his cell phone. He was on his way out to Naperville to interview one of a dozen families who'd been bilked by a fraudulent builder. "Nothing go bump in the night?"

"All serene. I did find out some interesting things."

"You, too? So spill. What deep dark secrets did you unearth?"

"I know who killed Beau Rendell and why."

"So, are you going to share this with me, Sherlock, or do I have to beg?"

"Normally I'd say begging is good, but I'm in a hurry to

get to the bank. I want to take a peek in Beau Rendell's safe-deposit box before my meeting with the bankers."

"If you find millions in hard cold cash, I'll split it with you."

"No chance," I replied, and told him everything I'd figured out about Harald Feiss the night before.

"Curiouser and curiouser," he replied when I had finished.

"Don't you mean 'bravo'?"

"Well, I didn't tell you, but I called a friend of mine who runs a P.I. outfit in L.A. and had him buzz over to the Regent Beverly Wilshire to see what he could find out about Jeffrey Rendell's last days."

"And what did he find out?" I asked, feeling rather deflated.

"Well, for one thing I learned that a luxury hotel is not a particularly good place if you want to keep a secret. They keep records of everything, and the staff doesn't miss a thing."

"So what secret was he trying to keep?"

"Let's just put it this way. Jeff checked in on Friday and met a guy named Ken Gunther, who I guess works out of your firm's L.A. office. Ken had already booked a room. The whole thing was comped, by the way. The hotel picked up the whole tab. According to the manager it was some kind of quid pro quo deal for the L.A. Stadium Commission.

"Okay, so on Friday they went out to dinner. According to housekeeping, everything looked pretty much like you'd expect. Records indicate Jeff made three calls, two to his wife and one to his office at the stadium. Jeff and Ken and Jack had dinner in the restaurant, a real power deal according to the waiter, who knows everybody and strings for the scandal sheets on the side. That's when things started getting interesting."

"What happened?"

"Well, first this guy Jack McWhorter gets an emergency phone call. Apparently there was some kind of fire at Monarchs Stadium where they cook the food, and he excuses himself, he has to fly back and take care of business right away."

"Is that it?"

"No. Then about an hour later the concierge received a fax for Jeffrey Rendell and delivered it to the table."

"I know. The cops showed it to us at the hospital. He had it in his pocket when he was shot. It said, 'If you want to catch them at it, try your father's house tomorrow at two.' The message was printed by hand in block letters."

"Well, according to our waiter snitch, the fax really upset Jeff, who immediately excused himself saying that he wasn't feeling well and headed back to his room."

"Let me guess. He wasn't really sick."

"He immediately made a string of phone calls, one to the airlines, one to his house in Milwaukee, and one to a taxi company. He left L.A. an hour later on America West flight 252 to Chicago. Apparently he stayed overnight somewhere near O'Hare, rented a car, and then headed up to Milwaukee."

"Okay. I'll bite," I said. "So who sent the fax?"

"I don't know who. All they could tell me is that it was transmitted from the Milwaukee Monarchs' offices at the stadium."

There is a kind of theater to safe depositories, an inherent drama in the locks and keys, the heavy vault door that swings so silently on its hinges, the solemn banking acolyte who ushers you into the softly lit private room and closes the door upon you. For me the mystery was heightened by the fact that I not only had no idea what I was going to find, but that I'd made the journey from thinking that whatever it was, was critical to irrelevant and back to critical again.

The fact that the fax had come from the stadium did not in and of itself blow my theory about Harald Feiss out of the water. After all, you'd hardly expect him to send something so potentially incriminating from his own office. However, it messed up my tidy theories, and I desperately wanted things to finally turn out neat. Indeed, I was starting to feel as though I deserved it.

I laid the box upon the table and pulled the key out of my bag, inserted it in the lock, and turned it. With a sense of anticipation that surprised me, I lifted the long flat lid.

Just as Jeff had said, the box contained documents. Manila envelopes, neatly labeled, contained the contracts of key personnel. I noted there was one for Darius Fredericks, the one that was as infamous for its lack of a morals clause as it was for its dollar amount, another example of Harald Feiss's incompetence. Jake Palmer's was there, too, along with Coach Bennato's and, interestingly enough, one for Jeff. I looked them through briefly and was forced to conclude that I'd chosen the wrong line of work. Football paid better than anything else I could think of, including robbing banks. Indeed, a quick scan of Darius Fredericks's contract revealed that if the wounded wide receiver ended up dying, the organization would find itself considerably richer.

There was only one envelope that was unmarked, and I pulled it from the bottom of the pile. It was also sealed, and after a moment's hesitation I loosened the flap and emptied out the contents on the table.

It has been a long time since I have been really, truly shocked. I stared and gaped, pushing my chair back instinctively from the table to gain some distance. They were a series of photographs, professional quality, of my friend Chrissy Rendell engaged in what could only be described as an astonishing variety of sex acts with a generously endowed black man who I did not recognize.

My stomach turned and yet I forced myself to take a closer look. In the pictures her hair was cut in the shaggy style she'd favored in her last year of college. A close examination of her face revealed that the pictures were, I guessed, at least a half a dozen years old. I wondered why Jeff had chosen to keep them in the team's safe deposit box and could only conclude that the decision had not been his own, but Beau's. If it was Beau who had been originally approached with the photos I would not have put it past him to use them as a tool for keeping Jeff in line.

No wonder Jeff had been desperate for the cops to not see these, I thought to myself quickly, sliding them back into their envelope and locking them back up in the box. He'd said Chrissy didn't even know what was there. No doubt someone had tried a spot of blackmail. I wondered who.

There was no pretense in Gus Wallenberg's office that morning, no bonhomie. Just the banker behind the bunker of his desk, a small smile of self-satisfaction on his face.

"I assume you have come to deliver a cashier's check for $18 million," he said, leaning back in his chair, enjoying himself.

"I had hoped to bring it with me today," I answered easily, "but you can understand that Jeffrey Rendell's murder has interfered with the family's ability to transact business."

"Unfortunately these personal issues are no concern of the bank," pointed out Wallenberg. "I'm sure you understand that, barring full payment of the default amount, First Milwaukee has no choice but to put the Milwaukee Monarchs Corporation into receivership."

"I'm not sure that would be in the bank's best interest," I suggested.

"If you can't make good on the default, I'm afraid that our business is concluded."

I looked at my watch. "I believe your secretary should be receiving a fax copy of a commitment letter for the funds from the newest shareholder of the Monarchs organization. A hard copy will be arriving via Federal Express later this morning."

He picked up his phone and punched the number for an internal line. "Stella?" he barked into the receiver. "Is there a fax coming through for me?" He nodded and released the switch. A few seconds later a primly dressed woman delivered the faxes.

"Paul Riskoff the real estate developer?" demanded Wallenberg, scanning the top sheet.

"Yes. As you can see, Mr. Riskoff is prepared to pay $50 million for an as yet unspecified number of shares. That's enough to cover the default, current payables, and a hefty contribution to renovating their existing stadium."

"I'm sorry, Ms. Millholland," declared Wallenberg, not looking sorry at all, "but you and I both know that this piece of paper is worthless and your client is still in default."

"Jeffrey Rendell died last night," I pointed out.

"And in the wake of her husband's death, Mrs. Rendell assumes the obligations of her husband's estate. The identity of the noteholder in no way changes the contractual obligations of this bank."

"I think it drastically affects your exposure," I pointed out.

"According to which accounting principle?" demanded Wallenberg.

"Oh, I'm not talking about anything you can put down in black and white on your balance sheet, but I guarantee you that if you call the Monarchs' loan, this bank will take a hit on the bottom line so big that it will take you six months to stop gushing red ink."

"Are you threatening me?"

"No. I'm merely pointing out what will happen should you elect to remain inflexible in this matter. First of all, I am prepared to see to it that Mrs. Rendell signs an agreement today with the Greater Los Angeles Stadium Commission, who will see to it that you receive your $18 million via wire transfer by the close of business today."

"Then the bank will be satisfied."

"Good. Because after that I'm getting on the phone to the producer of every single tabloid news show and I'm going to make sure that my attractive and highly sympathetic client not only parades her widowhood on television, but tells everyone who will listen to her that it was the actions of First Milwaukee that forced her to move the team. People will be standing in line to pull their money from the bank. When I'm done with them, they'll see it as their civic duty. You'll be lucky if you have six Christmas Club accounts by the end of the year."

"This is blackmail," sputtered Wallenberg.

"This is business," I replied coldly. "Don't you start turning all pathetic on me now. After all, you're the one who decided that we were going to be ruthless."

"Just tell me how I'm supposed to know that this Riskoff guy is for real? What guarantee are you willing to give me that he is going to make good on this letter?"

"How about a million dollars?" I suggested, pulling the number out of the air. I figured that at the end of the day the only thing that bankers understand is money. "I'll write you a personal check for $1 million right now as a good-faith payment against the team's obligation." I pulled my checkbook out of my briefcase. "Not only that, but should the team not make good on its obligation after ten days, I'm prepared to default the million. You give us ten days and if we don't come through, you get to keep the million. I'll even make it out to you personally if you'd like."

"The bank will be fine," replied Wallenberg, too stunned to be insulted by the implication.

I handed Wallenberg the check and got to my feet, offering up my winningest smile, and was out the door before I had the chance to even absorb the full impact of what I'd done. While it had been at least a couple of months since I'd had time to sit down and balance my checkbook, I could say one thing with certainty. There was nothing even close to a million dollars in that account.

CHAPTER

26

Mader's is a Milwaukee institution, a downtown German restaurant that looks like it was airlifted out of Bavaria. The main dining room is enormous and paneled in carved wood depicting alpine scenes. There is lots of stained glass, and wooden trolls peer down from every available vantage point. Before I went off in search of Jake Palmer, I stopped at the pay phone by the coatroom and, to the astonishment of the coat-check girl, made arrangements to have my check covered.

That done, I called Chrissy's house to tell her the good news. I was alarmed when no one answered until I remembered that we'd deliberately turned all the ringers off. I left her a message saying that I hoped to be back inside of an hour and went off in search of my personal Goliath.

Even though the place was still crammed with the lunchtime crowd, Jake was easy enough to pick out. Not only did he not blend in with the suits, but also there was a line of fans stretching respectfully for his autograph.

"Hey there," he said, rising to his feet and explaining with a big grin to his fans that his lawyer had arrived. He hopped over to the other side of the table and chivalrously pulled out my chair.

"What a great place," I declared, breathing in the sauerkraut-scented air. "I confess I wouldn't have thought that you'd be a big fan of German food." At this a buxom, dirndl-skirted waitress appeared bearing a stein of beer at least a foot high. He licked his lips. "I take it back."

"May I take your order?" inquired the waitress reverentially.

"Two sampler platters," announced Jake.

"Oh, good," I remarked, handing back the menu unread. "I'm starved."

"Then you'd better make that three sampler platters," Jake grinned.

The waitress disappeared, and a busboy took her place, materializing with a basket of hot rolls. Jake tore one in half like it was some hapless running back and popped it in his mouth like a doughnut hole.

"I'm so glad you called me," I said. "But I hope you aren't missing practice on my account." I remembered vaguely something I'd read somewhere about there being fines for missed practices.

"Nah, Coach let me out so I could speak at some booster luncheon across the street. I do about a dozen of them a season. I'm the Monarchs' dancing bear. The suits are always so-o-o impressed by how articulate I am. You want to know why?"

"Because you're black and they're racists?" I offered.

"Racists? Those motherfuckers expect that when I open my mouth, I'm going to grunt like a fucking chimpanzee."

"Are you telling me you already had lunch?" I asked, feeling a bit slow on the uptake.

"Yeah, sure, if you can call it lunch—a circle of weird fish and two grains of rice. Now this place here, they serve up some real food. A big man's got to eat big to play in the NFL."

As if to illustrate his point the waitress appeared with our sampler platters. She had to move the bread basket and shift the water glasses around to make room. I couldn't believe it. It was like six meals crammed onto one plate.

There was pork loin, schnitzel, goulash, beef roulade, an enormous potato dumpling, and two kinds of kraut.

Jake the Giant dug in with relish. I took a tentative bite of the potato dumpling and felt it instantly expanding in my stomach.

"So tell me about Darius Fredericks," I said. "My secretary said you had things to tell me about him that I should know."

"For one thing, he's not a killer."

"What makes you say that? He almost killed that Amber Cunningham. They pled it down to agg battery, but the original indictment came down as attempted murder."

"Batting some chick around and shooting somebody are two different animals," replied Jake.

"Violence is violence," I replied. "I don't want to get into a discussion of how many angels can dance on the head of a pin."

"I'm with you on that."

"So then you tell me what he was doing at Beau Rendell's house on Sunday?"

"Well, that's what I wanted to tell you about. I was in the locker room after the game yesterday and Hale Millon, another guy who plays on the offensive line with me, says he's heard rumors that Fredericks is coming back to play for the Monarchs."

"Rumors? What kind of rumors?"

"Millon and Fredericks, they use the same agent, a guy named Gorman out of New York. I guess Hale heard it from him."

"Do you know how I can reach this guy? The agent?"

"I got his number right here." He pulled his cell phone out of his pocket and handed it to me. In his palm it looked like a postage stamp.

I punched in the numbers scribbled on the sheet of paper while Jake attacked his lunch. Gorman's office picked up and immediately put me on hold. I listened to the insipid music while Jake cleaned his plate. As soon as he was done the waitress appeared with another.

"Got to keep up my strength," he whispered confidentially. "The team nutritionist has me on a ten-thousand-calorie-a-day diet."

The secretary came back on the line and told me that regrettably Mr. Gorman was in a meeting. I told her that it was an emergency and left the number at Chrissy's house as well as Jake's cell phone number.

"You know you're wrong," said Jake, judiciously cleaning the gravy from his plate with a piece of rye bread.

"Wrong about what?"

"Violence."

"In what way?" I asked, curious to see what a man who makes millions of dollars trying to knock his opponents unconscious had to say on the subject.

"Violence is not all the same."

"I agree. What I said was a generalization. Sometimes violence is necessary—in war, for example, or self-defense."

"It's more than that," he declared. "There's a place for violence. It's okay when it's in its place."

"You mean the football field."

"That's one place."

"What about what Fredericks did to that girl?"

"As far as I'm concerned he got what he deserved. Same thing with Coach when he choked that kid. That wasn't part of the game and he got called on it."

"Who did Coach choke?" I demanded, feeling the stirrings of something very much like fear in the pit of my stomach.

"Some kid back when he coached in Texas. A player. They fired him for it and he was banned from college ball for life. When Beau Rendell hired him I think he was working selling Chryslers."

"Tell me," I said, rising quickly to my feet and throwing down a couple of bills to cover my lunch, "do you remember what Coach Bennato's wife's name is?"

"Marie. Why do you ask?"

"And what about his daughter?"

"His daughter? I don't know. She's got some plain-assed name, I can't remember. Bonnie, or Debbie or something boring like that."

"Listen," I said urgently. "I have to go. But I also have to talk to this agent Gorman. If he calls you, I want you to try to reach me." I grabbed a pen that had been left behind by some autograph hunter and scribbled down the number.

"Where are you going?" he asked, surprised at my abrupt departure.

"I've got to get to Chrissy Rendell's house. It's a matter of life and death."

I couldn't believe I had been that stupid. It wasn't Feiss who was behind Debmar, it was Bennato. It was Bennato who owned the land. It was Bennato who'd waited patiently for Beau Rendell to make good on his promise to make him rich. Bennato who'd lost his temper and confronted Beau. Bennato who'd reached up in a fit of temper and choked the object of his displeasure just as he had on the sidelines so many years ago.

Bennato hadn't meant to kill Beau, but once he had, he'd done everything within his power to throw suspicion on Jeff. The sleeping pills, the whispered hints about dark secrets at the wake, the assurances that the police would get nothing out of him—all the while fitting Jeff for the noose.

Jeff had signed his own death warrant when he'd

angrily told Feiss that all the obligations that his father had made were canceled. He was a dead man just as soon as he'd announced he was moving the team.

Bennato was in a position to set the fire that brought Jack back to Milwaukee. He'd probably been whispering his suspicions about Jack and Chrissy in Jeff's ear from the minute he killed Jeff's father. It has been said that football was nothing if not a violent game of chess. Bennato had spent his entire career planning strategy and coolly moving men across the playing field. A master of a violent game, he'd been playing Jeff, Chrissy, and the police from the first move.

As I pulled into the driveway I felt the first wave of misgiving when I realized that there was no security guard on the street. I told myself that he might be making a tour of the property or taking a bathroom break. Otherwise, everything looked exactly as I'd left it that morning, a peaceful house on a quiet suburban street.

I parked the Jaguar behind the Volvo in front of the house and walked around to the side door under the porte cochere because I knew that's where Chrissy kept the key hidden. I lifted the mat, unlocked the door and returned the key to its place, and let myself in. The house not only seemed quiet but felt empty. I felt a shiver of dread and told myself that I was imagining things.

I went off in search of Chrissy. Finding the first floor deserted, I made my way upstairs, expecting to find her still asleep. Her bedroom door was ajar, but when I stuck my head in, I found it empty. The bed was still unmade and there were clothes on the floor. I noticed that the light was on in her bathroom and the door was open.

"Chrissy?" I called out. "I'm back." There was no answer.

I looked inside the bathroom. The floor was wet and the air was still humid from the shower. Makeup was spread out all over the counter, scattered not just next to the sink but in it. Several compacts had apparently been knocked on the floor, and I noticed that the rug was askew. But what really made my mouth go dry was the Milwaukee Monarchs' envelope that lay open on the counter. I quickly took a look inside. Where it had once contained dozens of pills it was now empty.

I ran through the house, calling her name, desperate to find her. Terrified, I told myself to get a grip. I was not just letting my imagination run away from me, but hypothesizing ahead of the facts. I hadn't even looked to see whether the car was still in the garage. For all I knew, she'd poured the pills down the sink and run out to get a cup of coffee while I was charging around getting ready to dial the suicide hot line.

I walked through the kitchen and opened the door that led from the house into the garage. I immediately knew that there was something wrong. The overhead garage door was closed, but the engine of Jeff's Lexus was running and the air was thick with exhaust. I fumbled in the dark for the switch to open the garage door, feeling the door to the house snap closed behind me as I worked my way along the wall, groping for the switch. I found it and immediately heard the garage door spring to life and begin to lift.

However, it had not risen more than six inches before it changed directions and closed again.

Panicked and beginning to cough, I hit the button again. The same thing happened, only this time the door opened only a fraction of an inch before reversing itself and moving down. Frantic, I groped for the doorknob to go back into the house, but was horrified to discover that it would not turn.

"Think," I told myself.

That's when I remembered that all automatic garage

door openers were required to have a manual override. The one on my parents' garage door looked like a small red handle on a rope that hung from the chain that controlled the door. Gasping and dizzy, I plunged into the garage, half climbed up the hood of the Lexus, and flailed in the general direction of the ceiling until my hand hit something that felt like string. I pulled as hard as I could and felt the mechanism release.

Then I slid down the passenger side of the Lexus and raced toward the entrance to the garage, scrabbling in the dark for the handle that I knew must be centered near the ground. I found it and I heaved, raising the door and letting in a tide of cold, clean air.

Bent over and coughing uncontrollably, I forced myself back into the interior of the garage, frantic to get Chrissy out of the car. I made my way to the driver's side of the Lexus. With the light from the open garage door I could now see Chrissy slumped over the steering wheel. Feeling nauseous with fear, I yanked open the handle, sobbing in frustration to find that it was locked. I ran around the back of the car to the other side, noting that the exhaust pipe had been neatly covered over with duct tape. I tried the passenger door, too. It was locked, as well.

I raced to the back of the car and clawed desperately at the tape until I was finally able to pull it off only to receive a lungful of exhaust for my trouble. I briefly contemplated going back into the house to look for an extra car key but immediately discarded the idea.

I had no time.

Instead, I looked frantically around Chrissy's immaculate garage, searching for something to use to break the windows. Unfortunately, it was not the usual repository of tools or garden supplies, but rather a yuppie car hotel. There were no rakes or shovels, instead a truckload of landscapers arrived for the yard's weekly manicure and departed again when they were finished, taking their tools with them. I opened cupboards and looked on shelves, searching for a hammer or a brick. Instead I found neatly labeled storage boxes containing flower-arranging supplies and bundles of old clothes labeled for the Salvation Army.

Finally, I spotted Jeff's golf clubs in the corner, each in its own furry shroud. I grabbed the first one that came to hand, ripped off the ridiculous cover, and swinging it like an ax, brought it down with all my strength on the windshield of the Lexus. I felt the shock of the impact reverberate up my arms, but the window remained intact and Chrissy did not stir. I continued beating against the glass, shouting with frustration. Suddenly the windshield gave way all of a piece and came raining down on Chrissy in a glittering hail of broken glass.

Immediately, I dropped the club and reached back through the shattered windshield to unlock the door. Then I opened the driver's door and reaching across the body of my unconscious friend I switched off the ignition. Without stopping to think about her still-wet hair or the fact that she was dressed in only a T-shirt and a pair of lace panties, I grabbed her by her shoulders and dragged her from the car and laid her down on the driveway. I pushed the wet hair off of her face and noticed with relief that she was still breathing. I examined her face carefully, struck by something and hard-pressed to decide what it was.

I looked again, closely. There was no doubt about it; there was something funny about her lips. She'd applied her foundation and her lipliner, but that was all. She had not yet begun to fill them in with lipstick. Chrissy Rendell had not tried to commit suicide. No one as disciplined about her appearance as she was would elect to kill herself halfway through her makeup routine. What I was seeing, like Beau's crumpled body at the bottom of the stairs, was a carefully staged scene.

I stood up and immediately saw Bennato coming at us slowly. He had a gun in one hand and a roll of duct tape in the other. I suddenly realized that I felt no satisfaction in having been right.

All I felt was fear.

CHAPTER
27

"What a shame about the Rendells," Bennato said, gesturing with the gun for me to step away from Chrissy. "They seem to be dropping like flies."

"Let me see if I get how you mean this to play out," I replied, moving slowly, unable to take my eyes off the hole at the end of that gray barrel. "Jeff, thinking that he's going to find his wife in bed with Jack McWhorter, stumbles upon a homicidal burglar instead. Then, distraught, his wife takes an overdose of pills and tries to take a ride to oblivion."

"Oh, she'll do better than try," he assured me.

"How did you get her to take the sleeping pills?" I asked.

"How does a man with a gun get anyone to do anything?" he replied coolly, waving me back into the house.

"Luckily for you Jeff remembered his father's gun in the drawer and shot Fredericks," I pointed out. For some reason the talking seemed to help keep me calm. As long as I was talking I was breathing.

"Fredericks would never have talked. Still, you know what they say. It's better to be lucky than good."

"You're right. This way is less messy. All the loose ends tied up."

Even with Bennato's gun trained on me I made my way into the house as slowly as I could. The farther I got from

Chrissy the more helpless I felt. Even though I was face to face with an armed man who had already killed twice, so far my fear was all for Chrissy.

Once I got to the middle of the kitchen, Bennato motioned for me to stop. I looked around the room and tried to assess my options. I was quite a distance from the stairs, the door, or the garage. Coach Bennato stood between me and the door into the rest of the house. The telephone was at his back.

"All the loose ends tied up except for you," he informed me with an elaborate sigh.

"Don't even think about it," I said. "Right now the evidence tells your story. It's doubtful they'd even have enough to arrest you, and if they did, with a good lawyer you'll walk," I assured him, trying to sound lawyerlike and reasonable.

"Oh, I think it'll tell the story I want even after I shoot you," he replied.

Normally threats like that are easy to speak, harder to honor. But Coach Bennato had already proved himself a killer. I had called it right. I was just another loose end that needed cleaning up.

My breath started coming in shallow, rapid little gasps that didn't seem to be doing a particularly good job of getting oxygen to my brain. My thoughts ran wildly from one subject to another. I found myself wondering whether it would hurt when the bullets hit me, whether Chrissy had inhaled enough carbon monoxide to cause brain damage, how long it would take her to develop hypothermia lying in her underwear on the driveway, and how many bullets were in the efficient-looking automatic whose barrel I was staring down.

I watched with a sense of horrible fascination as Coach Bennato's thumb traveled and came to rest on the hammer of the gun. It was a small gesture, less than a quarter of an inch. But if it's true that all acts of violence are committed twice—once in intent and the second time in action—I knew that I had just come a great deal closer to dying.

And then everything seemed to slow down. For the first time I knew that I was experiencing real fear. Not the fear of high places or the fear that comes with being alone in the dark. The kind of fear that is born from a thousand years of inbred instinct. The kind of fear that tells you what to do if you want to stay alive. Real fear will sometimes tell you to play dead or to stop breathing, tell you whether to run or stay and fight. What it told me was that there was no way out of that kitchen that didn't involve getting shot. For some reason I accepted this dispassionately—a fact.

I remembered my roommate's countless stories of patients who'd come into her emergency room shot five or six times. The important thing, I told myself, was to be sure to keep Bennato sufficiently off balance to prevent him from controlling where he hit me. I remember thinking that even if I could not take his gun away, I could take away his choice of how and when to use it.

I don't remember making the decision to charge. I'm sure it wasn't made consciously. I don't even remember being shot. All I remember is tackling Bennato around the ankles, his body falling on top of mine, and the two of us rolling around on the floor, scrabbling after the gun.

Somehow I managed to get on top of him and get my hands around his throat. It was then that I realized my entire left side was slick with blood and I was having a hard time making my hand work. I kept on telling it to squeeze, but it wasn't doing any good.

"Hey!" said Jake Palmer, walking in through the garage, carrying Chrissy, still unconscious, over his shoulder like a spoil of war. "What the hell is going on here?"

"Help . . . me," I managed to gasp.

"What the fuck," was all he said before he stepped up neatly and kicked Coach Bennato in the head. He pulled his cell phone from his pocket, pulled the antenna out with his teeth, and began to dial. "What are you doing here?" I gasped, slipping too rapidly into shock to seem appropriately grateful.

"When Gorman called me back, I tried you at the number out here, but nobody answered so I figured I might as well take a ride, you know. I mean, hey, I heard you say that it was a matter of life or death that you talk to this guy, but I never figured you meant it literally."

CHAPTER
28

Football season was finally over. The Monarchs had finished out the year in the toilet. The team was in shambles. Coach Bennato was in jail getting ready to stand trial for murder. His wife, Marie, and his daughter, Debra, brought him casseroles every day.

My shoulder had needed surgery. Luckily I drew the same crew who'd tried to patch up Jeff. Chrissy and I were even roommates again, this time in the intensive care ward, but only for one night. Her recovery was quick and complete. She brought baby Katharine to visit me every day.

Stephen came, too, but it was more obvious now than ever that without a business problem to chew on between us there was really nothing to say. He brought flowers and left sheepishly. He only came the one time.

As usual, Cheryl had been right. Not only that it was about time that I broke things off with Stephen, but that my partners would eventually forget about Avco and the $250,000. Gus Rolle, my nemesis on the management committee, was discovered to have embezzled something like $2 million from a client's trust account in order to feather a love nest for his twenty-two-year-old secretary. By the time the Brandt brothers were finally indicted on charges of selling child pornography, my transgressions had, for the most part, been forgotten.

The shoulder had turned into a real pain. Not only did I need surgery, but I had to wear it in a weird kind of suspension splint that kept my elbow above my ear. Wearing anything but a cape was nearly impossible, and sleeping was a real treat. Eventually it was replaced by an arm cast and now, finally, just a sling. I had reached the point where the temptation to use the arm was practically irresistible, and Cheryl had taken to scolding me whenever she caught me at it.

The new apartment was finished, gorgeous, and empty. While Paul Riskoff and I had become the best of friends, Stephen and I had been reduced to squabbling over the furniture. That's why I was at the apartment that Sunday morning, enjoying the thin January sunshine as it poured in through my perfectly arched windows. I was going through the apartment matching the furniture that had already been delivered to the checks that had paid for, trying to figure out who owed who what. I was surprised when the house phone rang and the doorman asked me if I wanted him to send Elliott Abelman up.

We hadn't seen that much of each other in the weeks since I'd been hurt. He'd come to the hospital, of course, and we'd resumed our phone-friend habit, but nothing more. I sensed a certain reluctance in him, a desire not to crowd. I think he was waiting for me to come to him. For the time being, I thought I might as well leave it at that.

Apparently Elliott had been out running. He appeared to be almost totally swathed in Gore-Tex, and his face was ruddy from the cold.

"I brought you a housewarming present," he said. "I was just planning on leaving it with your doorman, and then I saw your car out front." He pulled a flat paper bag out of his warm-up and handed it to me.

"Classy wrapping paper," I remarked.

"It's for your coffee table," he said, as I pulled the latest issue of *Milwaukee Magazine* from the bag. On the cover was a picture of a smiling Chrissy Rendell, her arms thrown around Paul Riskoff's shoulders. The title ran: MILWAUKEE'S NEW DYNAMIC DUO.

"Thank you," I said. "I shall treasure it always. Now all I need is a coffee table."

"You know, that Chrissy is quite a fox," remarked Elliott with a wolfish grin. "Now that she's single again I was wondering if you'd mind fixing me up with her."

I took the magazine and heaved it at him with my good arm. I only missed him by an inch.

A Conversation with Gini Hartzmark

Q: Describe Kate Millholland. How is she different from other female sleuths?

A: Kate is a young Chicago corporate attorney specializing in the kind of fast-paced, transaction-driven law that is only done in large firms like Callahan Ross, the staid and self-satisfied firm of which Kate is now a partner. She is also a Millholland, which means that her family is a big deal in Chicago in the same way that the Kennedys are a big deal in Boston.

Kate is smart, she is strong, and—like most other female sleuths—she is also an outsider. What makes her different is that the worlds that she stands outside of are those of the quintessential *insider*—old money and corporate law. She is not only independent but difficult. (Some would say impossible.)

Q: Is Kate modeled after someone you know?

A: Yes and no. Kate began life as a construct, a device. I knew that I wanted to write a series character and the premise of the series was that every book would take the reader inside a different business. I also knew I wanted to write a woman, but I didn't know enough about police work to write a credible cop and I felt uncomfortable with a female P.I., which has been done successfully by so many others. Given my background, a lawyer seemed a natural. Of course, back when I was making these decisions, Scott Turow had yet to write *Presumed Innocent* and John Grisham was just another plaintiff's attorney in Oxford, Mississippi. The choice of Kate's background—great wealth and old money—came directly from my experiences attending an exclusive girls' prep school. While I didn't share Kate's pedigree, I had classmates who did, and I was interested in writing about the narrowness of that world and the contradictory mix of unlimited opportunity and suffocating expectations that characterize it.

I used to reply incredulously to all inquiries about whether Kate and I were alike. After all, I sit alone in my office in a torn sweatshirt writing novels and taking care of a household that includes three school-age children and a husband with a very demanding career, while Kate, dressed in an Armani suit, deals with her glamorous clients and their high-stakes corporate problems. In her spare time she carries on with brilliant and impossibly handsome Stephen Azorini. Yeah, right. We have a lot in common. Of course, the truth is that we do. We share the same cranky outlook and have a similar disregard for what other people think of us. Neither of us has much use for authority, which is why I write books (my characters do what I want them to do or I kill them) and Kate is perennially in trouble with the senior partners at her firm.

Q: Why did you decide to write a series character?
A: I always wanted to write a series because those are the books that I've always loved best. I grew up reading about Hercule Poirot, Sherlock Holmes, and later Lord Peter Wimsey and George Smiley. As a reader it is wonderful to be able to spend time with a character you enjoy book after book. As a writer I enjoy having the

luxury of having the character grow and change over the course of many stories as opposed to just one.

Q: What are the challenges of writing a series character?
A: For me the hardest thing about writing a series is introducing Kate and the continuing characters in every book. It's not just that I know that the readers of the previous books are already familiar with them while others are meeting them for the first time, but rather that it is difficult to present the same information (Kate's background, profession, widowhood, etc.) in a fresh way each time.

There are also weird problems, like the fact that it always works out to be winter in the books. In part it is chronological, because the books follow one after another and the first book in the series, *Principal Defense*, begins in the weeks between Thanksgiving and Christmas, which put me on a certain schedule. After *Fatal Reaction*, I was determined to write a summer book, but because *Rough Trade*, the next book in the series, was about the business of major league sports, specifically a football team, it had to be fall. So here I sit in monotonously sunny Phoenix (*not* a conducive climate for a mystery writer—I crave downright gothic amounts of clouds and rain) with the air-conditioning set at arctic levels, writing about the snowy Chicago skyline.

Q: How do you keep track of Kate's characteristics and behavior (so you don't contradict yourself in later books)? Do you reread the previous books before writing a new one? Do you keep a written record? Or do you have an incredible memory?

A: After five books, a lot of Kate's characteristics and behavior are second nature to me. After all, when you think about it, I spend a lot more time with her than with my husband. I do reread the previous book before beginning the next one, but that's more a function of trying to get Kate's voice back in my head and wanting to avoid repeating myself. From time to time I also flip back through the well-worn copies of the previous books that I keep on a corner of my desk to check details. Still, I make mistakes, especially with names of very minor characters. For example, the name of the wife of the managing partner in Kate's law firm changes from Bitsy to Betsy from book to book.

Q: How does Kate change over the course of your books?

A: Kate changes like a real person, as a result of experience and the passage of time, but more slowly. Time in Kate's world passes only half as fast as it does in real life in order to give me a chance to write about this period in her life.

Still, she's changed quite a bit over the course of five books. Not only has she grown more confident in her professional life, but as she puts more years between herself and her husband Russell's death, she is beginning to face up to the issues of her personal life.

Q: Do other characters grow along with Kate?

A: I'm not sure that they grow, but they do seem to progress. Her secretary, Cheryl, will be finishing law school and moving on to her own practice, which will not only add a different dimension to their relationship but also make way for a new character close to Kate. Claudia, Kate's roommate, is also moving ahead with her medical training and bringing changes.

I think there's no question that in *Fatal Reaction* the pressures on Azor Pharmaceuticals have made Kate's boyfriend, Stephen, much more critical and demanding, which I think is only to be expected.

This interview originally appeared in a slightly different form in Murder on the Internet.

If you liked *Rough Trade*,
don't miss the other
Kate Millholland novels
by Gini Hartzmark

PRINCIPAL DEFENSE

FINAL OPTION

BITTER BUSINESS

FATAL REACTION